Vanquish

Vanquish

Triumph Series #1

S.J. McGran

Copyright © 2014 S.J. McGran

Editing by Tee Tate, Litstack.com
Proofreading/Blog Tour by Betsy at Book Drunk Blog

All rights reserved. No part of this book may be reproduced or transmitted in any form without written permission of the author, except by a reviewer who may quote brief passages for review purposes only.

This book is a work of fiction. Names, characters and incidents are either the product of the author's imagination or are used

ONE

Zhoe

Passing rows upon rows of gravestones, each one marking the place of a loved one, I think about the poetry you can find here. Some have been taken too soon; others were fortunate enough to live a long life but each one of those gray and black and white headstones holds a story, a memory.

Once I find Cole's grave towards the back of the cemetery I get out of my car and inhale a calming breath. Funny how a place associated with death and sadness allows me the first chance to really breathe. To really feel.

Strolling slowly up to the grey headstone, I run my hands along the curve at the top. It's smooth and cool to the touch. Plopping down in front of the headstone, I cross my legs so I'm sitting Indian-style.

The words etched on the marble, *Cole Dawson May 6, 1991 – September 10, 2009*, never cease to gut me. They rob me of breath. They tear the hole in my heart a little more each time. Even after five years.

Just eighteen years of life. I still don't understand how He allowed my brother to be taken so suddenly.

I'm not sure if I believe in God anymore. My faith was shaken that day and it still hasn't fully recovered. I've always believed in *everything happens for a reason*, but I hate that clichéd saying now. People say it just to make you feel better, to soften the blow.

What could the reason be for Cole being murdered? For him only living for eighteen years? For him never being given the chance to grow up and actually live?

After a few moments of wondering, I start my one-sided conversation with the headstone. "Hi, Cole. I miss you. You have no idea how much I miss you." My voice is quiet, soft.

I don't know why talking to a piece of stone makes me feel better, but it does. I always come here on the anniversary of his death, but I come a lot during the year, too. I come when I need to vent or to cry. I come when I feel like no one else in the world will understand what I'm going through or what I need.

Cole was two years older than me but we were as close as siblings can get. He never left me behind, never made me feel like I was stupid or inadequate because I was the younger sister. We shared all of our secrets and dreams. Nothing was left untouched. Cole knew me better than anyone. He was always the first person I would go to when I had a problem. He still is most times. He can't offer me advice or talk back but just knowing he's out there somewhere listening to me is usually enough to calm me down, or help me work through things.

"I started classes last week. They suck. I don't know why I allowed dad to talk me into this, why I allow him to control my life. I hate my classes. I hate this life they've chosen for me. But, I just don't know how to get out."

I'm crying before I even realize I'm doing it. Before I even realize I'm this upset about the path my life has taken.

I'm a business major at the state's most prestigious university; it's not Ivy League like Daddy wanted but it's a great school and one I wanted to go to. I figured if I didn't get a say in what I was majoring in, with Daddy paying for it and all, at least I could go to the school I wanted to go to.

Daddy wants me to take over his marketing firm someday. But, what I want is to work in the non-profit sector. I volunteer a lot in my free time now. It makes me feel useful, worthy. Really, it just makes me feel, when little else does these days. But, there's nothing prestigious about working in non-profit. Daddy always says it's nice to give back when you can, but you can't make a living out of it.

"How will you ever support a family? How will you ever find a suitable husband when you're slumming it with the rest of the city's scum?" Sometimes I hate Daddy. I hate his money and his view on life. Sometimes I wish I were born into a different family, a different life.

But, then I remember Cole and I wouldn't trade him for the world.

I sit in silence for a few moments to just remember Cole. Remember the good times, a happier time.

The slamming of a car door jolts me from my trance. Looking at my watch I realize it's time to get going. I have an 8:00 A.M. class on Communication. Awesome.

"I miss you Cole, everything was easier when you were here. I hope you're listening tonight while Ang and I tell funny and embarrassing stories about you. I love you."

Two

Jared

Stepping out of my beat-up piece of shit Chevy truck, I take a deep breath in. Today marks the fifth anniversary of the day my life went to shit. I hate today's date. I hate the memories and the decisions I made five years ago. I hate the person I was then.

I visit his gravesite on the anniversary of his death every year, and every year I pray it'll get easier to come here. I pray the guilt will have dissipated or at least lessened. It doesn't. If anything, it gets worse. Each year I'm getting older, while he's frozen in time at the age of eighteen. How is that fair?

Noticing a girl sitting in front of his headstone I stop my advance. She's gorgeous, even with her face masked in pain and tear tracks running the length of her face. Instantly guilt racks me – this is someone that cared about him. Someone missing him and I did that. I'm the reason she's sad, the reason he's gone.

Like the pansy I am I hide out behind a tree, watching her. I take in her pain because I deserve to feel every single ounce of it. Finally, once she's gotten into her car and pulled away, I walk up to the grave feeling insignificant.

"Hey man. Who was that?" I don't know why I ask I know he can't answer. "Listen, I'm sorry. I'm sorry for that night. I'm sorry for everything leading up to that night. I miss you man. I wish I could trade places with you. I would do it, you know? A thousand times over I'd do it."

I mean every word. I mean it when I tell him I would trade places with him. It was my fault we were there to begin with. Cole was a good kid until he met me. He had a family that loved him; he had hopes and dreams and everything he could ever want right at his fingertips. Me, on the other hand, I had no one – no family, no real friends, not even somewhere I could really call home.

It should have been me.

A few more minutes pass with me apologizing silently to the guy whose life I accidently took, before I head to work for the week.

On the drive to the jobsite I relish in the fact I can lose myself for a few hours. Construction is all I've ever known, and thankfully a job I actually enjoy. I got into some trouble in high school, and the owner of Porter and Son Construction saved me from a life I never wanted.

Stepping out of my truck I hear my name being called from across the lot, "Roman!" I turn to find my only real friend, Rico, running towards me. Richard Jones is the closest thing I have to family. We met in juvi and have been inseparable since. "How ya doin, man?"

Rico is the only person that knows what happened that night five years ago. Well, besides Cole and me. Needless to say he knows how rough this day is on me. "About as good as I can be today, I guess."

"I hear ya. We still on for tonight?" When I just nod he adds, "Cool. I'll see you later then."

"Cool." We leave it at that. We've talked about that day once before and once was enough. Now, instead of talking about it we go out to celebrate the short life he was able to live. It's become a tradition and one I oddly look forward to. It offers me a few minutes of reprieve, a few minutes to forget about the suffocating guilt.

THREE

Zhoe

Princess. That's what everyone calls me and has always called me. When I was a little girl I used to love it. Everyone in my family called me Princess, my mom, my dad and Cole. I especially loved it when my dad called me Princess.

I liked the idea of being somebody's something, the idea of being important to someone. Daddy would use it as a term of endearment, *"How's my Princess today?"* I would beam up at him like he was my whole world; then, I would run to my room and proudly wear my plastic tiara for the rest of the day.

In high school I learned to love the nickname for a different reason, especially when Daddy would use it. I learned rather quickly I could use his soft spot for me to get pretty much anything I wanted. Daddy would shake his head and smile at me telling me, *"Anything for you, Princess."* Yeah. I definitely used that to my advantage.

But now, I hate the damn nickname. I wish I'd never been burdened with it. Today when Daddy uses it, it leaves a sour taste in my mouth. *"Yep, sure, Princess,"* he'll tell me without even looking up from his computer. Or when my *mother* uses it it's like a curse, *"Whatever you say, Princess."* Of course this is always said with a sneer on her pretty face.

The worst, though, is when random strangers use it. I know what I look like. I know I look like the pretentious snob my family wishes I was. With my brand new Lexus that cost more than my entire tuition, more than most people make in a year's salary, and my perfectly done hair and nails, my designer clothes. I get why people feel the need to call me Princess, but they don't know me. They don't know how untrue of a description that is for me.

Pulling up to the university I slam my door behind me and take off running for my first class of the day, after losing track of time at the cemetery I'm running late. In my haste I manage to plow into a group of girls standing outside one of the sorority houses nearly knocking several of us off balance, mumbling an apology I turn back in the direction I was headed.

"Oh, I'm sorry Princess, was I in your way?" I hear one of the girls shout loud enough for the entire Quad to hear.

Just get over damn it, I chant to myself. It's just a bunch of catty girls trying to draw the attention back to them. Shaking it off I finally reach University Hall and shove through the doors, taking the stairs two at a time. The entire class shifts their attention to me when I burst into the classroom in a less than discreet way.

"Well, Princess. So nice of you to join us today," the professor unnecessarily acknowledges my presence.

Yeah. I hate that stupid nickname.

And today. I really fucking hate today.

Ignoring the stares and snickers I make my way to the back of the room and take a seat at an empty desk. As soon as I sit down I pull out my iPad and my cell phone. I am so not listening to this guy go on and on about proper presentation etiquette.

I look down at my phone when it vibrates with an incoming text. I smile a little seeing Angelica's name flash across the screen. Angelica and I have been friends since we were babies. Our mothers have been friends most of their lives so it made sense we would become besties, too.

We are exactly one week apart in age but are as opposite as two people can get; we always joke that they must have mixed us up in the hospital and sent us home with the wrong families.

Both of our families are well off but Daddy likes to spend his money hosting elegant galas and buying bigger houses and faster cars; whereas, Angelica's dad hosts charity events and sits on the committee for several non-profit organizations in the city.

Angelica would be the perfect daughter for my father. Where she is prim and proper, I am laid back and often times crass. She believes she is entitled to the money she was born into and can come across as a spoiled brat, where I like to spend my time at the local homeless shelters and other non-profits in the city. Ironically, even my nickname fits her better.

Regardless of our differences we are best friends and I wouldn't trade her in for the world.

Ang: Hi, friend. Are we still on for tonight?
Me: Obviously.
Ang: Whatever. I'll be at your place at five to get ready. Plan on heading out around 6?
Me: Perfect.
Ang: Love you.
Me: Love you, too.

Every year Angelica and I go out to celebrate Cole and the short life he was able to live. It started the year after he passed because I just couldn't sit in that house anymore.

Ever since Cole's death, Mother has been self-medicating with anti-depressants and sleeping pills. On most days she is little more than a zombie, but on the anniversary of his death it's like she's checked out and is ready to give up on life altogether. Daddy spends most of his day in his office or checking on Mother to make sure she hasn't overdosed and everyone forgets that I'm even there.

So, Angelica and I decided to get out of the house and head to one of the college bars where they don't ID. We sat around sharing good memories of Cole. It has become a tradition ever since and honestly, I'm not sure I could get through the day without it.

I sigh relaxing back into my chair. I just have two more classes to get through before I can go home and enjoy a nice night out with my friend. Just a few more hours. I can do this.

***

At exactly five o'clock, Angelica shows up pounding on my door. I don't know why she bothers knocking. She has a key and often lets herself in before I can even get my ass off the couch. As if to prove my point the door opens and her heels click across the tile in the entryway just as I start to stand from my spot on the couch.

My condo is two stories with an open floor plan on the first floor that consists of a giant kitchen, living room and dining room combination, a full bath and a laundry room.

Upstairs are two bedrooms and a bathroom. My bedroom has a balcony that overlooks the pool area; it's my favorite place in the world to be. I've turned the extra bedroom into a guest room and office combination. Angelica sleeps in there most weekends, unless we both fall asleep watching movies on the large sectional in the living room.

As much as I despise Daddy paying for everything, I do love my apartment. I absolutely love having a place to call home, one where my workaholic father and walking-dead mother are absent – a space just for me.

Angelica bounces up to me looking completely put together as always. Her long blonde hair is straightened perfectly and just brushes her waist; her green eyes are highlighted with purple eyeliner and shadow. She's wearing knee-high black boots, skinny jeans and a form fitting black long sleeve V-neck sweater that leaves very little to the imagination.

Angelica is tall, thin and has perfect skin and hair. She looks like a damn model. All the time. If I weren't so used to it, it would drive me crazy. "Hi, friend!"

"Hey, thought we were getting ready together?" I ask as I look down at my yoga pants and hoodie; my hair is still wet from my shower.

"I decided to save time. Now go dry your hair and I'll pick out an outfit for you." She skips off towards the stairs and my bedroom before I have the chance to say anything else. Shaking my head, I follow her because let's face it; I have little choice in the matter.

Angelica and I are just as opposite in the looks department as we are in personality. Where she's tall and thin, I'm of average height and a little on the curvy side. I have hips for days and large boobs that are more trouble than they're worth. I am proud of my body though. I work hard at maintaining my toned arms and legs and flat stomach, but sometimes I wish I had a little less to grab onto.

Once in the bathroom I focus on drying and straightening my shoulder length dark brown hair. I add a little blush to give some color to my nearly translucent skin, a little mascara to highlight my bright blue eyes and some clear lip-gloss finish it off.

I'm not one to wear much makeup, call me lazy but it seems like more work than it's worth. Aside from my minor insecurities about my curves, I'm comfortable with the way I look and rarely feel the need to embellish. Just another difference between my best friend and me.

Walking into my bedroom I laugh under my breath. For as different as we are, we sure get each other. Lying on my bed are skinny jeans, black ballet flats, a white long sleeve T-shirt and a billowy black and grey scarf. Perfect. After getting dressed I head downstairs, grab my purse, phone and keys and the two of us are out the door.

Four

Jared

"I was thinking of going to The Slip. Sound alright to you?" I ask Rico as soon as he gets in my truck. The Freudian Slip or The Slip as most locals call it, is a dive bar right off campus. It's one of our favorite hangout spots.

"Cool with me." Reaching over he rolls down his window letting in a cool breeze. It may be September in Ohio but it's an usually warm one and I'm thankful for the breeze. "I could use a cold one, man. It was a long day out there."

Nodding my head in agreement, I put the truck in park and climb out. As soon as we walk in we head towards the back grabbing a high top table near one of the pool tables. The bar itself is pressed along one wall and is surrounded with bar stools. There are several booths and small tables near the bar with four pool tables and high top bar tables in the back. For being a college bar it is relatively clean and features a great beer selection, one of the many reasons we come here.

It's early so I'm not surprised how dead it is in here, but it will most likely start to pick up in a few hours. "I'll grab the first round if you get the table set up."

"Cool. I'll take whatever they have by Great Lakes."

I can't help but watch as the pretty bartender flirts obviously with a few guys opposite me as she pours them shots of tequila. When she finally comes to take my order, I chuckle as she shamelessly shakes her ass for me as she walks away.

"These are on me this time, handsome," she gives me a wink as she leans toward me.

I'm about to give her a line when I'm interrupted by a couple of girls walking in; they are laughing, drawing attention to themselves. Though, they are both stunning so I probably would have noticed anyways.

The first girl is a tall blonde that reeks of money and snobbery, it's obvious she likes attention with the way she walks up to the bar plops down in a stool and shoves her cleavage in the male bartender's face. Her friend follows her laughing and shaking her head, she must be used to her behavior.

This girl is much more my speed; she's gorgeous – in a natural beauty kind of way. Her smile is soft and sincere.

The longer I watch, uneasiness, or maybe just awareness settles over me. There is something about her that seems to pull to me, maybe I know her from somewhere?

I stare at her like a fool for a few seconds too long; I know this because she catches me. She looks up and makes direct eye contact with me. As soon as she does my breath is knocked right out of my fucking chest.

It's her. It's the girl from the cemetery this morning; the same girl that was crying at Cole's gravesite. Holy shit. I thought she was beautiful this morning, but damn she's stunning now. Her blue eyes watch me for a long moment. I have to admire her confidence; most girls would have started blushing or would have averted their stares by now. But, not her. She just keeps on staring at me as blatantly as I'm staring at her.

I hear Rico yelling at me from across the room, "Roman, you coming man?" Shaking my head I turn away from the girl and make my way to my dumbass friend. All the while contemplating my next move. Part of me wants to talk to her, to get to know her, to find out who she was to Cole.

But the other part of me, the guilt-ridden side of me, wants to let her go on her way. She obviously cared about him and once she finds out who I am and what I did, she'll hate me. Might as well save us both the trouble.

Still, I find I can't keep my eyes off of her for too long. I'm following proper protocol for the night – I'm conversing, playing pool, drinking beer. But, I'm only partially paying attention; most of my attention is focused on the beautiful girl at the bar.

Five

Zhoe

"Zho, are you even listening to me?" Angelica sighs dramatically, her shoulders slumping on the exhale, as I snap my attention back to my friend. My eyes have been wandering for most of the night. This isn't the first time Angelica has had to do or say something to bring my attention back to her. "Who are you staring at? You've been distracted all night."

Turning in her barstool and starts to look around the bar for the guy that has stolen all of my attention. I can't help the chuckle that escapes – there is no way she'll pick him out. He is sexy – drool worthy sexy – but in a dark and dangerous way, not in the clean cut, Abercrombie model way that Angelica is so typically drawn to.

He's wearing dark jeans that fit to his legs and ass so perfectly I can almost see every muscle straining as he moves. His plain black T-shirt is tight across his broad shoulders and showcases muscular arms. Dragging my attention from his rock-hard chest I'm transfixed on his arms. His right arm is completely covered in tattoos - colorful, beautiful pieces of art. I find I want to trace each one and find out its story.

His dark brown hair is just long enough to give it that messy look from running his fingers through it, which he's done numerous times throughout the night, making my own itch with the urge to take their place. His strong jaw is shadowed by facial hair, it's more than a five o'clock shadow but I wouldn't quite classify it as a beard, either. The dark stubble calls to me. I want to run my fingers through it, and feel the roughness of it on my face and other sensitive areas of my body.

I have to suppress a moan at the thought.

I'd feel guilty for practically salivating over the man if he hadn't been watching me, too. On several occasions we've made direct eye contact. His deep, rich brown eyes colliding with my blue ones from across the room. I don't believe in love at first sight, this most definitely is not love; I mean I haven't even spoken to him. But lust at first sight? Oh, yeah this is definitely that.

Every time I catch his penetrating stare I squirm a little in my seat, not because I'm nervous, no I can definitely hold my own against this man. I'm anxious because I need *something* to relieve the itch; something to take the edge off. Preferably him.

"Oh! Is it that guy in the polo at the last pool table?" Angelica asks, finally picking out a guy she thinks I would have my sights set on. I can't help but laugh out loud. She picked the right table, just the wrong man. *My man* is playing pool with a guy that is so opposite him and right up Ang's alley.

I take a minute to appreciate the guy Angelica has now set her sights on. He's your typical tall, dark and handsome. He's wearing jeans and a white polo shirt, his hair is messy and falls across his forehead in a way I would assume he meant to look accidental but probably took the time to style it just right. He's attractive don't get me wrong; he's just not my type.

The guy he's with isn't my typical type either, but I've never felt such an insta-connection with anyone else before this man. Maybe that's saying something.

"No," I answer. "Same table. Different guy." I'm being vague I know but something inside me doesn't want to share him. He's my eye candy for the night, not hers or anyone else's.

I hear Angelica make a confused grunt. "Uh, the sexy, scary guy in the black and tattoos?" Sexy scary, yep that's him.

"Yeah," I answer quickly before taking another large gulp of my beer. I'm suddenly very thirsty. And hot.

"He's staring at you." I look up from my beer to find his attention trained on me again. All night we've done this. But neither of us has moved from our spots in the small bar, neither one of us has even offered up a smile. We just stare. Taking in the electric current that passes between us. Reveling in it. Soaking it up.

"I know." This causes Ang to flip her attention back to me. She looks at me like I'm crazy. When you've been friends as long as we have often times you don't need words to convey a message to each other and right now her expression is practically shouting, *you know he's staring and yet you're still sitting here with me?!*

"Let's go talk to them." Rolling my eyes at her, I snicker to myself…totally didn't see that one coming.

I've been enjoying myself tonight, talking about Cole, laughing with my best friend and eye fucking the sexy scary guy from across the bar. What I don't want to do is go over there and find out he's nothing like my imagination has made him out to be or worse – he's even better.

"I don't know, Ang. We've been watching each other all night and neither of us has made a move. Maybe he doesn't want me to talk to him. Maybe he thinks I'm crazy for eye-stalking him all night."

"Well, that does sound kind of crazy. But, what's the worst that could happen?"

"Uh. I don't know, he drugs us, takes us home and chops us up in little pieces?" Okay, that was dramatic. He's scary looking but not in the serial killer way. No, his scary is more like "I've been through hell in this life, I'm damaged but I'll still make you fall in love with me and then crush your heart into a million little pieces."

As much as I'd like to, I just really don't have time to get involved with someone that needs fixing. I have enough damage control to do in my own life. And I definitely don't have time to have my heart broken.

She laughs at me. "Or he takes you home and fucks your brains out. You need a good lay. You have such a pathetic sex life."

"Gee thanks."

"I mean look at him, Zho," she demands, like I haven't been staring all damn night. "He definitely knows what he's doing in bed. I bet he's huge, too."

I'd put money on it. Everything about him is huge. His man parts have to be huge, too, right? Before I have time to answer her, or before Angelica has time to standup from her barstool making the decision for me, I hear our names being shouted from behind us. Both of us flip around looking towards the door and the noise. In walks two guys from our classes, Brad and Chase.

Both of their parents run in the same social circles as ours; thus turning me off immediately. They think they are better than everyone, believing they deserve everything handed to them on a silver platter. Including Angelica and me. Unfortunately, Angelica has fallen into Brad's bed many times. Stupid girl.

Rolling my eyes I turn back around in my seat and take a long swig of my beer, eying Sexy-Scary over the rim. This time he shoots me a cocky smirk that is so drop dead sexy I almost choke on my beer. It's as if he knows I don't want to deal with these two guys; that I don't want their attention. I'd much rather have his attention. Maybe Angelica was on to something. Maybe I should go talk to him. It has to be better than dealing with these two idiots the rest of the night.

Six

Jared

Thanks to the douche bags that just walked in screaming it, I finally know her name. Zhoe. It fits her, equal parts sophisticated and sassy. I had to smile when she looked annoyed and disgusted, finding her beer much more interesting. Well, her beer... and me.

We've been watching each other all night. I feel like an idiot and a pansy for not making a move but there's something - okay this is cheesy - but something kind of special and interesting and different about what we're doing. It's like we know that once we talk whatever this is that's drawing us together will disappear.

But, now it's more than that. Cole had a sister. He used to talk about her, about how great she was and how close they were. I can't remember her name, but what if Zhoe is his sister? Her being so upset at the cemetery this morning would make sense then.

This is a fucking disaster. The one girl that finally catches my attention in however long and I can't have her. There is no way it would work if she knew who I am. I'm glad now I decided to take the pansy-way out and stay away from her tonight; she doesn't need any more heartbreak in her life.

Unable to completely let her go, I'm still watching her out of the corner of my eye and I see her shake her head at her friend. She looks upset, like whatever her friend is suggesting is something she definitely doesn't want to do. She must concede though as her friend makes one of those obnoxious girl squeals and throws her arms around Zhoe's neck. Zhoe laughs before pulling a pen out of her purse and bends over the bar top.

I watch her as she stands and makes her way towards me. I almost swallow my tongue watching her walk; her curvy hips sway with each step, but I'm not even sure she's aware she's doing it. All I can think about is grabbing onto those hips, kissing her plump lips and running my fingers through her hair. Everything about her seems soft and sexy.

She walks directly up to me stopping only inches away, wrapping me in her soft vanilla scent. I could lean down and kiss her she's so close. My six feet frame towers over her, her head comes chest level and makes me want to wrap her in my arms and protect her. My primal instincts seem to have kicked in around this girl; though if I'm being honest I'm the thing she needs protection from.

She stares up at me, her blue eyes piercing for several long seconds before they roam the length of my body. I want to laugh or make a cocky remark about the way she's shamelessly checking me out. But, when she sucks her full bottom lip into her mouth, her teeth biting roughly into the smooth skin, all thought flees my mind.

Snapping her attention back to my face she offers me a small smile, grabs my hand and pushes a piece of paper into it. Then, without a word she turns and walks away from me.

I'm still standing there staring after her when Rico walks up to me. "Damn. Who the hell was that?" Rico asks titling his head to the side to get a better view of her ass. I want to punch him for being a pig but I realize I was doing the same exact thing. Her skintight jeans leave little to the imagination, cupping her voluptuous ass perfectly.

Straightening my head and turning my attention back to my friend I answer, "Not sure. But quit staring at her ass, you douche." I give him a shove to his shoulder for good measure.

It's only a small lie; I know a few things about her. I know her name is Zhoe. I know she knew Cole. I know she's gorgeous even when she cries. I know she drinks beer and when she laughs she does it loudly and tends to throw her head back and I know she has the most piercing blue eyes I've ever seen. I know she smells like vanilla and has a body I'm dying to feel wrapped around me. I also know I should stay far away from her.

He looks at me like I'm crazy. "Well what did she give you?"

I really didn't want to do this with an audience; I was hoping Rico wasn't paying close attention to us. I open my palm to find a bar napkin with her first name and phone number written in perfect handwriting on one side. I must be grinning like an idiot because I hear Rico laugh before he nudges me in the side. "You got it bad, dude."

I just roll my eyes at him. How can I have it bad for a girl I've never even talked to? I mean I didn't say a single fucking word when she walked over to me, not "hi" or "thanks" or "you're gorgeous." Or "why were you crying this morning?" or "who was Cole to you?" Nothing. I just stood there staring at her, lost in her perfect blue eyes like a moron.

I'm not going to lie - I'm impressed. It took a lot of balls, more than I have, to make the first move. She never backed down from my stares all night and then she walks over to me all sexy and confident and just gives me her name and number and walks away. She has to know I'm going to call her. She has to know she's appealing as hell.

Shaking my head I turn back to Rico. "Whatever, man. You going to re-rack or what?" I try to get us back to the present and our game. That girl, Zhoe, has taken up enough of my concentration for one night. I'd much rather think about her when I'm alone in my bed tonight.

Seven

Jared

My life may not seem like much to most people, but I'm happy. When you come from the life that I did - a life surrounded by drugs and abuse - it's hard to make something of yourself but somehow I did. I may have made a few mistakes along the way, there were times I almost fell into the life my parents bred for me, but I didn't. I got out and I'm proud of who I am now.

That doesn't mean I'm free and clear of my past. Every Wednesday evening after work I head down to a local church and attend a Narcotics Anonymous meeting. I've gone through the twelve steps and I truly don't believe I was addicted, but I can admit I *was* abusing drugs at one point in my life and I don't ever want to go back to that place. The NA meetings help keep me grounded and on track.

Taking my usual seat near the back I take a look around as I wait for the meeting to start. It's amazing to me how each one of us can be so different and come from such different backgrounds and yet battle some of the same demons.

I've been going to this same meeting for about three years, while most members tend to come and go and there are always new faces, there are several of us that are in it for the long haul.

I notice one of the long time member's walk in and I can't help but compare our stories, our lives. He came from a similar life as me - neglectful parents, surrounded by drugs - but once he met his wife he decided to quit that life, to get clean. They are expecting their first baby soon and truly I couldn't be happier for the guy, after everything life dealt him in the past he deserves to be happy now.

I can't help but wonder about my own future when I see him though. The whole wife and kids thing has never really appealed to me. It's not that I'm 100% against it, it's just something I never thought I'd have, something I never allowed myself to hope for.

When you come from a life of darkness, it's easy to have nightmares but dreams are few and far between.

When I was able to dream I could only focus on one thing - getting out. Make something of myself. Live. Breathe. I was too focused on those things to able to dream of anything else, so love and marriage and a family never even crossed my mind.

Maybe one day I'll meet a girl that makes me change my mind, my outlook. Maybe I'll meet a girl that knocks me on my ass so hard I can't imagine life without her.

Maybe Zhoe is that girl for me, or could be if I allowed myself to give her a chance.

I'm so damn torn on what to do about her. Most of me wants to call her, to get to know her - even if it is just as friends. The rest of me is afraid it's selfish of me to want those things. I obviously took someone that meant a lot from her, is it really fair for me to step into her life, now?

For years, I've tried to repress my memories of Cole. It's not that I want to forget him; it's just too painful to remember. I'm afraid this girl will stir up those memories and emotions, but I'm more afraid of what she'll think of me when she finds out what I did.

Eight

Zhoe

My cell phone rings just as I'm about to get out of my car and Angelica's perky voice greets me on the other end. "Hi, Friend!"

"Hey. What are you doing?" I ask even though I know before she answers me.

"Ugh," she grunts and I can't help but smile, "I'm just pulling into Mom and Dad's. Who decided Wednesday's were family dinner night again?"

"Pretty sure you did, so that you can still have your weekends free."

"Right," she answers. "I wish I didn't have to do them at all. What are you doing?"

"I just got to the Y. Since we went out Monday night I decided to see if they needed any help with dinner tonight."

"Such a good Samaritan." She's making fun of me but I don't care. Every Monday night I head down to the local YWCA and volunteer. Usually I help serve or make dinners, but sometimes they need help doing laundry or cleaning. I do whatever I can to help.

My favorite part of volunteering here, though, is the children. I hate seeing all the babies and kids that have to grow up in a life like this, but those are my favorite nights, too. The kids always smile at me, they always want to play and it helps ground me. It reminds me that if these kids can smile with the hand they've been dealt, surely my life isn't so bad.

"You know the offer is always open to come with me sometime. You can bail on your parents tonight and help me instead." I always invite her to come, but she never has. To each their own, I guess.

"Nah. I'll see you tomorrow night though, right? Are we still going to The Slip? Oh and by the way has Mr. Sexy-Scary called you yet?"

Thanks for the reminder, I think to myself. I don't understand why he hasn't called. I may have misread whatever the hell was happening the other night but I was confident when I handed him my number I'd be getting a call from him. "Yes to your first question, and not yet to your second. But, that's why we're going out tomorrow... I need a new victim."

She cackles, as I knew she would. Angelica is never one to turn down a manhunt. "Perfect. See you then."

Hanging up, I head down the street towards the YWCA, passing an old church on the way. As I'm turning towards the entrance of my building I hear my name being called from across the street.

"Zhoe?" I turn just my head to look over my shoulder at the deep, rich voice calling out to me. As soon as I see him I stop dead in my tracks. It's Sexy-Scary.

He's standing on the other side of the street with one hand on a beat-up old Chevy truck. Does he always look so damn good? He's wearing another T-shirt stretched taut across his impressive build – I'm not complaining because I love how his tight shirts show of his delicious body, but does he know they come in a bigger size?

His beard is a little thicker than it was two days ago, making my fingers itch again. How is it possible for someone I know nothing about to affect me so much? I'm sweating and anxious; my breathing is coming a little faster - especially as I watch his gaze move up and down my body several times.

I can't read his expression; he's just staring at me like he was the other night - no smile, just pure heat and lust in his eyes. I have no clue what to do. Do I smile and wave? Do I yell hi back? I mean I don't even know his name! Panicking because I have no clue what else to do, I turn and hightail it into the Y, all the while berating myself for being such an idiot.

Just minutes ago I was upset because he hadn't called yet. Then, when I see him again I run away from him? What the hell is wrong with me?

***

"I'm sorry. You did what?" Angelica is looking at me like I've grown three heads. Her jaw is dropped and her eyes are wide. Meanwhile I'm focused on the beer in front of me. Desperately avoiding her eyes.

As planned we met up at The Slip tonight. We're sitting in our usual spots at the bar and I'm telling her all about my major blunder from the day before. "I, um. I ran away."

I spent the rest of the night analyzing exactly what happened. I cannot believe I just turned and ran away from him like that. What the hell was I thinking?

Angelica bursts out laughing. Like full-on belly laugh. I feel my cheeks tint pink with the embarrassment. Only I would do something like that. Angelica would have walked right up to him and planted a kiss on his perfectly, plump lips, or slapped him for not calling her yet. I, however, run away. "Oh, friend. You are so clueless."

"Gee, thanks for the moral support, *friend*." I exaggerate the last word. I know she's just joking with me and really it doesn't bother me as much as I'm pretending it does.

"Oh, I'm sorry, did I hurt your feelings?" she asks rolling her eyes at me. "If you see him again, do yourself a favor and don't run, okay? He looks like he could be a good time."

That he does. The thing is I'm not really a fun-time, just a fling, type of girl. I've only been with two men my whole life, both of which were pretty serious. Well, at the time I thought they were serious.

After a few more beers and a few more jokes at my expense we notice the bar is starting to fill up.

On Monday the bar was occupied by a few college students in jeans and hoodies just looking to have a few beers, play a few games of pool and unwind. On Thursdays a DJ is brought in with the tables being cleared to make room for an impromptu dance floor. The guys all have a little extra gel in their hair and might even don a polo or button up with their jeans instead of just a T-shirt. The girls are dressed to the 9's in skimpy dresses and skirts, sky-high heels and more makeup than the cosmetics counter at Sephora.

Though, I can't be too judgey. Angelica and I are both much more put together than we were on Monday. We're both wearing tight dresses that cling to our bodies showcasing every curve we have, which for Ang isn't many.

Angelica is wearing four-inch heels that match her emerald green dress perfectly. Her hair is down and curled to perfection and her makeup is even more flawless. I opted for an LBD and another pair of ballet flats; I'm just not much for heels. I also left my hair down and curled. I feel sexy and pretty but still me. I'm okay with being the only girl here not in heels that could cause me to break an ankle.

The DJ starts Lady Gaga's "Do What You Want" and immediately all of the women in the bar flock to the dance floor. "Oh! I love this song," Angelica screeches in my ear. "Let's dance!"

Grabbing my hand she pulls me onto the dance floor. I may act reluctant but I secretly love letting loose and dancing, especially to a song as sexy as this one. I close my eyes and swing my hips to the beat, letting it wash over me. I feel Angelica grab my hips and press into me.

I can feel people staring at us, watching us. It isn't surprising considering our dresses hide only the essentials and we're rubbing against each other provocatively. Even though I expect to be gawked at this feels like something else. A prickly sensation runs down my spine causing goose bumps to breakout across my exposed arms. I open my eyes and turn my head towards the bar, immediately I see the deep brown eyes that have been haunting me the last several days.

Sexy-Scary is leaning against the bar, one elbow propped on the smooth surface, his other hand holding a bottle of beer. His ankles are crossed giving off a cool, calm and collected vibe. Though, his eyes are anything but.

I watch him drag his gaze from my face down my body. He doesn't rush; instead, he takes his time running his gaze all over me. Every inch of my body he devours feels like it's on fire. I can almost imagine what his strong hands would feel like making the same path as his eyes.

He pays special attention to my breasts and the ample cleavage hanging out of my dress top. When his gaze drops lower, I give a little twist of my hips enjoying the way his eyes widen and his nostrils flare as I do it. I've never felt sexier, more wanted and more wanton than I do in this moment.

By the time his dark brown orbs make it back to my face, I'm breathing hard, my chest rising and falling in deep, shallow bursts. I'm sweating not from the heat of the dance floor but from the heat of his gaze. My panties are soaking wet and he still has yet to touch me, smile at me, talk to me.

My past sex life was always a means to an end... most times I got off, but other times I was left hanging, relying on my own hand or my B.O.B. It was never interesting or adventurous, and it certainly wasn't dirty. But, Mr. Sexy-Scary looks like the answer to my lackluster sex life. He looks like every fantasy I've ever had come true.

Yes, this is a very, very dangerous man. Good thing I'm feeling a little daring myself tonight.

Nine

Jared

I down the rest of my beer in one long gulp, reveling in the way the cool liquid feels going down my throat. I'm suddenly very parched. What is it about that girl that pushes all of the right buttons? Reaching behind me to grab the new beer the bartender just sat down, I use the distraction to adjust my unexpectedly too tight jeans.

I hear Rico let out a low whistle of approval and turn to see his attention drawn to Zhoe and her friend as well. "Holy. Fucking. Shit." My sentiments exactly. "Is that the girl from the other night?"

I just nod at him, not taking my eyes of Zhoe. I couldn't even if I tried. "Yeah." My voice feels weird- raspy and low with my arousal. How insanely sexy do you have to be to turn me on so much I can't think straight, making my dick hard enough to pound nails, from across the room?

"What the hell are you waiting for, man? She gave you her number and she's dancing like that just for you. She hasn't taken her eyes off of you. You better get out there before someone else does." *If only it were that easy*. My body is literally aching for me to go to her, to wrap my palms around her hips and pull her perfect ass into my throbbing groin, feeling her grind against me. But, my mind is telling me to back off and let the poor girl be. Just enjoy from a distance.

As though he heard every dirty thought I just had, some douchey looking frat-boy walks up behind her and does exactly what I was imagining I'd do. "Told you," Rico says beside me. My hand tenses around my beer bottle. I'm watching her, waiting for her to push him off of her but instead she leans back against him. Her body flush with his.

Then, she does the one thing I'm not expecting. She opens her eyes and stares right at me. Her eyes never leave mine, her teeth biting into her fleshy bottom lip, as she grinds her perfect body against his. It shouldn't turn me on, but it does. But, more than that, it spurs me into action.

I cross the room in a few strides not stopping until I'm directly in front of her. I grab both of her biceps pulling, with more force than was probably necessary, her body into mine and away from his. As soon as I touch her skin my body feels like it's on fire. I need to touch more of her, feel more of her. There's just something about this damn girl that knocks me right on my ass.

The guy she was dancing with finds his balls, stepping up close to Zhoe's back looking me in the eye with what he probably thinks is an intimidating stare. "Back off, man. She's with me."

I let a sly grin take over my face. Gently sliding my palms down her arms I grab her hips and pull her even closer, until there's not even a centimeter of space between us. "Are you with him, Zhoe?" She shakes her head at me, taking her bottom lip between her teeth. So, Zhoe has a shy side, huh? Interesting.

"Fuck you, whore," the dumbass responds to Zhoe's answer.

At that I step around Zhoe pushing her body behind me protectively. "What the fuck did you just call her?"

For long seconds we stand there in a testosterone fueled stare-down. I see the exact moment it clicks in his brain that he's not going to walk away from this in one piece if he doesn't shut his mouth and walk away. Which is exactly what he does – silently. Turning on his heel he walks away with his shoulders slumped and his tail between his legs. *That's what I thought.*

Turning back around I grab Zhoe again, bringing her sexy body back into mine. With one hand wrapped around her hip and the other tilting her head back, I ask if she's okay. Her only response is to nod at me.

"Good," I whisper against her neck. "Because I really want you to keep dancing, Pretty Girl." I hear her breath catch and I can't help but smile at that. Good to know I affect her too.

Ten

Zhoe

Taking a deep breath I steady my erratic heartbeat. *You started this*, I remind myself. I can't believe he wants me to keep dancing. The only thing I want to happen here is for him to go all caveman on me; picking me up, throwing me over his shoulder and walking out of the bar with me… not stopping until we get somewhere with a bed. Especially after he went all alpha just now. So. Fucking. Sexy.

What is happening with me? I've never wanted a one-night stand or a random hookup but with this sexy stranger there is nothing I want more. I feel him remove his hands from my hips only to place them on my ass, kneading it gently, causing me to fall into him even more.

There is not an inch of space between us. My chest is flattened against his taut stomach, my thighs pressed against his, his hands are on my butt and mine have magically wrapped themselves around his neck. I can feel his erection through his jeans against my stomach, fueling the fire that has overtaken my body.

Regaining a little composure I start to move. Slowly I move my hips from side to side grinding into him, after a few beats he starts to move with me. There is something so sexy about a man that can dance, like *really* dance, and this man can. There is something equally sexy about the way we watch each other.

Typically in this situation I would have my ass pressed against the guy's front when dancing, but I can't bring myself to turn away from him. I can't drag my eyes away from his for even a second.

Okay, that's a lie; they may have strayed for a second or two when his tongue snuck out to wet his lips. In the heat of this moment, that was the single most erotic, sexual thing I've ever seen. That's how turned on I am by this man. Just the sight of his tongue is enough to elicit a moan from deep in the back of my throat. I can't take my eyes off of his lips. They are so full and pink and they look so soft. I want to dig my teeth into his bottom lip and never let go.

Deciding tonight is my night of rebellion, of living life a little dangerously and playing games, I take a chance. My fingers skate along his neck moving up to cup the back of his head. I push it down towards my face at the same time I raise up on my tip-toes. Why didn't I want to wear heels again? I bring his lips down on mine, just a light brushing at first.

His lips are equal parts hard and soft. He tastes like mint, beer and man and it is addicting. Needing more, I press my mouth a little harder, opening a little more. I hear him groan, I feel it vibrate through his chest. I'm not even aware we were moving until my back hits a wall, but at some point he must have moved us across the dance floor to the other side of the bar.

He leans down just slightly, enough to grip my thighs in his strong hands, and hoists me up. Of their own accord my legs wrap around his waist. I don't care that we're in the middle of the bar, I don't care that people I may know are here or that those same people are getting a free show.

All I care about is how sexy and delicate this man makes me feel, as he holds me in the air with one arm, the other running a titillating path along one of my thighs with his warm, calloused palm.

His mouth comes down on mine. He doesn't hold back, he doesn't hesitate. He knows exactly what he wants and he takes it. I'm helpless to his assault. Opening to him he takes my tongue in his mouth, sucking and stroking expertly. I feel like I'm drowning; his mouth is literally devouring mine. And I fucking love it.

My hands are wandering along his upper body, taking in his broad shoulders and thick biceps. Moving them back up I grip the hair at the back of his neck I pull his head back, the second his eyes meet mine I want to die. I would give anything to be able to blink my eyes and be somewhere else. I'd give anything to be in a bed based on the look in his eyes alone.

His dark brown irises are nearly black, his pupils dilated with his desire. He looks hungry, feral, like he could eat me alive and still not feel satisfied. My look must mirror his, then, because I feel the exact same way.

His head dips, breaking eye contact again. "Please tell me you live close," he whispers against my neck. All I can do is nod, my head too foggy, and my throat too thick with desire to speak. "Do you need to tell anyone you're leaving?"

At first I just nod at him again, but then I find my voice when something dawns on me – I'm getting ready to leave with this guy, and hopefully have the best sex of my life with this guy and I don't even know his name. "Um. Who should I tell her I'm leaving with?"

His head snaps up from my neck, leaving me feel a little bereft until I glance back at him to see a huge grin plastered on his face. He lets out a light chuckle that reverberates through my body before gently placing my feet back on the ground. His hands glide gently down my hips sliding my dress down with the movement – at least one of us thought to make me decent again. My thoughts are already planning on how quickly we can get *undressed*.

He offers up two words, two words that for whatever reason send chills down my spine. "Jared Roman." I give a hard nod and force my shaky legs to move away from him, to seek out Angelica. To tell her I'm leaving with Mr. Sexy-Scary, Jared Roman, and we're going back to my place.

Holy. Shit.

Eleven

Jared

I stand facing the wall for a few moments trying to regain some composure; concentrating on my breathing, hoping my hard on isn't too obvious. When I turn around I immediately scan the bar looking for Zhoe. I find her at the corner of the bar, close to the front door standing with her friend. She reaches up and grabs the beer from her friend's hand downing the entire thing in one long gulp.

Seeing her need a little liquid courage makes me smile, knowing I've affected her. Lord knows she's affected me.

That was by far the hottest make out session I've ever had, and not one I'm likely to forget anytime soon. For a fleeting second I feel guilty about hoisting her against the wall like that, especially seeing how nervous she is now that the heat of the moment has passed.

But, then I remind my conscience – she started this.

What else did she expect to happen after we practically eye-fucked each other again? All that chemistry was bound to catch fire sooner or later. I'm thinking we need to get home, get naked and find out just how explosive it really is.

I could feel her heat and wetness soaking through the tiny scrap of panties she had on, while I had her center pressed against my straining erection. I can't wait to feel her softness under me again. Those luscious curves of hers aren't just great for looking at; I loved the feel of squeezing her hips and ass in my hands.

I watch her animatedly point in my direction while speaking with her friend. Her cheeks are still flushed either from embarrassment or arousal. Her friend looks at me, making direct eye contact and I take that as my cue to head over to them.

"So, Jared Roman. What are your intentions with my friend?" Wow. This girl gets straight to the point. I'm not really sure how to answer that loaded question though. It's clearly a trap. Would it be wrong to tell her I plan to give her the best orgasm she's ever had?

"Angelica!" Zhoe screeches beside me before I even have the chance to say anything. This time when I look down and see her pink cheeks I know it's from embarrassment. I can't help but chuckle at that.

"Angelica, huh? Well I'm not sure what Zhoe's intentions are but mine are to get to know a beautiful girl a little better." This girl intrigues me so it's not a lie, entirely. I want to get to know her but right now I'm more interested in getting to know her body.

"We're leaving," Zhoe speaks up, reaching for my hand. "I'll call you in the morning, Ang." They give each other a quick hug before I find myself being dragged out of the bar.

As soon as we're outside Zhoe turns to me. "I'm sorry about that. We've been friends for a long time so it's natural for her to worry about me."

"I take it you leaving the bar with a random guy isn't normal behavior for you then?" I don't know why I asked her that. I also don't know why I care. It's not like this is new to me, picking up girls in a bar, but I've never asked one of those girls a question like that. I don't know when I started acting like such a chick but this doesn't feel like a typical pick-up. It's definitely more.

How can it be more though when I don't even know her? I don't know her last name. I haven't even been inside her. But, something tells me that once isn't going to be enough with this girl, I'm going to become addicted, I can feel it. Already I'm craving the feel and taste of her lips. I want to press her against another wall until her tiny body climbs up me like a pole all over again.

"Uh, no. I've actually never had a one-night stand or a random hook up. I don't really know what got into me back there. I've never done that. Oh my god, everyone in that place probably saw all my goods. Oh shit. What the hell was I thinking? I wasn't thinking obviously." She's pacing, words spilling out of her faster than I can process them. "If you weren't so damn sexy I would have been able to think, I would have stopped that. Damn you and your lips."

A huge smile breaks out across my face as I reach for her. I grab her shoulders and pull her close, not close enough that our bodies are touching but close enough we can feel each other's body heat. "Zhoe." She looks up at me through her insanely long eyelashes, her face turning bright red.

I can't help the laugh that escapes my throat. This girl is too much. One second she's walking sex, turning me on without even touching me, and the next second she's blushing so hard her face is bright red. At my laugh she glares at me, making me laugh even harder – this girl is a walking contradiction. "You think my lips are sexy?"

"Oh, like you don't know you're sexy." She rolls her eyes at me, pulling out of my grip.

I'm having none of that though. I'm desperate to keep touching her. I take a step towards her, causing her to move backwards until her back is pressed against the brick wall of the bar. Placing my forearms on the wall beside her head, I lean into her – pressing our lower bodies together.

"Relax. We don't have to do anything you don't want to do. I'm not going to lie to you though, that," I nod my head toward the bar hoping she knows I mean us together against the wall inside, "was the hottest thing I've ever experienced and I want more. I want more of those juicy lips, I want to feel your sexy legs wrapped around my waist as I hold onto all those luscious curves of yours."

She just nods her head at me. She doesn't move away from me, instead I feel her lean into me a little bit. It wasn't much but it was enough for her breasts to rub against my chest. Taking her cues I grip her chin in between my thumb and forefinger, forcing her gaze to stay locked on mine. Our lips are centimeters away but I don't make another move. I stay like that for a second, restraining myself with more self-control than I knew I had. I told her we would go at her pace and I intend to keep my word, but damn it if she isn't making it difficult.

Finally, after what seems like a short eternity, she leans up and plants her lips against mine softly. She lets out a soft sigh that I take full advantage of. My tongue finds its way into her soft, warm mouth. I could live there it's so perfect.

"I want that, too," she whispers so quietly, so sweetly I'm afraid it was just my imagination.

Pulling away while things are heating up, but before they get out of control, again, I smile at her and plant a chaste kiss on her forehead. "So, Zhoe. What's the plan?"

She smiles softly at me, the pretty pink tint back on her cheeks. "I only live a few blocks away." I let out the breath I didn't know I was holding as I reach for her hand and let her guide me back to her place.

TWELVE

Zhoe

This is your night to be rebellious, remember? You wanted to play with fire. You wanted this dangerous man. It's obvious he wants you, too. Go get him. Show him exactly what he's been drooling over all night. Give him something he'll never forget. Stop being such a little girl, pull up your big girl panties (the sexy ones, of course) and enjoy a night of steamy hot sex with Mr. Sexy-Scary. Jared Roman. Oh my god, even his name is sexy.

The walk back to my apartment is made in complete silence except for the inner monologue in my head. It's a good thing he can't read my thoughts because if he could, he'd definitely be running in the opposite direction at this point.

The whole way, he never lets go of my hand, rubbing his thumb in gentle caresses back and forth. It's a soothing gesture, which is ironic to me considering how hot and heavy this night started and will more than likely end up. It's an effective move, though I'll give him that. By the time we're walking up to my front door I'm so turned on I can hardly see straight.

I'm fumbling through my small clutch purse frantically searching for my key when I feel Jared's strong hand apply pressure on top of mine. He pulls my purse out of my hands pulling the key from inside. I know my face has to be beet red for the tenth time tonight. He must think I'm so nervous and inexperienced when in reality I'm shaking because the fire he started at the bar is burning me from the inside out agonizingly.

The fire is burning so hot and slow it feels like I'll die if he doesn't put it out. I take the key from his hand and thankfully manage to insert it in the lock quickly and gracefully. As soon as the door closes behind us though, the grace ends.

Before I can even process what happened, I find myself in the same position I was at the bar. My back pressed against the wall and my legs wrapped around Jared's waist. I've always been a little envious of Angelica's height but right now I'm so glad I'm small enough for this man to be able to pick me up.

We only stay like that for a few minutes tasting each other before Jared turns and heads towards the living room. He walks through my place like he's been here before, like he knows exactly where the couch is. As soon as he finds it he sets me down in front of the large sectional, taking a step back to look down at me.

"Take off the dress, Zhoe." His voice his low and raspy and the command sends a rush of wetness to my panties. I've never been with a controlling man, especially in the bedroom.

Oh, I've read about plenty of them and the fictional bad-boys never fail to turn me on. But, I've never been privy to having a real life bad boy in my bed, or living room before. I can't believe how fucking hot it is.

Not wasting another moment I reach behind me and pull down the zipper letting the dress fall to the floor and pool around my feet. Thankfully I thought to wear some sexy underwear. As I stand before him in my red lace bra and matching thong I've never felt sexier.

Jared rakes his gaze up and down my body numerous times. With one finger he reaches into the cup of my bra fingering one nipple lightly. My eyes close and my head falls back on a light moan, who knew just that simple touch could feel so good.

Apparently just a finger wasn't enough for him because Jared's giant hands pull the cups down enough to expose my nipples, pushing my breasts high on my chest. Almost instantly his mouth closes around my nipple, licking and biting in the most painfully gentle way.

I let out a soft whimper when he pulls away, his eyes reluctantly move from my partially bare chest to my eyes. "The bra, Zhoe."

Again, I don't hesitate. For some reason I'll analyze later, I desperately want to please this man. Much the way I did with my dress, I unhook my bra and let it fall to the floor. I start to reach for my panties, assuming he'll want those gone next but his strong hands stop me. "Let me."

Jared traces a light pattern on my lower belly, just above the band of my panties with the tips of his fingers causing goose bumps to rise on my skin. Finally, his fingers sneak beneath the band, stopping just before he touches me where I really need him, causing me to growl out in frustration.

With a cocky grin he removes his fingers and grabs the side of my panties slowly dragging them down my legs, moving down with them until my panties are off and he's on his knees before me.

I look down my body to see him staring back up at me with lust filled eyes. Holy shit, that is a fucking sexy sight. So sexy in fact I may have let out a little whimper. "Sit down, Pretty Girl. I've got you," Jared says with a cocky smirk on his beautiful face.

Once I'm seated he lifts my left leg placing soft, wet kisses from my ankle to the inside of my thigh where he spends a little extra time sucking and biting before placing it over his shoulder. He repeats his actions on the right leg. With both legs draped over his shoulder I'm very aware of how open and vulnerable I am at the moment. But, fuck it! Everything he's doing feels so damn good and he hasn't even touched me in my most sensitive spots.

There is no way in hell I'm stopping him now.

Thirteen

Jared

    Jesus. This girl is so insanely sexy. She responds to me like no one else I've ever been with; with her legs draped over my shoulders and my nose pressed against her center the sight of her wetness is enough to make me almost explode in my pants. I run my nose against her folds scenting her. "You smell so good, Pretty Girl. Tell me what you want."
    "You. Please. Touch me. Lick me. Do *something*."
    Her response amuses me. Her voice is barely more than a whisper, her throat thick with arousal. I will gladly lick her clean, especially if she tastes as good as she smells. I flatten my tongue and rub it across her clit once. Her head falls back on a loud moan before her hands reach down desperately trying to find purchase in my hair.
    She gives up trying to grab my hair and instead palms the back of my head and pulls my face back down to her core, at the same time she uses her heels to push my upper body closer.
    "More," she's practically growling. I love being in control in bed and I love a girl that submits, but a girl that knows what she wants is equally as hot.
    Deciding I've tortured both of us enough I spear my tongue, finally getting inside of her wet pussy. It's everything I hoped and more. She's hot, warm and so fucking wet. She tastes like honey. I can't get enough.
    "Oh god. Yes. Don't stop." Not that I want to stop, but there is no way I could. She's practically holding me captive to her body. Her hands are putting pressure on the back of my head making sure I don't leave where she needs me most, her heels are painfully digging into my back telling me how much more she needs and her back is arching off the couch trying desperately to get closer to my mouth.

Slowly I lick my way around her lips, making sure to caress every single inch of her sex. When I reach her clit, I bite down before sucking it into my mouth, causing her to scream out. Her moans aren't words, just sounds of pure unadulterated pleasure and it's so fucking sexy. My cock jumps at the sound, it's so hard it's damn near painful. I let out a growl of my own.

Watching her body react to my touch so violently is the sexiest fucking thing I've ever seen. "Open your eyes. I want to watch you come," I growl onto her lower lips. As soon as she opens her eyes I insert two fingers and use my tongue to massage her clit. I can see her fighting to keep her eyes open, trying to fight against her orgasm, "let go, Pretty Girl. I want you to come all over my mouth."

"Oh God!" She's screaming now, her body writhing so much I have to remove my fingers from her center using both to apply pressure to her thighs, holding her in place. My mouth has to take over doing all the work but still I don't stop. I can't stop.

I continue lavishing her with my tongue. Alternating between licking and sucking her clit and fucking her sex with it. When she can't take anymore she lets out a loud whimper, her hips grinding relentlessly on my face, as she comes against my lips just like I told her to.

Even as the aftershocks of her orgasm die down I can't bring myself to remove my mouth. She tastes and smells and feels too good.

I don't stop until I feel her hands on my shoulders practically shoving me away, "Jared. Oh my god. You have to stop. It's too much." With one last wet kiss on her little bud, I pull away. Still on my knees, fully dressed I look up Zhoe's delicious body to find her breasts moving up and down with each rapid breath she takes. Her eyes are closed, her head lulled off to one side of her body. Fucking gorgeous.

As badly as I want to be inside her tonight, I know it's not going to happen. She's spent. I pick her up from the couch, cradling her to my body. Her arms automatically wrap around my neck, her head on my shoulder, her eyes still closed. "Where's your room, beautiful?"

"Upstairs, on the right," she mumbles against my chest. I couldn't help but kiss her head. She looks so sexy and sated and innocent, such a heady combination. There is something about this girl that calls to me. I know now that I'm not going to be able to just walk away. I need more. Way more.

Pulling the covers back with one arm, still holding her weight with the other, I gently place her on the bed and cover her delicious body with the blanket. Again I lean down and place a few soft kisses on her forehead and cheeks. "Sleep, Pretty Girl."

I stare down at her for a few moments categorizing her face; noticing things I hadn't in the dark bar. Her nose is covered in freckles; her eyelashes are so damn long they are practically resting on her cheekbones. I'm well aware of how her skin feels under my hands now, but I hadn't noticed how creamy and perfect it is. This girl is so gorgeous and I'd be willing to bet she doesn't even know how stunning she really is.

Grudgingly, I make myself take a few steps back from the bed. How odd that I want to stay all night. I've been with plenty of women over the years, never once have I wanted to spend the night with them.

Deciding it's best that I leave I find a notebook on her dresser, leaving a note on her nightstand – hoping she understands this was not a one-night stand. With one last gentle kiss I walk out, knowing it won't be long before I see her again.

Fourteen

Zhoe

It's been two days since Jared gave me the best orgasm I've ever had, carried me to bed and left me a sweet note to wake up to. Since then though, it's been radio silence. I can't contact him since I don't have his number or any information about him except for his name. Jared, however has my number and still has yet to call me.

His note led me to believe I'd be hearing from him, which only confuses me even more when I think about the fact that he hasn't. I woke up that morning feeling sore and satisfied, a feeling I haven't felt in far too long. When I first rolled over I was disappointed to find the other side of my bed empty. But, then I noticed his note:

I can't wait to see you again, Beautiful. –J

I mean it's not like the note was cryptic or I'm some stupid girl reading too much into things. He spelled it all out for me - he wants to see me again. So why the fuck hasn't he called?

I will myself to stop thinking about him, to stop obsessing over his call. I definitely need to stop dreaming about the way his tongue felt pressed against me and getting angry at the fact I didn't get to see an inch of his rock hard body.

Remind me again how I ended up naked and spread-eagled on my couch, letting a stranger lick me to the best orgasm I've ever had while said stranger remained completely clothed? Probably not the classiest moment in my life. Though, it was definitely the most satisfying.

Growling my frustrations I throw back the covers and storm into the guest room to wake up Angelica. "Ang!" I shake her a little knowing there is no way she heard me call her name, that girl could sleep through a bombing. "Ang. Get your lazy ass up. We're going to the gym." I desperately need to work out these frustrations.

"No," she growls into her pillow. "I don't wanna."

"Please?" She may come across as a hard ass but she has never been able to turn me down when I result to begging. She rolls over to face me, giving me the most evil look she can muster considering she only opened one eye.

"Fine. But only because you asked nicely. I'll be ready in ten." Smacking her ass and thanking her for being the best friend ever, I head to my room to get ready, too.

Angelica and I joined a kickboxing gym a few months back. We usually only go once or twice a week but today it's exactly what I need. I'm eager to relieve some of my anger, and I'm hoping a session at the gym will do the trick. I waste no time throwing a few warm-up punches as soon as I grab a bag.

"Whoa. You okay there killer?" Angelica shouts to me over the music and rhythmic punching of dozens of fists pummeling punching bags.

"Perfect," I grunt out while laying into my bag as hard as I can. I may or may not be picturing a certain sex-god's face while doing it. I mean seriously, how dare he go down on me, not ask for anything in return, leave me a sweet note and then not fucking call me. Asshole.

"He's going to call, Zhoe. Give him a few days." I just glare at her over my shoulder before turning to land a roundhouse kick into the bag. Obviously my friend knows me too well. Mental note: remember to never give the dirty details to Ang next time you're *not* bringing home another random guy from the bar. Lesson learned.

After a hardcore forty-five minute workout beating the shit out of something, I'm feeling much better. I've decided I don't care if he calls. It was a successful night on my part. I rebelled, I had fun, I had a damn good orgasm thanks to a sexy guy and I didn't have to return the favor. All and all, the night was a win for me. Now, I can forget about Jared Roman and move on with my life. It's his loss anyways.

"Feel better now?" Angelica asks as I wipe my face with a towel.

"Yep." I down a huge gulp of water before turning back to her. "I've decided it's his loss. Moving on."

"Yo! Roman, what's up man?" *You have got to be kidding me.*

"Well, you may want to disappear then. And fast," Ang informs me.

I turn towards the voice calling out the name I just swore I was going to forget, just to make sure he isn't talking about *my* Roman.

But, of course that's not how my life works. As soon as I turn I see a sweaty Jared barreling across the room in my direction. How the fuck can he look so great after working out? I want to smack him and then lick the sweat off his massive biceps that are on display under his black workout tank. *Great, just great.* I probably look like ass; it's no wonder he didn't call.

"Zhoe! Wait up!" I turn and push my way through the few people trying to get out the front door. As soon as I make it outside, I take a right and start power walking towards my apartment hoping he doesn't follow. I don't turn back to check. But, then again I really don't have to.

I only make it about a block before I feel his strong hand grip my elbow effectively bringing me to a halt in the middle of the sidewalk. "Why you running, Pretty Girl?" He turns my body to face his. But before I can think of a witty come back about how I always run from guys that know how to work their tongues but apparently not a phone, I'm pressed against a brick building and Jared's large body is covering me. Again.

Seconds after that, his lips come down on mine, crushing them in a brutally carnal, wet kiss. I can't help but react to this man. My body and my head are operating on two different wavelengths. *You're supposed to be pissed at him, damn it! Play hard to get for once will you?* My brain is literally screaming at my body. But, he's too good. My body knows what he can offer and wants more. Always more.

"God damn, Zhoe. I've missed those lips of yours."

At that, I shove him back with every ounce of strength I have left. Why did I use so much energy pretending to punch his face again? If I knew he was there the whole time I would have punched the real thing.

"As long as I'm not using them for talking?" I challenge him, quirking one eyebrow at him.

After a long pause I turn to walk away from him again, but his arms come around me from behind successfully stopping my escape. I feel his breath on my neck before I hear him whisper, "I'm sorry. I planned on calling today. Do you forgive me?" His lips managed to find their way to the sensitive skin under my ear where he shows me all over again just how talented that mouth of his is. "Do you forgive me, Zhoe?" God, that voice.

I'm powerless to this man; all I can do is nod my assent. "Good girl. I don't mind having your body pressed against mine but do you think you can behave yourself if I let you go? Are you going to run away from me again?"

Behave myself? Good girl? Who the hell does this man think he is? And why the hell am I suddenly so fucking turned on I can't even stand on my own? I clear my throat a few times before I'm finally able to speak. "I won't run." With one last kiss on my neck Jared releases his hold on me.

I'm almost knocked flat on my ass once I turn around and get a good look at him. If I thought he was gorgeous in a dark bar, it's nothing to how stunning he is now. His eyes are such a unique color brown, they remind me of milk chocolate. His muscles and tattoos are mouthwatering; his arms are so huge it would probably take both of my hands to wrap all the way around them.

The workout tank he's wearing fits him like a second skin leaving very little to the imagination. I can see the ridges of his abs – I'm pretty sure there are six of them, but I remind myself to do a thorough investigation later when the shirt is gone. His legs are strong and covered with dark hair. Everything about him screams "man!"

When my gaze finally makes its way up his body, I see him taking in me, too. I feel more self-conscience now than I did flat on back two days ago. I'm wearing black compression capris and a bright pink yoga tank, with a built in bra. Yeah, my workout gear isn't leaving much to the imagination either. Plus, I'm a hot, sweaty mess from my workout. It can't be an attractive sight.

"Do you even know how fucking sexy you are?" Jared asks, breaking me out of my reverie. I scoff at him; just add that to my not-sexy qualities list. Who scoffs? Jared reaches out grabbing my hip and dragging me back into him. "You are too sexy for your own good."

Now that I'm fully pressed against him, Jared wastes no time taking advantage of the situation. His hands once again dig into my ass as a sexy growl leaves his lips. I press up on the balls of my feet at the same time he leans down, our lips meeting perfectly in the middle to tangle in a sexy, too hot for the street kiss.

"Come to dinner with me tonight," he breathes against my lips barely pulling away from me.

It's not really a question. He knows I'm going to say yes. "Okay."

He flashes me the same cocky smirk he was wearing the other night. "I'll pick you up at seven." With that he places a closed-mouth kiss on my lips and walks away, leaving me standing in the middle of the sidewalk staring after him with my mouth wide open like an idiot.

I hear Angelica before I see her. I have no idea how long she was standing there since I left the gym without saying a word to her in a mad dash to get away from Jared. Unsuccessfully. "Close your mouth. We've got work to do!" She pulls me behind her toward the apartment. "Shower first, then lunch and shopping. You desperately need some new panties. I know you had on your only sexy pair the other night and he cannot see you in the same ones. Then I'll help you do your hair and makeup for your hot date with Mr. Sexy-Scary. Deal?"

I just nod and smile at her. God, I love this girl. What would I do without her?

Fifteen

Zhoe

I'm exhausted. After spending several hours shopping for the perfect outfit for tonight's date all I want to do is curl up in bed and sleep until I have to leave. Jared saw me at my worst this morning – no makeup, hair in a messy bun on top of my head, in sweaty workout clothes – surely he won't mind taking me out for pizza in jeans and a hoodie, right?

"No. Nope," Angelica chides me for trying to sit down. "I didn't spend all day shopping so you could bail out. Get up and get in the shower." Grunting I manage to get my ass into the shower. "Oh and make sure you shave… everything." I hear my friend's sing-songy voice through the bathroom door.

This better be a damn good date for all this trouble I'm going through. I couldn't make a decision to save my life today so I ended up buying three different outfits: a cobalt blue wrap dress with three-quarter length sleeves and a plunging neck line; red skinny jeans with a black blazer and sky high black stilettos, or the same blazer paired with high-waisted grey shorts and black tights. Ang said she'd make the decision for me while I was in the shower.

I hate when a guy asks you out but you're not sure where you're going so you have no idea what to wear. If I wear the shorts and we're going to some high-end restaurant I'll stick out like a sore thumb. The same goes for the dress if we're going to a sports bar. It would be nice if a man could look at your outfit and change the plans to fit what you're wearing, but they just don't understand those things.

I take my time in the shower letting the hot water ease some of the tension in my shoulders from today's shopping excursion. I take Angelica's advice and shave… everything. Well, okay not everything, but mostly everything. Once I'm buffed, polished and shined I walk into my bedroom.

As if she could read my mind I see the jeans and blazer lying on the bed when I emerge from the bathroom, "I figured this is a pretty safe choice, no matter where he takes you. Plus, it seems like his style. So..."

"It's perfect. It's actually the one I was hoping you'd pick. Thanks." I sit down in front my vanity in my bedroom and close my eyes trying to calm myself before tonight. I think I'm nervous because I've built him up in my head – sexy, good in bed, strong, great dancer, controlling – but tonight is my chance to actually get to know him. What if I don't like him? What if he doesn't like me?

Dating has always been easy for me before tonight probably because I knew the two relationships I entered weren't going to last the long haul, not that I'm thinking Jared and I are meant for each other either. But, tonight is different. He's different.

My first serious boyfriend was in high school. We met through our parents, since I attended an all-girls school. His family was wealthy and snotty and he was the same, but I was sixteen and he was a senior with a fast car and good looks. Plus, he was the guy all of the girls wanted which made me want him, too. We dated for two years, until I visited him in his dorm room and found him sleeping with someone who obviously wasn't me. I probably should have been upset or hurt but I felt relieved – clue number one he wasn't the guy I was supposed to end up with.

My second boyfriend and I met my freshman year in college. Ang and I went to a Frat party on campus at his house. He was tall and thin but well built. He was intelligent and seemed to have a good head on his shoulders – I was instantly drawn to him. After a year or so of dating we just fell apart. We realized we were more friends than boyfriend-girlfriend. It was a mutual breakup and drama free. I still see him on campus every now and then and we're friendly to each other, but never once have I thought to myself *I miss him, I want him back*.

So here I am, two years later, in my junior year of college completely single. It's never bothered me before. I mean I have Ang and we have other girlfriends, we go out and party and I don't have to answer to anyone. I have my B.O.B. so I don't really need a man for that either. But, ever since Jared blew into my life this past week I can't help thinking about how nice it would be to have someone in my life to care for me and make me smile and love me.

"Okay, all done," Angelica's voice snaps me out of my thoughts. I open my eyes and smile through the mirror at my best friend. My hair is swept to one side of my head and secured in a ponytail with a few pieces left out to fall around my face and ears, making it look like I meant for it to be messy. My makeup is done perfectly, black eyeliner and mascara, light blush and bright red lipstick.

I finish off the look with the skin-tight red jeans, white silk blouse, black blazer and black pumps, and a matching set of black pearl earrings and drape necklace. Taking one last look in the mirror I decide I'm good to go. I feel sexy and edgy, but still classy and put together.

"Damn, girl. You'll have him eating you out in no time. Oh wait…"

"Oh my god! I'm never telling you anything again!" I feign annoyance but I have to admit that was a good one and can't help but laugh at my friend.

"Yeah right. After all the work I put into getting you ready today, I deserve details…lots and lots of juicy details. I'm talking, don't hold anything back. I want to know the length, the girth, the…" Before she can say anymore the doorbell rings.

"Saved by the bell," I mumble lamely. A quick glance at my clock tells me he's right on time. I wonder how long he sat in his car so he wasn't early? I smile at the thought; maybe he's just as anxious and excited as I am.

Sixteen

Jared

I just about swallowed my tongue when Zhoe opened her front door. I dropped the small bouquet of purple flowers unceremoniously on the floor, dragging her body into mine so I could taste her before either of us even got a word out.

Moving my lips against the soft skin under her ear I hum, "I'm not going to kiss your perfect lips because I don't want to mess up your fuck-me lipstick…yet. But I have to taste you. You look absolutely delicious."

I move my lips from there, then down her neck, to her collarbone that is just barely visible under the top of her shirt. Moving back up I nip at her jaw, traveling back to her ear I suck her lobe between my lips, "delicious."

Zhoe still hasn't said a word, not "thanks," or even "hi." She just stood there and let me ravish her neck. Once I had enough to hold me over, I grabbed her hand and drug her to the car, afraid we'd never leave if we didn't right that moment.

"Don't worry, I'll clean up this mess, and lock up. Have fun you two," I hear her friend call out to us.

It's not until I have her tucked into the truck and am backing out of the parking spot that she finally speaks. "So are you going to tell me where we're going?"

"Oh good. I thought maybe I rendered you speechless back there."

"You're good, but you're not *that* good," she jokes right back with a smug grin on her face. I know I affected her, but there's no way she's going to admit it. I also know she's still upset with me for never calling her. I plan on making it up to her all night.

"I thought we'd start at the Ale Shack, if that's okay. If not, we'll go wherever you want." The Ale Shack serves the best burgers in town and brews their own beer. She seems like a burgers and beer kind of girl, so I'm hoping I pinned her right. *Please don't let her be a five-star restaurant type.*

I hear her moan her approval causing my dick to jump. Holy shit, she cannot make those noises all night. All I can think about now is what she sounded like as I ate her to oblivion the other night. Fuck, now I can't stop thinking about the way she tasted on my tongue. Think about the Reds, about last night's win and Joey Votto's walk-off home run. Think about freaking anything but the way this girl makes my dick rock hard without even trying.

"Oh my god. I love that place." She's really talking about food right now? All I can think about is fucking her in the cab of my truck and she's talking about burgers. What the hell? "Their Lonestar burger is by far my favorite thing ever." When I glance over at her catching sight of her smile I swear right then and there to do whatever I can to keep it on her face. I must have some sort of goofy look on my face because she asks, "Why are you looking at me like that? Can't handle a girl that actually eats?"

"Actually it's really fucking sexy watching girls eat." I hate girls that pretend to want a salad. No girl actually wants to eat a fucking salad, especially when they can have a juicy burger instead.

"Glad to hear it, because I can eat you under the table."

I lean over, trailing my hand from her knee up her thigh. "That's okay. I'd much rather eat you anyways." She turns away from me a blush coloring her cheeks, this makes me laugh – this girl is too much.

Zhoe isn't the type of girl to let me have the last say though, looking over at me with her lip between her teeth, her eyes hooded she purrs, "I can't wait, handsome."

A strained growl leaves my mouth, as I shift uncomfortably in my seat trying to adjust my now way too tight jeans. When she busts out laughing I realize she just beat me at my own game. I only stew on that thought for a moment though, too lost in her laugh.

If I thought her smile was perfect, her laugh is even more infectious. She doesn't hold back. She full out laughs at her own joke. That laugh might one of the sexiest things she's done yet. Sexier than the tight red pants and the red I-want-to-fuck lipstick, sexier than the way she moaned my name the other night, sexier than the way she moves on the dance floor. Fuck it, this girl is sexy – everything about her.

"You have a great laugh." For a girl that just belly laughed at her own awful joke and is proud of how much food she can eat, I wouldn't expect a compliment to embarrass her, but it does. Her cheeks tint a beautiful color pink before she ducks her head and mumbles her thanks. If her laugh was sexy, her blush is damn cute. I want more of both from her tonight and I intend to get them.

Zhoe reaches out to turn the radio up as if the music will protect her from my attention and my compliments. She flips through the stations until she finds one she likes. She closes her eyes, her head bobbing back and forth, her lips are moving to the words of the song. I am definitely more of a rock guy but watching her sing about dancing in skintight jeans and getting some is almost enough to sway my tastes to country.

At a red light I reach over, unbuckling her seat belt and grab her thigh, sliding her across the bench so she's sitting in the middle seat right next to me. Needing her close to me.

"What the hell?"

"Keep singing, Pretty Girl." As expected she blushes and stops singing and dancing. I let out a little laugh. "What song was that?"

"'Get Me Some of That' by Thomas Rhett."

"Mmm. I liked it. It's fitting." She laughs lightly and relaxes back into my touch.

Placing the truck in park I squeeze her thigh to get her attention. "Don't get out." As soon as I'm standing, I reach back to grab her around the waist, sliding her towards me. I lift her out of my door and into my body.

"I could have done that myself, Jared." She glares up at me, but with the hint of a smirk on her lips.

"I know, but I wanted an excuse to touch you."

"What made you think you needed an excuse?"

Again, I growl pressing her into the side of the truck. "You're killing me, baby. You have to stop saying things like that." She just winks and shimmies out of my grasp, leading the way into the restaurant.

Once we're seated, we ordered right away, neither of us needing to look at the menu. As promised Zhoe ordered the Lonestar burger which is topped with BBQ sauce, cheese and bacon. There is no way she can eat all of that. She surprises me by ordering a dark beer. I also ordered a dark beer as well, but I stick with a plain cheeseburger, to which Zhoe calls me out.

"I can't believe out of all those choices you choose the one thing on the menu you can get from McDonalds." She's visibly upset by my choice in food which makes me laugh.

"First of all, I can't get a pound and half burger at McDonalds with aged cheddar and provolone. Second of all, the burgers here are so good you don't need to mask them with all that other crap that's on yours."

"Whatever. Have you ever even tried the Lonestar burger?"

"Nope. I get the same thing every time I come here. Have you ever tried their plain cheeseburger?" I throw her question back at her.

"Nope. I eat that every time I grill out." Her snarky response makes me grin. I love that she's not afraid to offend me or put me in place. This girl is definitely not shy.

"Okay," I say, trying to smooth things over, "how about we agree to disagree?"

"Deal." She takes a large drink of her beer, glancing around the restaurant before focusing her attention back on me. "So, how long have you been going to Five Rounds? I'm surprised I've never seen you there before."

This surprises me, too. I've only been going there for a few months but the classes aren't overly large maybe 10-12 people per class. I definitely would have noticed her tight little body before.

"Just a few months. I only go on the weekends though, maybe that's why we've never seen each other?"

"Probably. Angelica and I rarely go on Saturdays, they are our sleep-in days."

"What made you decide to go today?"

She looks at me for a minute trying to decide what to say. "I needed to work out some frustrations."

"Well, it's a good thing you were there today. Otherwise we may not be here right now."

I see it in her eyes before the words come out of her mouth. She's getting ready to let me have it. I knew she was still upset that I hadn't called yet, which is exactly why I brought it up.

She's insanely sexy when she's upset.

"Or you could have just called me and asked me out like a normal person." She quirks one perfect eyebrow at me, like she knows I'm going to give her some lame excuse.

"Zhoe, I'm sorry. You're right, I should have called and made plans but I'm new to this. I haven't dated anyone in, well in ever really. You'll have to cut me some slack, okay?" I'm a pro at one-night stands but real relationships have never been on my radar. Until now.

"Why should I cut you some slack? You left a note practically promising a phone call and you didn't follow through on your word." Her words seem clingy and needy, but the tone of her voice and body language tell me she's anything but. She's not telling me these things to make me feel bad; she just wants me to know how she's feeling. She's honest and blunt and it's a refreshing change from the girls I usually deal with.

"Isn't it enough to know I want to be here with you? I couldn't stop thinking about you. I couldn't stop thinking about how you felt and tasted and sounded when you came on my tongue. I've been dying to see you again." The more I talked, the more prominent her blushing got.

"Shh." She looks around to see if anyone heard what I'd said. "I forgive you, just keep it down." Fuck that blush she's wearing has me hard as a rock, well that and remembering the other night.

"In all seriousness, I'm sorry I didn't call, Zhoe. You intimidate me. You're so damn beautiful. You're sweet and sexy and confident. You overwhelm me."

"That was a pretty good line, Stud." She smiles at me and I feel like the whole room just got a little brighter.

"It wasn't a line, baby. It's the truth. I guess the smashed flowers in your entryway are something else I should apologize for, huh?"

She laughs again and I feel like every man in the bar watches her as she elegantly drops her head back and lets out a loud, throaty laugh. I completely forget what we're talking about; suddenly all I can focus on is the column of her neck. I want to put my lips on it, again, kissing her from the base up to her jaw, then over to her plump lips. Over and over again.

She clears her throat and when I move my eyes back up to hers I see my emotions reflected back at me. "I forgive you for the flowers, especially if you keep looking at me like that." As if that's going to be an issue. Sex seems to be all I can think about when I'm around this girl.

"Look at you like what?" I challenge. I wonder what side of her I'm going to get – the cocky, sexy girl or the shy girl who's afraid our dirty words are going to be overheard.

"Like you want to devour me." I shift in my seat, trying to relieve some of the pressure in my jeans. Apparently she chose to go with the sexy side.

"Mmm. That's because I do. You're dessert." I expected her to blush again but instead she looks at me from under her insanely long eyelashes, as she pulls her bottom lip into her mouth. *Fuck, why is that so damn sexy*? I lean toward her across the table. "You better let go of that lip, Zhoe, before I take you out to the truck and give you everything you're asking for and more."

Immediately her lip pops free as she lets out a soft little whimper. This girl is driving me insane. I reach down adjusting my jeans, trying to prevent the zipper from digging into my rock-hard cock. I just smile at her and shake my head. I need to get us back on safer ground; all this dirty talk is too dangerous for a public setting.

Thankfully our server dropped our food off then. Giving me a minute to adjust my pants for what feels like the tenth time tonight.

With the sexual tension brewing on the backburner we were able to move to lighter subjects. I learned that she and Angelica had been friends since they were babies. Her favorite color is purple and her favorite flowers are tulips.

We never really touched personal subjects, choosing instead to stay to lighter ones. We laughed and joked – I love that she can take a little ribbing. Every time I'd tease her about something she'd find something to tease me about right back. As promised, Zhoe finished her entire burger and most of her fries, shocking the hell out of me. She even took a bite or two from my burger, claiming hers was much better. It was fun and relaxed and enjoyable – I hope our night won't end here.

Seventeen
Zhoe

I have no idea how I managed to get through dinner. Every time Jared looked at me I thought my clothes were just going to magically melt off of me. Secretly, I kept wishing his clothes would magically disappear, too. Aside from the scorching looks we kept giving each other the date went wonderfully; there were never any awkward moments, even the silence was comfortable.

Even when things were new and fresh and exciting with my ex, I never felt like this. It's disconcerting the things Jared is already making me feel.

Jared makes me feel sexy and special and interesting. He actually listens to me when I tell him something and when he asks a question it's because he's genuinely interested in my answer, he's not asking it because it's what you do on a first date.

He also makes me feel safe and protected. As we made our way through the restaurant and parking lot, Jared held his hand firmly on my lower back. I felt as if no one could get to me, except for the one guy I desperately wanted to.

"So, what would you like to do next?" he asks once we're both buckled in to his beat-up Chevy truck.

"All you planned was dinner?" I ask him sarcastically.

He actually looks a little sheepish before answering. "Yeah. Sorry. Was I supposed to plan more?"

I can't help but laugh at him. This big, macho, controlling man is asking me what he's supposed to do on a date. He looks so unsure it's quite entertaining. That is until I turn to see him glaring at me. "I'm sorry. It's just ironic how such a big, scary guy can look so insecure. Why don't we just go back to my place? I have a few beers in the fridge, we can just relax and hang out a bit."

After a few moments where he doesn't make a move or a sound I start to feel bad for laughing at him. Riding the high of how he makes me feel, I scoot towards him on the bench seat with more confidence than I usually have. I lean towards him and mumble against his mouth, "I'm sorry for laughing at you." I place few wet kisses on his lips. God, his lips are addicting. "Want to go back to my place or do something else?"

He lets out a manly growl before gripping the back of my head in one of his palms. His hands are so big I swear my whole head fits in his palm perfectly. His tongue massages my bottom lip a few times demanding I let him in. I can't help but comply; my body is completely powerless to this man.

With a final kiss placed firmly on my lips he backs away from my face, his signature smirk in place. Turning away from me he turns the car on and puts it in gear, acting completely unaffected. Meanwhile, I'm staring at him longing for more, begging the traffic gods for clear roads.

"Your place it is, gorgeous," he brings me into his side with an arm wrapped securely around my shoulders. I let out a little giggle that I try to cover with my hand before Jared notices. I've never giggled in my life, what the hell is this man doing to me? "Did you just giggle?" Jared asks me like he can't believe it either.

Straightening my back I look straight ahead before answering. "Absolutely not. I do not giggle."

He busts out laughing at me. "I made you giggle. Do it again!"

I look at him like he's lost his damn mind. "What? First of all, I don't giggle and even if I did, I can't do it on command."

We're stopped at a red light now. I can feel his gaze on the side of my face. He leans down towards me and I can feel his lips in my hair. "Sure thing, Pretty Girl. I'll get that cute-as-hell sound out of you again. Don't worry."

At that I roll my eyes. I'll be damned if I ever giggle again in my life.

***

"Do you want a beer?" I ask once we're in the door. I'm already heading to the kitchen needing a bit of distance between the two of us. I talked up big game in the car, but now that we're here I'm feeling a little nervous. I know we've already done quite a bit but I'm not sure I'm ready to go any farther than we already have.

The problem is, I can't seem to stop things once we get going. It's obvious we're attracted to each other. It's even more obvious he wants to have sex with me. I mean, he practically spelled it out for me at dinner. I just don't think I'm ready to go that far, just yet.

As if he can hear my thoughts, Jared walks up behind me placing both hands on the closed fridge door, trapping me against his chest. *So much for distance*, I think to myself.

"Relax, Zhoe. We don't have to do anything you don't want to do. We don't have to do anything at all. I just want to spend time with you, okay?"

I try to clear my throat a few times but it's not working so I just nod my head at him instead. See, this is exactly that I'm talking about. The second he touches me, it doesn't matter where or how, my brain shuts down. The only thing I can do is feel.

Right now all I feel is him. The way his hard chest is pressed against my back, the way his strong arms are caging me in, the hotness of his breath on my neck, and the smell of his musky, manly scent; he kind of smells like a combination of soap and sawdust. Whatever it is, it's delicious.

I don't know how it happened, it wasn't a conscious decision, but it happened anyways. My head has fallen back to rest on Jared's shoulder, my hands are gripping his strong thighs and my ass is pressed against his groin.

I can feel his erection in my lower back, one of his hands is gripping my hip so hard it's borderline painful, like he's trying to keep from moving it elsewhere. His other hand is resting on my lower belly. I desperately want him to move it lower. I can feel his hot breath on my neck, especially when he whispers against it. "Tell me what you want, baby."

On a groan, I start to move. I start to grind against his hard body. The way we're wrapped around each other, moving together, is more fitting for the dance floor of a trashy club - not for the middle of my kitchen with no music. Yet, here we are, moving seamlessly together.

"Jared..." I'm not sure what I'm asking for, or even if I'm asking for anything at all. I could stay like this all night. I feel safe and sexy at the same time.

"What do you want, Zho?" Jared whispers against my neck. His lips have started marking a trail from my ear down to my collarbone. "Tell me, baby. I'll give you anything you want, you just have to tell me."

He makes it sound so easy.

With my brain no longer operating, my body takes over. "Take me upstairs, Jared." My voice is low and raspy but I know he heard me loud and clear.

The second the words are out of my throat Jared takes a step back, pushing me in the direction of the living room. "Lead the way."

I walk quickly to the stairs, eager to get to the bedroom. I look longingly at the couch as we pass by it; the bedroom is just so damn far.

"I want you in bed, Zhoe." Jared's voice growls from behind me, giving me a smack on the ass. I take the hint and hustle up the stairs and down the hall. Stopping in front of the bed I turn in time to see Jared take a few more steps into my space.

His hands wrap in my hair as he consumes my mouth. His kisses are hard, hungry and almost desperate. He holds nothing back as he tastes every inch of my mouth, alternating between sucking my tongue and nibbling my lips.

Once he's taken his fill of my mouth, he looks down at me with a deadly quirk of his lips and a dangerous gleam in his eye. He makes quick work of undoing and removing my jeans. Deciding to help him out, I remove my jacket and blouse. I'm left standing in front of him in my new lingerie and my long pearl necklace that is resting perfectly in my cleavage.

He takes in my matching set of black lace bra and boy shorts for several moments, at one point he licks his lips, causing me to moan. "You are too fucking sexy, Zhoe. Do you know how sexy you are?"

"I want to see you." I ignore his compliments, too eager to see his body. "Please." I reach up grasping the hem of his T-shirt and pulling it over his head. "Jesus."

"What?" He looks down at me, confused. I realized I said that one word like something was wrong. But there is absolutely nothing wrong with the sight in front of me. He is fucking ripped. His shoulders look massive with nothing covering them. His pecs hard and defined and holy shit don't even get me started on his abs.

Flattening my hands on him I run them slowly down his washboard abs, counting all six ridges as I go. "You're beautiful." One arm is completely covered in vibrant, beautiful works of art. I want to take the time to admire each piece but now is not the time. Later, I remind myself.

"I think that's my line," he says as he pulls my chin up to look at him. He places several closed-mouth kisses on my lips. "You are stunning. Fucking perfect."

Removing my mouth from his, I trail kisses down his chest and stomach until I reach the waist of his dark jeans. Without hesitating or bothering to ask for permission, I unbutton them and lower the zipper.

Jared must be getting anxious because he clutches the waistband in his hands and pulls them down his legs. Leaving him standing there in nothing but skin tight, black, cotton boxer briefs that leave little to the imagination.

His briefs are tented very obviously where his massive erection is straining to be freed. Deciding to help it out I reach into his boxers and pull him out, reveling in the way he feels in my hand. I knew he'd be big, but he's fucking huge. Swallowing the lump in my throat I look up at him and am met with eyes dark and hooded.

"Jared…" I hesitate. "I'm, I'm not ready for this to go all the way just yet."

Eighteen

Jared

Jesus. A man only has so much self-control. Fighting the urge to throw her pretty, little body onto the bed and fuck her senseless I will myself to slow down. If she isn't ready, I can wait. I can go at her pace. Even if it feels like it's going to kill me.

"I told you we don't have to do anything you don't want to," I breathe against her neck. Her grip on my cock tightens as she runs her tiny hands up and down my length. Moving a half-step back my cock thankfully falls from her hand, reaching down I tuck it back into my boxers.

"Why?" Her bottom lip comes out in the cutest pout.

"If you want me to go slow, you can't touch me like that." Dropping to my knees in front of her I kiss her stomach from hip bone to hip bone. Her fingers grip my hair pushing my face closer to her core. I can't go there yet, though. "Lay back on the bed, baby."

Doing as I asked she lies on her back, her hair fanned out behind her head, her legs spread and her fingers gripping the sheets. She's like a fucking dream come true. I've never seen a sexier sight in my life. I move up the bed until one knee is between her legs, the other on the outside of her thigh - effectively keeping her trapped beneath me.

Reverently, slowly I graze my palms over every inch of skin I can. Her shoulders, her arms, the tops of her breasts barely visible beneath her bra; her eyes close as I grip her breasts in my palms.

"Jare…"

Needing to taste her I drop my lips onto hers. My kisses match the rhythm of my stroking, soft, slow. I kiss every inch of her lips, licking every inch of her mouth until I'm short of breath. Pulling back my words vibrate against her lips, "you're so fucking beautiful, Zhoe."

Zhoe moves her legs out from under mine, bringing them up to wrap around my waist, effectively bringing my body into hers. Thrusting my hips once the head of my cock hits her clit causing a sexy moan to escape her lips. Like a man crazed I slam into her over and over desperate to hear that sound again.

It's my turn to call out when her nails dig painfully into my back. This moment is so amateur - us still partially clothed dry humping on her bed. Yet, when she digs her nails into me, likely drawing blood it becomes erotic, sexy as hell.

Lowering my head I take one of her hardened nipples into my mouth sucking it, pulling back I let it go with a pop before moving to the other. This time I bite down gently, and judging by the loud moans leaving Zhoe's lips she likes the pain.

Looking up at her with her nipple still firmly in my moth I catch her looking down her body at me, her lip between her teeth trapping her tortured sounds. I twist my hips hitting her clit with each rotation and watch in awe as her body starts to tremble beneath mine.

"Oh my god."

Repeating the motion I hit the same spot, sending her spiraling over the edge. Her words are unintelligible as she comes for me. Watching Zhoe come is the most beautiful sight in the world. Her eyes are closed, her head thrown back and her back bowed off the bed; her chest is flushed, her breasts rising with each rapid breath.

"Holy fuck." Collapsing on top of her, I roll quickly to my side wrapping her in my arms.

"Jare, you didn't, um…" Her cheeks blush and I can't help but chuckle at her.

"Shh, that was all for you baby." I place a few soft kisses on the back of her neck. I'm going to have blue balls for days but it was so worth watching her fall apart underneath me like that. The way she responds to my touch is almost too much.

She rolls over placing a few gentle kisses on my lips before trying to sneak out from below me. Grabbing her waist I throw her back on the bed, back underneath me where she belongs. Squealing she does her best to get away but I've got her caged in. With my fingers I start tickling her sides.

"Stop! Oh my gosh, Jared, stop!" She's screaming and laughing and writhing; trying desperately to get away from my touch. After several minutes of torture I finally relent, rolling off of her onto my side. Once she's caught her breath she turns just her head to face me, she's still smiling and I can see a few tears left over from her hysterics. "You're a jerk," she says playfully slapping me on my arm.

Leaning over I kiss her on her nose with a giant, goofy-ass grin on my face. "Sorry."

"No you're not." She's rolled over on her side now, too. We're lying in her bed, me completely naked and her in only her under garments smiling at each other like we've known each other forever. It feels surreal, and comfortable and a little intimidating. I've never felt anything like this with other girls. Actually, I've never really felt anything for other girls, but with her it all feels different.

"No, I'm not sorry. I love hearing your laugh." As expected her face flushes, which only eggs me on. "You have a great laugh. I could listen to it all day."

Choosing to ignore my compliment she starts mindlessly tracing the patterns on my arm. I typically kick the girls I sleep with out of my bed rather quickly, but the one's that have managed to stay for a few hours all felt the need to touch and analyze my tattoos. I don't know why they do it. Maybe they hope they'll gain a little insight into my soul when I tell them what they mean.

What I do know is that I've never told anyone what they mean, not even the tattoo artist inking them on me. But, with Zhoe I find I want to tell her their story, my story. I want her to know me. I'm actually preparing myself mentally to share a small part of my soul with her when, as usual, she does the one thing I'm not expecting her to.

Leaning forward she places her lips on the one tattoo that means the most to me; the one tattoo that connects us in some way. The tattoo is an ink jar and a quill pen; most of the quills are falling off the pen and are stained red. It sits right over my heart. I got it in remembrance of Cole. He dreamed of becoming a famous writer one day, but since I couldn't protect him, I couldn't save him, that dream died right along with him.

Without a word, she removes her lips from my chest, places a soft kiss on my lips and curls her body into mine. I know it's stupid to think like this, but it's as if she knows what that tattoo means to me, that it saddens me to have it and because she knows these things, she doesn't ask the questions I could see in her eyes. Instead she just holds me. Providing comfort in her touch instead of with her words.

I hesitate for only a moment before wrapping my arms around her small frame and brining her as close to me as possible. It's not long before Zhoe's breathing evens out, but my mind is far too preoccupied to let me sleep. I can't stop thinking about the way this girl makes me feel. Part of me wants to hold her close and never let her go, the other part of me wants to run the other way.

I know I don't love her yet, but there is no doubt that I could love this girl. I could fall head over heels for her. I could love her with every ounce of my shattered soul if I'm not careful.

Nineteen

Zhoe

It's been several days since my first official date with Jared, several days since I woke up in his strong arms as he kissed me goodbye before he left for work in the morning. It was all I could do to let him go; even now the memory brings a smile to my face.

Jared's arm that had been acting as my pillow moving from under my head wakes me. I open my eyes enough to see where he's going. Leaning down, he places a soft kiss on my forehead before whispering, "shh, go back to bed, Pretty Girl. I didn't mean to wake you."

"What time is it?" I asked groggily.

"Early. I have to go to work. Go back to bed; I'll call you tonight when I get off," before he could leave my bed completely I reached out, grabbed him around his thick neck to bring his lips back down to mine.

"Come back to bed, it's cold without you in here." I smiled at him in what I hope is a sexy-sleepy way, hoping I'm not coming across as needy.

Lowering back down he pressed his body on top of mine. "Don't tempt me." He kissed me sweetly for several long moments, until I felt myself melting back into the mattress. "Have a good day, gorgeous." With a wink and an adorable grin he pushed up off the bed, left me lying there with a love-struck smile on my face. Le sigh!

Who knew that a man that appears so scary and dangerous and hard could be so soft and sweet? I haven't been on many first dates but I'm aware that was one for the record books. Even Angelica – who's been on many first dates – agrees with me. Everything was perfect, starting with him reading me well enough to take me to a burger joint rather than a fancy restaurant for dinner, calming my nerves and making me laugh continuously and then ending in my bed wrapped around each other. Fucking perfect.

I haven't seen Jared since then, as we're both crazy busy during the week. He works eight to ten hours every day and by the time he gets home and showered, I'm usually in my pajamas doing homework. But, we manage to talk everyday either on the phone or through text.

I've woken up to an adorable text message every morning that usually start out sweet: "good morning, pretty girl" or something along those lines, but as the day goes on they get a little dirtier. Kind of like the one I'm reading now:

Jared: Six days without tasting that sexy body of yours is way too fucking long. I can't wait till you're sitting on my face, screaming my name again tonight.

Holy shit. Thank god I'm at home alone. My face has to be flaming red. I've never had a man speak to me like that so my initial reaction is to be embarrassed but once I start picturing the image Jared so eloquently painted I start to get hot for another reason.

Wiping my now sweaty palms on my jeans I muster up the courage to respond to him, hopefully driving him as crazy as he's making me.

Me: My turn again, huh? Too bad. I was really looking forward to feeling the tip of your cock against the back of my throat.
Jared: Wish fucking granted. I'll be there in an hour, be ready.

Shivers race down my spine at his command. Who knew I'd be into controlling men? But I'm *into* it; I'm *so fucking into* it. Racing upstairs I hop in the shower trying to both cool myself down before I combust from the arousal coursing through me and to start primping for tonight's date.

I have no idea what he has planned for tonight so once again I have no idea how to dress. Feeling a little risky and provocative, I do something I've never done, I go commando. I put on a red lace pushup bra, and pull a plain black shift dress over top of it. I finish off my look with light makeup, pulling my hair back into a ponytail. I throw on a pair of black wedges and decide I'm ready to go.

As soon as I hear the doorbell the calmness I found in the shower dissipates. My heart is beating erratically, my breathing is faster and my palms are sweaty. How insane that I'm turned on just from the idea of him being on the other side of my door, with full intentions to follow through on the promises we made each other earlier?

With one final deep breath I open the door to find Jared standing there holding a bouquet of purple tulips and wearing the biggest shit-eating grin I've ever seen. Reaching up with his free hand he runs his thumb along my cheekbone. "What's with the blush, Pretty Girl? Thinking dirty thoughts?"

Pulling out my inner wanton daredevil I just nod my head at him slowly, while raking my teeth against my bottom lip, as I brazenly look him up and down. Jared steps into me pulling my body into his. His free hand wraps around my ponytail causing my head to tip back before he roughly covers my lips with his. The other hand is still tightly gripping the flowers he brought. We stand like that for several minutes feeling each other, tasting each other, my front door wide open.

"Let me set your flowers down, Pretty Girl," he says, pulling away just slightly so he can mumble against my mouth. "I don't want to owe you again."

The flowers? He's worried about the damn flowers? All I can think about is how quickly we can get to the couch and get undressed. Grabbing his thick forearm I pull until he moves the few steps I need him to into my apartment, reaching around him I close the door and shove his back against it. I grab the flowers from his hand and throw them to the floor. "Screw the flowers."

Instantly, Jared growls and presses his hands into my ass bringing me flat against his body. I reach between us to undo his belt buckle and lower the zipper on his jeans. Pulling his pants down just far enough to free him, I pull him out running my hands along his hard length several times before dropping to my knees in front of him.

"Baby, quit. You don't have to...." I cut off that train of thought quick; wasting no time I take him all the way into my mouth as deep as I can. "Holy shit."

I love the way he feels in my mouth. He's so thick and long and smooth. But, I love the way he reacts to me even more. Knowing I can affect this big, strong man so much is a heady thought; it's a thought that turns me on greatly.

Reaching down I lift the hem of my dress up a few inches, just enough to get my fingers between my thighs. I'm soaking wet just from the taste of him in my mouth. I'm desperate for release.

With one hand I massage my clit, with the other I work with my mouth on Jared's cock, bringing us both to the edge. "Fuck. Yes, baby. Touch yourself. That's so sexy."

Working him harder, I take him deeper and deeper until I feel like I could gag on his size. I promised him the tip of his cock would be at the back of my throat tonight and I am definitely holding up my end of the bargain. After a few more strokes I feel him swell and his whole body stiffen.

I work myself faster, too, desperate to come at the same time as him. The moment I feel my body start quaking I hear Jared shout, "fffuuuccckkk," muffling my own moans, as I taste his salty, sweet come run down my tongue and throat.

Once he's finished, he halls me up to my feet. "Come here, gorgeous." He wraps both arms around me, holding me close, resting my cheek against his chest and I revel in the feeling of being held by this man. It feels so good and safe and right. I never want to leave.

"Have I told you how fucking beautiful you look tonight?" he says into my hair.

I let out a little giggle, mumbling into his chest. "Uh, no. I think we got distracted before you could get there."

He pulls me back so he can look me in the eye. "Well you look stunning." The smile on his face is so beautiful and carefree that I can't help but smile back at him. A thought wrecks my whole world: I never want him to leave. I want to stay like this wrapped in each other's arms, smiling up at each other forever.

"How's about we just stay in tonight, instead?" Jared asks. "I don't want to waste this pretty outfit, but I don't want to share you, either."

He always says the perfect things. I feel my heart opening up to him a little bit more each time I see him. "Okay," I whisper back simply.

"Why don't you go put on something a little more comfortable and I'll order us a pizza?" See? He says the perfect things. What girl doesn't want to be told you look stunning but I'd much rather you put on something more comfortable? I'd trade my heels for yoga pants any day; thankfully I've found a guy that doesn't mind.

He lets me go then and I start to make my way towards the stairs to go up to my bedroom, looking forward to throwing on a pair of yoga pants and a comfy shirt. "Oh and Zhoe?" Jared calls out to me just as I'm about to step on the first step. I look at him over my shoulder catching sight of his gaze. He looks me up and down, his eyes burning me from the outside in. "Don't bother putting any underwear on."

The sexy, knowing smirk he gives me is enough to make me wet all over again. Who needs dinner anyways? I mean can't we just sustain on each other's bodies?

My thoughts must be written all over my face because suddenly Jared's voice breaks through my thoughts. "Food, Zho. You need to eat. You'll need energy for what I have planned for us later, so quit looking at me like that."

Twenty

Jared

That girl is going to be the death of me. First she presses me against the door and gives me one of the best blowjobs I've ever had, while bringing herself to orgasm. But knowing she planned on leaving the house in a sexy little dress and no underwear? That's enough to bring any man to his knees.

But Jesus, the look she was giving me just now? Like she'd much rather dine on me than on food was enough to make me lose it right then and there. The feeling is so fucking mutual, too. I have no idea how I found the willpower to walk away from that offer, well to table the offer anyways. I fully intend on getting my share of her sexy little body later.

When she comes back downstairs in skintight black leggings and a baggy white T-shirt that hangs off her shoulder, I get hard all over again. It looks like she took her makeup off and pulled her hair back into a messy bun instead of the sleek ponytail she had it in earlier. Damn it if she still isn't the sexiest thing I've ever seen.

"You're so fucking beautiful, Zhoe." The blush I love so much makes an appearance and has me smiling. "I love when you blush." Pulling her into my arms I study her face for a moment before asking, "Which one are you? Shy or bold?"

"What? I can't be both?" Her retort comes in the sarcastic tone I've become used to with her.

"I didn't think it was possible before, but it is with you. Which one do you think you're more of though?"

She pulls a face like she has absolutely no idea how to answer my question. I'm also not really sure why I'm so interested in her answer, but for some reason I need to know. I feel like she's the confident girl I met at the bar, but part of me wants to believe she's only shy around me, that side of her is reserved only for me.

"I'm definitely more confident than I am shy. Actually, I never would have described myself as shy until I met you." She says this while looking straight in my eyes but with a blush on her face, giving me the exact answer I was hoping for. "What about you, huh? How would you describe yourself?"

Well if that isn't a loaded question if I've ever heard one. "Damaged," I answer honestly. I don't know why I told her that. I don't know why I was so blatantly honest with her. I'm trying to impress this girl, not scare her away.

But, in true Zhoe fashion she doesn't respond like most girls would; she doesn't run the other way or ask a million questions about what damaged me, she just simply answers, "aren't we all," before placing a kiss on my chin and turning to walk to the couch making herself comfortable.

Part of me wants to know why she doesn't ask questions, because for some reason I want her to know me as much as I want to know her. But, the other part of me appreciates that she doesn't ask; she just lets things fall into place naturally without digging for information.

"Want to play a game?" she asks out of nowhere. I sit down next to her on the couch, pulling her legs over my lap. I must look at her quizzically because she goes on without me having to ask. "I'll give you two words and you just answer with the one that comes to mind first, don't think or hesitate or answer the way you think I want you to – just use your instincts."

"Okay. Do I get to ask questions, too?" I don't want this to be a one sided conversation. I have no idea what kinds of questions we're going to ask each other but I know I want the opportunity to ask questions, too.

"Of course. We'll take turns. I'll go first." She pauses as if she's trying to decide what her first question should be. "Color, or black and white?"

Seriously? Okay this will be easy, "Color. Romance or Action?"

"Romance. But don't worry, I won't make you watch too many chick flicks with me." She laughs and it makes me laugh. She makes me feel lighter, like life is easy and not the cruel life I've always known. It's a welcomed change. "Vanilla or chocolate?" she asks.

"Neither. I'm not much for sweets." She looks at me like I've offended her in some way, which inspires my next question. "Dinner or dessert?"

"Dessert. I would so skip dinner if I could have ice cream instead."

"Ice cream, got it. Does that mean you won't eat the pizza I called in?"

"Oh no, pizza is the exception to the rule. I will always be in the mood for pizza. Okay, what about you? Pizza or burgers?"

"Pizza. Like you, I'll eat pizza any day. Islands or mountains?"

"Mountains. Not much for sitting on a beach all day."

"Too bad. I'd love to see you in a little bikini." I flash her a wicked grin.

"I'd just bet you would. Jeans or dresses?" Is this a trick question?

"Leggings?" I ask back, getting the response I wanted. Zhoe giggles, again, and reaches over to slap my arm.

"Not one of the choices. But, nice try."

"Okay, definitely jeans. Clothes or no clothes?" I know I'm pushing my luck with that one but I'm hoping confident Zhoe makes an appearance here and does something crazy and unexpected… like taking all her clothes off.

"No clothes." She answers without even flinching. She doesn't blush or back down but she doesn't take her clothes off either. Damn. "Slow and sensual or fast and hard?"

I whip my head back around to look at her. No wonder she answered my last question so calmly, she had a better one up her sleeve. "With you?"

"Why? Are you thinking about other girls right now?" She pulls her loose fitting shirt over her head, leaving her in only her skintight, sorry excuse for pants and that's it. She's not wearing a bra and I know for a fact she's not wearing any panties.

My mouth goes dry. Her tits are so fucking perfect; round and soft and just enough to fit in the palms of my hands. Her stomach is flat but still soft and feminine. All I can think about is getting a taste of that skin she's tempting me with. "You going to answer?"

"Right now all I can think about is fucking you so hard we break your couch." I finally find my voice and give her the crudest answer my brain can come up with without lifting my eyes from her perfect breasts. *Real fucking smooth*, I think to myself.

But I'm only able to think for a second as Zhoe climbs up onto my lap, her luscious breasts right in front of my face, enticing me, turning my brain to mush. "So hard and fast, then?"

"Mmm," is the only response I can come up with as I take one of her pink nipples into my mouth. My hands find their way to her hips groping and pulling her body closer to mine. "Fuck, baby. I want you so bad."

"I want you, too," she whispers against my jaw. Her lips moving down my face slowly, as her hands reach for the hem of my shirt yanking it over my head roughly. "Now, Jared. Take me now."

Who am I to deny the girl? "Hold on to me."

I start to stand up with her in my arms and wrapped around my body when the doorbell rings. "Fuck." Her head drops to my shoulder as her entire body starts shaking with laughter. Grabbing her hair in my hand I pull her head back so I can see her face, her eyes are full of tears from laughing so hard, her smile so huge it makes the room seem brighter.

I can't believe I'm laughing with her. I'm going to have the worst case of blue-balls I've ever had and yet I can't stop laughing with her. She places a soft kiss on my lips before untangling herself from me. "This isn't over you know." I slap her ass as she walks away from me to prove my point.

She stops in the middle of the room, looks over her shoulder and calls back to me, "promise?" With a wink she grabs her shirt and slides it back over her head. So not okay.

Growling, I make my way to the door to the pizza delivery guy with the worst timing in the world. I swear that girl is going to kill me.

After paying the kid, and tipping a couple bucks shorter than I normally would, I walk into the kitchen with the pizza boxes. "Did you seriously just short tip him?" she asks with her hands on her hips.

"He's a cock-block. That's what happens."

She just rolls her eyes at me, in what I'm starting to notice is a habit she doesn't even realize she has. "It's not his fault, Jare. He didn't know you were about to get lucky."

I growl at her before reaching into the cupboard above my head. "Don't remind me."

"Aw, poor baby." Zhoe saunters over to me, her flattened palms slide slowly down my body, stopping only once she has a firm hold on my junk. "Want me to kiss it and make it better?"

She doesn't wait for a response; instead she drops to her knees for the second time tonight. Only this time she doesn't give me a mind-blowing blowjob. Puckering her plump lips she places a sweet peck on my jean-clad dick, "patience, little one. It'll be worth it."

With a growl I grab her roughly by her upper arms, dragging her to her feet. "You're a tease." I step into her space until she's flush against the counter, deliberately rubbing my erection against her belly, "and he's not little."

My faux-scowl falls from my face at the sound of her laughter. Leaning into me she kisses me thoroughly, fully, until we're both panting. "Sorry, baby."

I give her a smack on her ass as she walks away from me. "You're forgiven. For now."

Zhoe grabs napkins, carrying the entire pizza box to the living room. I follow behind her with my hands full of beers; apparently we're both too lazy to go to the kitchen for round two.

Plopping down next to her I take a huge bite of the hot slice before turning to her. "So, what do you want to do with your life? I know you're in school for business, what's next?"

"Where'd that come from?" she asks. We've been talking and seeing each other for a little over a week now but we've never really hit on super personal subjects. I've decided we need to change that tonight. I'm not ready to open up to her completely about my sordid past, but I want to get to know her more.

"I don't know. We just haven't really talked about this stuff much."

She looks at me for a few long seconds before answering. "Do you want to know what I want to do with my life or what my dad wants me to do with my life?"

"You don't want the same things?"

She shakes her head and I can't help but notice the sadness that clouds her eyes. "I'm actually only a business major because my dad is forcing me to be. He said he'd pay for school and my apartment if I went to school for business. He wants me to take over his marketing firm someday."

"If you don't want that, why didn't you tell him no? Find a way to pay your own way?"

"I don't know. I'm weak."

"Zhoe, you are anything but weak. Tell me the truth."

She sighs, turning her attention toward the TV for a few long moments. I, too, direct my attention to the football game that's on, giving her space and time. I've never been one to talk about my feelings and open up and Zhoe's never made me, so I'm going to give her the same courtesy.

After a while she lets out another long sigh, setting her plate down on the coffee table. She doesn't look at me when she starts talking, "I started college not long after my brother died. My parents were, and still are, having a hard time with his death. So was I; I guess in that moment I really wasn't strong enough to fight him."

I follow her, placing my plate down, before pulling her into my arms. I wrap my arm around her shoulder as her head rests on mine. "I'm so sorry."

Twenty-One

Zhoe

Jared doesn't ask what happened but he doesn't have to, it's always the first question people ask. They always want to know what happened, why it happened, and how I'm doing.

His arms tighten around me as he mumbles. "We don't have to talk about it, baby."

I just shake my head at him. We do have to talk about it. It's part of me. Part of my past. "He was murdered," I pause taking a deep breath. "Sorry, that sounded really blunt. I guess I've just become almost numb to saying it. It's been five years; five long years to get over it but slowly I've come to terms with it. He's not coming back, you know?"

I know I told him I've become almost numb, but that is so far from the truth. Every single day I hurt. I miss Cole so damn much. He was not only my big brother he was my best friend.

"Daddy was always trying to control our futures telling Cole and me what we should want out of our lives. But, Cole had this fun, easy going spirit and more times than not he was able to put Daddy in his place. He always had my back telling Daddy I should do what I wanted, what would make me happy."

I feel tears fall from my eyes as I think about my brother and the way he could make my dad laugh without ever really trying. If I was Daddy's Princess, Cole was definitely his pride and joy. Cole was a good student and a hard worker, but he also had a great sense of humor and the biggest, kindest heart.

"Everything fell apart when Cole died. Daddy lost his ability to laugh and love, and Mother lost the desire to feel, to live. I just want to live, Jared."

"Shh, don't cry baby." He breathes into my hair, as his hands run up and down my spine. I take comfort in his arms, loving the way they feel around me. They make me feel safe, secure, loved.

"I miss him, I miss him so much. I miss the way he had my back. I miss the way we used to be a family, we weren't perfect but still–" I pause taking in a shuddering breath.

After long seconds of reticence I push my way free of his hold, suddenly needing space from his suffocating silence. I get it, it's not an easy conversation to have but say something, *anything* to let me know you're here with me.

Needing a distraction I start cleaning up our mess hoping a few seconds to collect his thoughts will snap him back into reality. Back with me.

"Now that you've got me all sad, I need to watch a chick flick! "The Notebook" it is, lucky you!" I let out a humorless laugh hoping to lighten the moment as best I can.

He tries to smile but it feels forced. Ignoring it I just nod my head returning the smile. "Anything for you, Pretty Girl."

I curl up next to him, placing my head in his lap. He pulls the blanket off the back of the couch draping it over my body. It's an almost reassuring, comforting action and I take a tiny bit of comfort in it.

I barely watch the movie. My thoughts lost in memories of Cole, in Jared's aloofness. I need Jared's strength right now but he's not there. He's lost in his own thoughts and all I can do is hope and pray that he'll come back to me. I really need him right now.

Twenty-Two
Jared

It's been a few days since I've seen Zhoe. I've been distant and cold and I know she's wondering what the hell is going on, but I just needed the time to get my head on straight.

When she told me her brother was murdered I knew without her even having to say his name that it was Cole. The coincidences were too much. I mean I had my suspicions all along, but having them confirmed? I fucking panicked. I had no idea what I was supposed to do with that information.

I watched her as she fell asleep on my lap, she looked peaceful in her slumber; meanwhile my heart felt like it was literally being ripped from my chest. Zhoe is the best thing that's ever happened to me in my shitty fucking life. I can't lose her, but is it fair to keep her when I'm the reason for her heartache?

For years I've wished it were me that died that night, but even more so now. Cole had Zhoe: he had the most beautiful, funny, perfect sister that loved him and I took that from him. I took that from her. I caused five years of pain for this beautiful girl and I'm going to cause more if I don't walk away from her now.

But, I'm a selfish son of a bitch. I don't think I'm strong enough to walk away from her. I know it's the right thing to do. I know it. But, I just can't.

For days I've been battling internally with my decision. What's right and wrong? Should I stay or leave? Do I tell her who I am? Unable to come to a conclusion on my own I've decided to pay Cole a visit. I need him to know just how much I care about his sister, how much she means to me.

I take several deep breaths trying to calm my nerves before I get out of my truck and make the short walk to Cole's grave. It's really kind of pathetic how crazy nervous I am, considering. If this situation was normal I'd be scared shitless to get his approval but he can't really give me that. Maybe that's why I'm so nervous, because I feel guilty and twisted up inside.

I plop down on my ass, sitting with my arms resting on my knees in front of his grave. I just stare at it for a few before finding the courage to speak up. "Fuck, Cole. Every year I come here and I tell you how sorry I am and how much I wish it had been me that day. How much I wish I wasn't such a damn coward."

I take a minute to gather my thoughts, little good it does me. All I see is Zhoe's face; her big blue eyes, her gorgeous smile, and her infectious laugh. Her sexy body.

"I met Zhoe, Cole. I met her and I'm fucking falling for her, dude. She's beautiful and funny and smart; she's fucking perfect. And I'm going to break her all over again."

I pause letting my emotions settle before trying to get back into my one-sided conversation. "What do I do, Cole? I know I should walk away from her before she finds out, before she gets hurt, but I just don't think I can. I need her. I need her so damn much. She's the only thing that makes me smile. She's the only thing that makes living this shitty life worth it."

I growl out in frustration, gripping my head in my hands. "Give me a sign, anything to let me know you're okay with this, to let me know we're supposed to be together."

I drop my head between my shoulders blowing out breath after breath trying desperately to find some composure. I asked him to give me a sign – I've never really believed in religion and life after death, but fuck if I don't need it to be true right now.

I sigh, resigned to losing Zhoe. The world was silent for too long for him to be able to give me that sign I was so desperately seeking. Pushing myself off I dust off my jeans, I start to walk away from him – again – before turning back. "I'm sorry, Cole. You'll never know how much."

Just then my phone dings, alerting me to a text message. I pull it out seeing Zhoe's name flash across the screen.

Zhoe: I know it's only been a short time since we started seeing each other but I need you to know I need you. I miss you. Don't just walk away from this, whatever this is. Please.

I snap my head up in the direction of Cole's headstone. Is this the sign I was looking for? I haven't heard from Zhoe since I walked out the other night, but this is so out of the norm for her. She's not the type of girl to beg, and definitely not the type to put her feelings out there like that. But for me, she did.

I can't help the smile that crosses my face. "Thanks, bro. I'll take care of her, I promise." At that, I walk away determined to get make this right. Somehow I have to find a way to tell Zhoe the truth. I was a coward once and it turned out to be the worst day of my life; it's time for me to find some damn courage and tell her the truth.

I won't be able to handle it if Zhoe leaves me, but I won't blame her. I'm too selfish, too weak to walk away from that girl. But, I'm also not going to stop her if she wants to leave me after she finds out the truth.

First though, I need to hold her and tell her I'm sorry for leaving her when she needed me. I need her to know how much she means to me. Selfishly, I want her walking away from me to be hard. I want her to *want* to work this out. I need feelings on the line.

Twenty-Three
Zhoe

"I'm so excited!" Angelica squeals as we get out of the cab. The four of us – Jared, Angelica, Rico, and I – decided to meet up at a new bar downtown. It's the first time all of us have gone out together. Really it's the first time Jared and I have gone out as a couple.

It's also the first time Jared and I have seen each other since he left a few days ago. I am still puzzled at his silence and distance. As far as I know everything was okay, both of us actually talking and sharing and then he shut down. Once I broke down, Jared closed up. He was there for me, comforting me by holding me and playing with my hair, but he wasn't actually there.

I could see it in his face that he was somewhere else, thinking about something else. I should have asked him what was wrong. I should have been there for him, but I was too wrapped up in my own self-pity that I couldn't think beyond that.

The next day I waited for his usual good morning text that never came. I decided to let him have his distance, hoping he could work it out on his own, but he never called. I reached out the next day and when he responded, he suggested a night out with the group. I would have much rather had some alone time with him but as long as he wants to see me again I'm okay with the plans.

I laugh at my friend who is always so excited to do or try anything new and who is completely oblivious to the distance between Jared and me, "Have you heard much about this place?" I ask as we get close to the front doors. The bar is called Rebel's and from its look it seems to be upholding its name.

The entire building front has been painted black; the huge double doors a bright red. The sign above the door is red neon, the end of the L curling to look like a devil's tail. Loud rock music explodes from inside whenever the door is opened.

"I haven't heard a lot, other than it's awesome! Come on, let's go find the guys." She grabs my arm pulling me behind her as fast as my heels will let me.

I grin at the thought of my outfit and what Jared's reaction to it is going to be. I picked out a new dress today when Ang and I went shopping with Jared in mind. I figured if he was going to try and freeze me out I was going to make it a hard decision – show him what he'd be missing if he walked away.

From the front the red, sequined, long-sleeved dress looks respectable, excluding the shortness of it. But, it's the back that drew me to it; it's completely open back, the material draping strategically at my lower back just above my ass. I fucking love this dress. I've paired it with sky-high black stilettos. I look like a girl on a mission and I am.

For days I've been freaking out thinking Jared is walking away from this, from us. I know we're new, I know we haven't really talked about feelings or labels, but I know without a doubt what we have is real and could be amazing if he gave us a chance. So, I picked out a sexy dress hoping to show him what he'd be missing out on if he walks.

It takes a few minutes for my eyes to adjust to the dim lighting when we enter the bar, but when I do I'm surprised at what I see. The place is packed with people fighting to get attention at the bar. There is a small stage near the back with two cages on either side of it; girls scantily clad are dancing extremely provocatively inside them. For a few minutes I have a hard time taking my eyes off them. The walls are lined with plush booths and high top tables line the large dance floor that is already crowded.

This place is definitely different from any other club I've been in. It's loud, dark and crowded but it still sends off a certain vibe that I can't deny appeals to me. It's sexy and dangerous. Suddenly, I'm eager to find Jared.

"I don't see them yet," I tell Ang as I do a quick scan of the room. It's so crowded I doubt I'd be able to see them anyways.

"Let's walk around, see if we can find a booth." I just nod at her letting her lead the way. We do a quick sweep of the room still not finding the guys but finding an empty booth towards the back of the bar close to the stage and dance floor.

Once we're seated I pull out my phone to shoot Jared a text letting him know where we are and Ang orders us both a Cosmo from the waitress. "Want to play gay or straight?" I ask Ang.

Gay or Straight is a game we started a long time ago at one of our parent's boring galas to pass the time; we pick out a couple and try to guess if they are gay or straight, sometimes we go even farther and try to come up with their life story. We don't do it to be hurtful or judgmental, but sometimes when you're sitting at a fancy, boring gala you need some form of entertainment.

"Oh my god, yes! It's been so long. Okay, I go first." She scans the room, finally picking someone out. "Okay, the two middle-aged guys at the end of the bar. The one guy has a polo shirt on with the collar popped, the other guy is wearing a suit and tie."

I look in the direction she pointed, finally spotting them. I watch them for a few seconds, taking in their mannerisms and the way they interact with each other before I make my judgment. "Straight. I think the guy in the polo can't let go of his college days and the guy in the suit just had twins, so he needs a night out without the ball and chain." We both bust out laughing at my ridiculous appraisal.

"I'd have to agree with that one, definitely straight. Your turn."

I spot two girls at a booth directly across from us. The one is wearing a dress so short I'm shocked her goods aren't on full display, the other girl has on an outfit I'm actually jealous of. She's wearing high-waisted wide-leg black pants and a billowy sheer-white tank. They are sitting close to each other, whispering and laughing – though Ang and I are also sitting close because of the noise level in here.

"Hmm," Ang picks up her drink to eye the couple from over the rim of her glass. "I'm tempted to say gay but I don't think they are gay together. Maybe they're in an experimental stage?"

"Ooh, that's a good one. We've never found swingers before, maybe their husbands are the guys at the bar?"

"Yes! They are going gay for the night!"

We are laughing so hard neither of us notices Jared and Rico standing in front of the table staring at us like we've lost our damn minds. "What the hell are you girls talking about?" Rico asks sliding into the booth next to Ang.

"Inside joke," she dismisses him quickly but with a sexy smile on her face letting him know it's not him. We've never let anyone in on our game so I'm not really surprised by her closed lipped response.

I look up at Jared who is still just standing there looking down at me. Damn, he's so sexy. "Hey, Stud." He's wearing dark wash jeans that cling to him in ways that should be illegal and a tight Young & Reckless t-shirt and a black ball cap on backwards. Simple, understated, drool worthy.

Finally, he slides in next to me, placing a sweet kiss on my temple. "You look amazing."

Twenty-Four
Jared

Holy fuck. Zhoe looks delicious. Her red dress shows off all of her curves, her hair is partially pulled back but mostly down and as usual she's wearing little make-up, save her red lipstick. What is it with this woman and red?

"You look pretty good yourself, handsome."

As if my lips have a mind of their own they find their way to the hallow of her throat, after placing several inappropriate kisses there I move my way back up her neck ending with a simple peck on her cheek. Looking at her causes me to laugh as her face now matches her dress. "What's with the blush, Princess?"

Before I can even think about what I've said, Zhoe is pulling away from me, the blush gone replaced with a look of irritation. "Don't call me that."

"What? Princess?" She just nods at me.

"It's a long story," Angelica pipes in from across the booth. "She's just sensitive. She doesn't like the negative connotations behind it. She doesn't like people referring to her money and status." I look at Zhoe who is glaring at her friend.

Trying to salvage the situation I put an arm around her shoulder bringing her back into my side. "Sorry, Pretty Girl." I continue quietly for her ears only, "You have to know when I say it I don't mean it that way. When I say it I picture a stunning princess trapped in a castle and I'm your prince charming, your hero coming to rescue you."

She looks at me like I'm crazy before she busts out laughing, a full on Zhoe laugh with her head tipped back and all. Exactly the reaction I was shooting for. "You're so corny." We sit there smiling at each other like lovesick fools for long moments, and for once I don't really give a shit what Rico or anyone else thinks. This girl makes me happy and I don't care who knows it. "I missed you," she whispers in a sad voice as she reaches up to run her fingers along my jaw.

Grabbing her hand I place several soft kisses on her palm and fingers, before entwining them and dropping the pair onto my lap. "Missed you, too, Zho. So damn much." She smiles softly at me and I know for the moment I'm forgiven, but damn it if seeing her sad face didn't tear me in two.

"Who wants to dance?" Angelica shouts loud enough for the three of us to hear her over the music, effectively breaking up the moment Zhoe and I were having.

"Me!" Zhoe exclaims. She looks over at me. "Come on, Stud. It's been a while since you've showed off your dance moves," she says with a wink, her elbow digging into my side as she nudges me out of her way.

Standing up so I can let her out of the booth, I turn her down. "Nah. I don't want to steal the show. Besides, I haven't even had a beer yet." Zhoe sticks out her bottom lip in a pout and it's too damn adorable. "I'll meet you out there in a few," I say unable to resist her.

I turn my back on them as they take off for the dance floor, but before I can even sit down fully I hear Rico's explicative. "Fuck. You're going to let her go out there alone dressed like that?"

I look up at my friend with a confused look on my face. "Trust me, Zhoe can handle herself."

"Dude, look at your girl for one second, you won't be so sure of that."

Turning my head toward the dance floor I spot Zhoe immediately, seconds later I'm out of my seat charging her on the floor. Once I reach her I grab her around the waist dragging her back into my chest. "Change your mind?" She looks back at me suggestively.

"I didn't really have a choice." She tries to turn in my arms to get a better look at me but I hold her still. "I just saw the back of your dress." I'm growling and I'm sure the look on my face isn't very friendly either.

Zhoe looks at me, her eyebrows scrunched together and her lips turned down. "You don't like it?"

Splaying my hands on her lower belly I start to move with her to the beat of "Va Va Voom" by Nicki Minaj. After a few sways of our hips I lean down, placing my lips on the base of her neck just behind her ear. "I fucking love it. I just don't want every other guy in this bar to see what's mine."

"Yours?" She finally manages to escape my death grip on her hips, turning in my arms so she's facing me. "I'm yours?"

I take a second to answer not because I'm unsure of what I want the answer to be but because the conviction in my answer is enough to shock even me. "You know you're mine, Zhoe." Never had I wanted a woman to be mine. I've never felt possessive or jealous but with Zhoe I am all of those things. I don't want to share her. I want her with me and only me.

Zhoe presses up on her toes to lay her lips against mine, even with her heels I'm still several inches taller than her. "And are you mine, Jared?" she questions, our lips still pressed lightly together.

"For as long as you'll have me, baby."

That admission rocks me to my very core. Not only have I never wanted a woman to be mine, but I've damn sure never wanted to be owned by a woman. Zhoe owns me though, she completely fucking owns me.

Zhoe kisses each corner of my mouth, my nose, and my chin. Slowly she moves her mouth down the base of my neck, sucking and biting hard enough I feel it throughout my entire body. I grab her ass in both of my hands huddling her into me, letting her feel my erection as I press it into her stomach.

Zhoe wraps her arms around my neck moving in even closer to me, her hips moving in synchronicity with mine to the beat of the music. Our eyes stay locked on each other; the rest of the room fades away until it's just her and I on the dance floor. I forget about Angelica and Rico, I forget the outside world even exists because truly nothing matters but the girl in my arms.

I have no idea how long we dance like that but eventually Zhoe looks up at me snapping us out of our trance. "Take me home, Jared."

Fuck. This girl is pushing all of my buttons tonight. Taking a second to look around I realize the once nearly empty dance floor is now completely packed; we are being bumped into on all sides by drunken dancers. Both Zhoe and I are covered in sweat, breathing hard; how long were we out there anyways?

Reluctantly, I pull my hands off Zhoe's ass, opting instead for one of her hands as I guide her back to the booth where Ang and Rico are still sitting. I planned on going over there long enough to say goodbye, desperate to get my girl home and in bed. Naked.

"So glad you could pull yourselves apart long enough to join us again," Angelica says in her typical snarky attitude.

Zhoe's only response is to stick her tongue out at her friend before reaching for her drink and downing its remains in one long gulp, causing all of us to break out in laughter.

"Come to the bathroom with me, Zhoe?" Angelica asks her and I have to stifle a groan. I just want to get out of this place. I'm desperate to get her underneath me.

"Yeah, sure."

"I'll go with you," I say still leery of the tiny dress she's wearing and wandering eyes.

"We'll be fine." She throws her hand on her hip and looks up at me with a cocky smirk on her face. I know she can take half the guys in this bar, I have seen her at the gym but it still makes me nervous. "We'll be right back, Jared." She leans up whispering against my jaw, "then we'll go home and get even sweatier. Deal?"

She doesn't give me the chance to respond before her and Ang are diving through the crowds to get to the bathroom on the other side of the bar. I stand there staring after her like a complete moron. I know this because Rico calls me on it.

"You've got it so bad, dude." He laughs before slapping me on the back and walking in the direction of the bar. "I'll grab us another round, save our table," he yells back to me.

After several minutes Rico walks back with his hands full of drinks, I reach up grabbing a few bottles of beer out of his hand setting them in the middle of the table. "So, what's up with you and Ang?" The two of them were looking awfully cozy at the booth before we walked up.

He snorts into his beer. "Abso-fucking-lutely nothing. Girls like that want nothing to do with guys like me."

"What the fuck's that supposed to mean? You're a great guy."

"Nah. She's too good for me. She'd never want anything to do with me and I wouldn't want her to get wrapped up with a guy like me anyways, you know?"

Fuck. "Yeah, man. I get you. I feel the same about Zhoe. She's so much better than I'll ever be, but I'm not man enough to let her go."

For long minutes Rico just looks at me over the rim of his bottle. "You're better than you give yourself credit for, man. And that girl is good for you, plus she cares about you, too. A lot. Don't let her go. You're one lucky son of a bitch."

"Don't I know it," I tell him. I shouldn't have a girl like Zhoe but I know we both meant what we said on the dance floor, I can feel it in my bones, in my veins. I'm hers and she's mine. For as long as we'll have each other. I just don't know how much longer Zhoe will want me. I do know I'll never not want her, I'll never have enough of her.

Twenty-Five
Zhoe

"Do you even know how disgustingly cute the two of you are?" Ang asks as we're waiting in line for the bathroom. I never understood the length of the women's restroom lines, I mean half of the time we fit two or three girls per stall, how can it possibly take so long to pee?

I just look at my friend with a huge grin plastered on my face. I'm so fucking happy right now I don't care how dopey I look. That is the most Jared's ever revealed about his feelings for me, for us, and whatever this is we're doing.

"I mean seriously," Ang continues, "it was just the two of you out there, you didn't even notice the rest of the world. I feel like I want that someday."

At that I look at her a little closer; my friend has never had a serious relationship with a man. It's something I've never understood because unlike my parents, her parents have a great relationship - one full of love and friendship and laughter. But, Angelica has always said she doesn't want someone else dictating what she does, holding her back. I'm such a hopeless romantic that I've tried endlessly over the years to explain to her that when you find the right guy they don't hold you back but encourage you to grow.

I think Jared does that for me. He makes me feel sexy, secure, strong and interesting. Who knew a man making you feel interesting could be such a turn on?

"What about Rico?" I ask. The two of them seem to be getting along rather well. "Nah, he's sexy as sin but he's not the kind of guy you settle down with. He'll be the first to tell you that."

"Yeah, but Jared was that way, too. I think part of him still is afraid of commitment."

"No way, that boy loves the shit out of you. He might be afraid of those feelings and afraid to tell you, but I see it in the way he looks at you. He definitely loves you." At that she walks away from me to take her turn in one of three stalls in the tiny bathroom – no wonder the line was so long.

I can't help but dwell on her words. Does Jared love me? Sometimes I feel like he does. Sometimes I, too, see it in his eyes, but other times I wonder if I want to see it and feel it so desperately I'm imagining it. I guess only time will tell.

Eventually we make our way out of the restroom, and as we're heading back to the booth Christina Aguilera's "Ain't No Other Man" blasts from the speakers. Both of us fall into a fit of giggles and squeals; we spent hours in high school dancing to this song in my bedroom.

Ang grabs my hand pulling me onto the dance floor and I follow her easily. No way am I going to pass up an opportunity to bust out our dance moves. I fall into place next to her and we start to step to the moves we made up so long ago. We're moving our hips provocatively, one finger wiggling back and forth to emphasize the *no other* part. We can't stop laughing. I'm so wrapped up in the moves and the memories, I don't notice for a second the strong hands that have attached themselves to my hips.

For one second too long I think they're Jared's strong palms, but then I take inventory of the way they feel different than the comforting, controlling, sexual way Jared touches me. Turning quickly I come face to chest with the biggest man I've ever seen in my life, which is saying something because Jared is a large man.

Placing my palms flat on his chest I shove him away from me with as much strength as I can muster up. "Back off," I warn. But the guy only smirks at me before taking a giant step up to me grabbing my hips again pulling my body flush with his.

"You like it rough, baby?"

Ew, seriously? What a fucking perv. "Get off of me. Now." I try again to warn him away from me before I really start getting physical, or more importantly before Jared notices what's happening.

The skeezeball only presses into me closer, this time moving his hands lower until they rest on the swell of my ass. Fuck this. Lifting my right foot I bring it up and slam it back down on the instep of his foot, taking extra care to use my stiletto heel to cause the most pain.

"Ow. You fucking bitch." He lets me go for one second, and that's all I need. I pull out of his grasp grabbing Ang and making a beeline for our booth.

But the guy only follows; grabbing my arm and yanking me back so harshly I fall on my ass. He leans down pulling on the arm he still has a tight grip on. "I'll make you pay for that bitch," he hisses in my ear. His grip is so hard on my upper arm I can feel it bruising already. All I can concentrate on is the pain and trying to get out of his death grip, when suddenly my arm is free.

Moving until I'm on my knees, I take in the sight in front of me. I see the guy flat on his back on the floor and a huge figure looming over him. Jared looks up from the guy's already bloodied face to stare at me. "You okay, baby?"

I just nod my head at him. Jared looks me over once more from head to knee, as I'm still sitting on them, as if making sure I'm really okay before he turns his attention back to the douchebag he just laid out. Jared raises his fist pounding it into the guys face over and over again, for a second I just stand there staring at him.

Angelica frantically screaming Jared's name is what finally snaps me out of it, especially as I turn to see the panic on her face. Seeing her fear snaps me back to life. Turning toward Jared I quickly take stock of what's happening in front of me. The guy is lying on his side, his body curled in on itself, his arms protecting his face. Jared is straddling him raining relentless blows to the guy's face, stomach, side, and back. A small crowd has started forming around us with some guys yelling *"Fight! Fight!"* while girls are either standing stock-still or screaming.

Moving quickly I jump to my feet and charge toward Jared. Reaching around the limp body, I make sure my face is directly in front of Jared's.

"Baby. Stop! Stop! I'm fine, please stop." For several long seconds he continues his beating until finally I've had enough. Reaching out, I place my hand on his shoulder willing him to look at me. After what feels like forever, he finally does. "Stop. Please."

Suddenly Jared stands up straight, his balled up fists dropping limply to his sides. He stares into my eyes, not moving a single muscle until his breathing slows to normal.

Finally, Rico appears pushing his way through the crowd. He takes one look at the scene in front of him before jumping into action. "We have to get out of here." He grabs Jared around his shoulders pushing him back a few steps until he can freely move him toward the front door.

Running over to Ang, I grab her wrist dragging her with me as I follow the guys out. Once we're all outside Rico and Jared continue their brisk pace for several blocks until we're far enough from the bar we feel comfortable we won't be recognized.

"Fuck!" Jared suddenly lashes out at the air in front of him.

Angelica and I stop several feet back, both of us leaning against the cool brick wall of the warehouse we're standing in front of. I'm still gripping her wrist tightly in my hand, needing the connection because I'm freaking the fuck out.

"What the fuck just happened, man?" Rico asks getting in Jared's face. I'm afraid that's only going to set him off again, but I have to trust Rico knows what he's doing after being friends with him for so long.

I'm a little worried though. Deep down I think I knew Jared had a temper, but I was not expecting anything like that. He was like a man possessed and I have no idea how I managed to get him to stop but for a minute there I was truly afraid he was never going to stop his brutal beating on that man.

As if just remembering I'm here and why he got into that fight to begin with, Jared takes several meaningful strides towards me, dropping to his knees in front of me he begins inspecting my body for any sign of injury. "Are you okay, baby?" I'm still a little freaked out by everything that happened so my reassuring words get stuck in my throat, instead I just nod at him. "I'm so sorry I wasn't there to protect you."

"Jare," I say finally finding my voice. I keep it low and calm despite the nerves wreaking havoc on my system. "I'm fine, okay? I'm fine."

He moves his hand up to cup my face and instinctively I flinch away. Turning my head to the side I press my cheek against the brick, closing my eyes. As soon as I realize what I've done I turn back to him, all I see in his eyes is regret. "You're scared of me." It's not a question, just an observation.

"No," I croak out. Clearing my throat I try again. "I just... I didn't think you were going to stop."

Jared says nothing, just looks at me for a few long, painful seconds before nodding his head once. He stands, pulling his phone from his pocket. He calls a cab company and asks for a cab for two; as soon as he hangs up I'm on him. "What are you doing?"

He ignores me though and instead turns to Angelica. "Make sure she gets home. We'll stay until the cab gets here but just go with her, okay?"

"Okay," she responds.

"What the hell, Jared?" I demand. Walking up to him I get in his face. "What are you doing?"

"Just go home, baby." He mumbles, placing a soft kiss on the top of my head before turning to walk a few feet away from me. I start to go to him but Rico puts a hand up to stop me.

"Just give him some time to cool off, Zhoe," he says to me. I stand there completely at a loss for what to do. This was so not how I planned on tonight going.

Twenty-Six

Zhoe

I wake up even more pissed off than when I went to bed last night. I'm tired, lonely, and annoyed. I was up all night tossing and turning, worrying about Jared. I probably checked my phone for missed calls or text messages at least a hundred times and debated with myself to call him at least a hundred more.

Resolving to fix this, whatever the hell the problem is, I decide to take matters into my own hands. After showering and changing into a pair of jeans and a long-sleeve navy blue Henley shirt, I make my way downstairs. I have to wake Ang to have her call Rico for Jared's address.

Add the fact that I've never been to his place another issue on my ever-growing list of things to be pissed about.

Once I pull into a parking space in front of his apartment building, I sit in the car for a few seconds trying to gather my thoughts. I'm not really sure what the hell happened last night. The only thing I do know is that I'm fucking pissed. I'm pissed he pulled away from me like that, pissed he made the decision for me to go home without him and pissed that he's probably sitting there thinking he's not good enough for me and trying to find some way to push me away for good.

Getting out of my car, I slam my door and march to his front door. He lives on the first floor of the building and his door faces the parking lot. I raise my fist and pound on the door repeatedly for a few minutes until he finally opens it for me.

Standing there in nothing but his boxers, I almost forget what I came over here to say. My mouth is suddenly dry and all I can focus on is his insanely sexy body. His hair is disheveled, his eyes heavy with sleep and damn it if I don't want to jump his bones right then and there. Which brings me to another issue, why the fuck hasn't he slept with me yet?

Finally finding my anger again, I push the door open wider making my way past him and into his place. It's small but it's clean. The front entryway is really just a small box with the kitchen off to one side that bodes a breakfast bar with two tall barstools. The living room is directly in front of me; it holds a large brown sectional sofa, matching end tables and a coffee table, the flat screen TV is mounted to one wall, the other wall is a large sliding glass door that leads to the porch. A hallway is off to the left of the living room that looks like it leads to a single bedroom and bathroom.

Jared clears his throat behind me, "Zho," he starts to mumble but I cut him off.

Twenty-Seven

Jared

Zhoe turns on me, she stalks towards me with a glare painted on her pretty face. Once she has my back against the wall she jabs her finger into my chest. "No, you don't get to say anything. You will listen and only talk when I'm done. Got it?"

I feel my mouth twitch as I fight to smile at her. She's fucking sexy when she's pissed. I love her shyness, and even her sexy boldness, but it takes a confident woman to get in the face of man three times her size. But, in true Zhoe fashion she doesn't back down. She glares into my eyes waiting for me to acknowledge her question.

Part of me wants to challenge her, push my luck, but the look on her face warns me otherwise. Choosing to take the smart, safe way out I answer quietly. "Got it."

"You scared me last night," she starts, getting right to the point. Fuck, I know I did. I scared myself. I haven't felt that angry in a long time, but she's mine, which means it's my responsibility to protect her from douche bags like that guy. "I wasn't scared for me, Jared. I know you'd never hurt me – I was afraid for you. I've never seen someone that angry, that out of control."

She pauses taking a big breath, her voice had softened during her speech but as she brings her eyes back up to mine I know her fear for me has taken a backseat again to her anger. "That being said, you don't get to make decisions for me. I wanted you to come home with me. It would have been nice for my boyfriend who's so hell-bent on protecting me to also be there to comfort me."

Shit. I know I messed up last night. I was up most of the night trying to find some way to make it right. "Zhoe," I reach up removing her finger still planted in my chest so I can hold her hands tightly. "I'm sorry, baby."

"For what exactly?" she asks, ripping her hands from mine to cross them over her chest. "Why are you sorry?"

"Um," is this a trick question? "For everything. For anything. For whatever you want me to be sorry for."

"Don't push me away, Jared." Her voice softens again and I know I have her now. I know her anger is dissipating. But, now what?

"I'm trying not to. I need you, Pretty Girl." I move to her again, this time wrapping my arms around her, bringing her head to my chest. "I was up all night missing you, missing the way you feel wrapped in my arms."

"Then don't let me go."

"I don't plan on it." With one finger under her chin, I lift her head back seeking access to her mouth. Placing my lips on hers I move from one corner to the other placing soft kisses as I go. I sneak my tongue out desperately asking her to open to me, to let me in. On a small sigh I make my move, our tongues dancing in perfect harmony for a long while. I feel her soften against me. Swooping down, I grab her by the back of her knees and carry her to the couch, wrapping our bodies around each other.

Fuck, I am so screwed. I have never needed anyone before – I've always relied on no one but me, but this girl has me so tied up I can't think without her in my arms. I need her. I've survived a lot of shit in my life, but I won't survive her leaving me.

I send up a silent prayer to a God I'm not entirely sure I believe in, to please let me find the strength to tell her the truth and for Zhoe to be strong enough to love me anyways.

"You're mine, Zhoe," I mumble through kisses on her neck. "I'm not letting you go."

And that's how we spend the rest of the day. Napping, making out and petting each other like horny teenagers. We taste and lick and suck until our mouths are swollen, it's sweet and unhurried – like we're savoring each other. It's comforting and simple and easy and fucking perfect. But, damn it, I need to be inside of this sweet, sexy girl soon before I go crazy.

Twenty-eight
Zhoe

"Seriously!" Angelica is literally shouting at this point, her voice at such a high decibel I can hardly make out the words, just the sounds. Looking around I notice most people at the bar are looking in our direction.

"Will you keep it down?" I admonish her, secretly hoping she'll take it down a few notches, but I know she won't.

"I'm sorry. I just don't understand how the two of you still haven't slept together. It's been almost a month. What the hell is wrong with you?"

I can't help but roll my eyes at her. Like waiting a little while to have sex with someone is so awful. "Well, technically we *have* slept together," I reply with a cheeky grin on my face.

"Oh don't get cute with me. He is a walking orgasm. How the hell haven't you jumped that yet?"

"Ang, not everything has to be about sex." I try to say this in the most believable way possible, but even I don't believe my words. Looking into the *whatever* face Angelica is giving me I know she doesn't believe me either. "Ugh! Okay, it's been awful. I want him so fucking bad. I mean we've done plenty of other things, we just haven't gotten there yet, for some reason."

"I just don't get it," she says with a thoughtful look on her face. The second she stops chewing on her bottom lip I know I'm in trouble. I see the light flicker in her eyes and I know she's come up with an idea. "I think we need to up the ante. What do you say?"

"I say hell yes! But, first why the hell are you so worried about my sex life?" We've been best friends our entire lives so it's not like we haven't talked plenty about sex, but this is the most involved she's ever been.

Downing a shot the bartender placed in front of her, she looks at me completely dejected. "I've hit a bit of a dry spell." She flashes me a wicked grin and before I can start to panic, I'm being drug out the door.

"What are we talking about here? One day? Two?" I joke with my friend. Finding an easy lay has never been a problem for my slutty, beautiful friend.

"Ha.Ha." She rolls her eyes at me. "But, yes if you must know, it's been three days."

"What happened to him?"

Angelica gives me a sheepish look and immediately I'm afraid to hear her answer. "Um, well. Rico and I kind of slept together."

"What?" It's my time to screech loudly.

"Will you keep it down? We're all adults and two of us are having sex." She shoots me a knowing grin and I can't help but roll my eyes and stick my tongue out at her. Rub it in, bitch. "But, don't worry, I'm not sure it'll be happening again. We've somehow found ourselves friend-zoned. So like I said… I need you to have a wild sex life so I can live vicariously through you."

I chuckle at her as she pulls out of the parking lot like a madwoman. "Uh, where are we going, crazy?"

"Shopping!" I can't help but laugh at her enthusiasm. This should be very interesting. We're both borderline drunk, both horny and on a mission. On second thought, this could work out wonderfully. I love my best friend!

***

I have been a nervous wreck all day today. After last night's shopping excursion I came back with an arsenal of goodies that will hopefully leave Jared panting and begging for more. More of which I'd be happy to give him.

I know he wants me and it's obvious how much I want him it just hasn't worked out. We keep getting interrupted or distracted or lamely falling asleep cuddling. But, not tonight… tonight Jared officially becomes mine.

"Zhoe?" Jared's raspy timbre echoes through my house. I texted him earlier telling him what time to come over and that the door would be unlocked. I know it's cliché and kind of lame but I'm waiting for him practically naked on my bed. If he doesn't pick up this clue, he's hopeless and I'm getting rid of him.

"Up here!" I call downstairs, hoping I don't sound as nervous as I feel. I know I just said it's lame, and it is, but it's still kind of scary. I mean I'm putting it all out there for him. What if he really doesn't want me? What if he's just been messing with me all this time? What if we haven't had sex because he doesn't want to have sex with me?

All of these questions and insecurities fly through my head in the matter of seconds it takes him to get upstairs. I'm still panicking, trying to find my inner sex-goddess, the confident girl he met at the bar, when he walks in my bedroom.

Any insecure thoughts I had vanish when I see the look on his face as he drinks me in. My bedside lamps are turned low, candles are lit and scattered around the room, and Rise Against is playing quietly in the background. Something about their gritty, dirty sound is like an aphrodisiac for me.

I'm lying in the middle of my white bedspread, wearing a black lace demi-cup bra, cut so low it barely covers my puckered nipples, and a matching black lace thong. I finished my outfit with a matching garter belt, thigh high stockings and black strappy stilettos. My hair is down and a little messy. Angelica painted my eyes in smoky, sexy colors but we opted to leave my lips bare.

Jared's eyes widen to take it all in, licking his lips he walks into the room a few steps more, his gaze never leaving my body. I feel it caress my figure from head to toe and back again and I imagine his hands trailing the length of me, making my panties get wet from the image.

"Holy shit," it's barely a whisper, almost like a prayer leaving his lips. Finally his eyes lock on mine and in them I see so much. I see the desire I've been dying to see from him, the heat and the want. Suddenly the room seems too hot.

"You're a little over dressed," I smart, hoping he'll get the hint. Really I want to scream at the top of my lungs "Take your fucking clothes off and fuck me until I can't walk straight, damn it!"

Reaching down, he grips the hem of his shirt in his hands, ripping it over his head. Kicking off his shoes, he removes his socks and jeans. Within a matter of seconds he's left standing before me in nothing but tight grey boxer briefs, showing off his massive erection.

I can't help but lick my lips at the prospect of having that in my mouth again. He tastes and feels so damn good I think I've become addicted to giving him head. I crook my finger at him as I move up on my knees, hoping he'll come to the edge of the bed so I'll have better access to him.

After a few seconds pause, where he drinks me in again, he finally starts to move the few steps towards me, stopping at the foot of the bed. Instantly his fingers tangle in my hair, tilting my head back giving him access to my lips and throat. I feel him drag his tongue along the column of my neck, stopping to bite my jaw before moving his lips closer to mine.

I can't take it anymore, as much as I love his lips on me, kissing and sucking and teasing, I need more. "Jared, please. I need you."

"Greedy girl. Have I deprived you of something you want?" His tone is harsh, but so damn sexy it sends another gush of arousal into my already soaked panties. Unable to find my voice I just nod my head at him. "Tell me, Zho. What do you want?"

His hands are exploring now, one finger dips into my bra just enough to tease my nipple, causing me to moan and arch into him farther. "You. I want you."

His warm palm slides down my body, leaving an aching, burning fire in its wake. "Is all this for me?" he asks, one hand fondling the edge of my thigh high, the other stroking my center over my panties. I let out a little whimper, hoping he understands I'm trying to say yes I just can't find my voice.

Grabbing me by the hips he picks me up off the bed and sets me on my feet directly in front of him. "You're so fucking sexy, Zhoe. I'm torn though…"

Circling me like I'm prey, he whispers in my ear. "I can't decide if I want to keep you just like this, looking like a sex-goddess…" he runs his hands from my hips down to my ass slapping it crudely, causing me to yelp in surprise. Holy shit, that was hot. I've never been spanked before but fuck I want more of that.

"...Or if I want to tear those skimpy panties from your body with my teeth." He finishes his thought by nipping my earlobe between his teeth, a preview of the promises he just made.

"Please." He's reduced me to whispered pleas. I'm not even really sure what I'm asking for. I just need more. I can feel him behind me, his chest brushing my back with each breath he takes, but he's not touching me anywhere else and I need so much more than this.

"Please what, Pretty Girl?"

"All of the above. Damn it, Jared. Tear my panties off, smack my ass, and fuck me hard. Just fucking do it already." I'm practically shouting but I can't seem to control myself. My hormones are taking over every logical thought I've ever had. I sound like a hussy, but I don't care. I need him and I need him now.

Still, he pauses – he's not moving, not breathing. He just stands there completely fucking motionless and silent. "If you don't rip these damn panties off and fuck me until I can't walk straight, I'm getting rid of your ass," I growl in his direction, my head turned enough that I can see his eyes.

At least he can't say I was giving mixed signals. I think it's pretty obvious what I want at this point. I can't wait one second longer. Done with his games, I decide to take things into my own hands. Turning around I place my hands on his chest and shove. He only stumbles back a step or two before regaining his bearings.

With my wrists locked in his large palms, he yanks on me until I'm flush with his body. He reaches up with one hand and brushes away the tears I didn't even know were falling. I don't even know why the hell I'm crying. Sexual frustration, maybe? Is that a reason to cry?

When Jared Roman has been haunting all of your sexual fantasies, giving you small glimpses of what he's capable of but never giving you the real thing, I say yes. Sexual frustration is a damn good reason to cry.

"Shh. I've got you," he whispers against my lips. "I'll give you exactly what you're asking for, baby. I'll kiss you until you have to come up for air. I'll smack that pretty little ass of yours until it's red and I'll fuck you so good you'll be begging me for more. Is that what you want?"

Fuck, that was hot. I'm powerless to do anything but whimper at his words, my knees and my pussy turning to liquid. I want him, I need him to do everything he's promising and more. He kisses me softly for a few minutes, holding my face between his palms, my own palms flat against his chest. When he's gotten his fill of my lips he moves south, licking and sucking his way down my jaw and neck.

"Turn around." It's an order and I submit like the good little girl I am. As soon as my back is facing him, his hands slide from my shoulders, down my sides and land on my hips. He pulls me back against him until his erection is settled between my ass cheeks. "Do you feel what you do to me?"

Again I just nod my head, letting it fall back against his shoulder. His hands finally move, slowly trailing a path down the front of my thighs, unhooking my garter belt from the stockings. He slides the belt and my panties down my legs letting them pool at my feet. "Step out."

Lifting my right foot and then my left, I kick the discarded undergarments across the room. His hands are once again in motion, this time they move north, over my belly up to my breasts. He takes a few moments to fondle each one, growling his appreciation in my ear. When he's had enough, he moves back a step to give himself room to reach the hooks on the back of the bra. Undoing it and sliding the straps down my arms, he tosses it onto the floor.

I'm left standing in nothing but my thigh highs and stilettos and I've never felt sexier in my life. Moving around so he's standing in front of me, Jared's eyes trail up and down my body, taking in his fill slowly. "Jared," I whisper.

Bringing his gaze back up to mine, he smirks at me. It's devilish and sexy as hell. I squeeze my thighs together hoping to find some sort of relief. "Get on the bed, on your back and open those sexy legs for me." Sitting down, I slide back until I'm in the middle of the bed. Once I'm there, I lie back and open myself to him.

Twenty-Nine
Jared

Holy. Shit. I think my tongue actually fell out of my mouth when I walked upstairs and found her waiting for me, practically begging me to fuck her. I know she's frustrated with me right now. Anger is simmering in her eyes, just barely disguised by the lust, and need.

But, if I don't force myself to go slow, I'm afraid I'm going to hurt her. I've never wanted anyone so badly in my life. Not to mention it's been a long fucking time since I've sunk into a warm, soft pussy. And the way she was yelling at me, telling me exactly what she wanted and how she wanted it? That was enough to bring any man to his knees.

Shedding the rest of my clothes and grabbing a condom from my jeans pocket, I stand at the foot of the bed admiring the view. How the hell did I get so lucky? She's sweet and innocent and smart, but damn it if she isn't a sex-goddess tempting me in the most delicious ways.

"Jared." Her voice is throaty, laced with desire. She watches me eagerly as I sheath my cock with the condom, whimpering. "Please. You're driving me crazy."

I smile down at her. "Hmm, payback, Pretty Girl." I stroke my length a few times, loving the way her eyes take in every motion. "I walked in here with you dressed like a walking wet dream earlier. I think it's *you* who's driving *me* crazy." Knowing I'm just torturing both of us, I decide to give in.

Placing one knee on the bed, I lean down kissing all the way up her right thigh, my hand blazing a hot path up her other leg. Once I reach her center I kiss and nibble and bite for a few seconds, unable to control myself – she tastes so fucking good. "Are you ready for me?"

"Damn it, Jared. Please!" I don't wait for her to finish her thought, rearing up on my knees I grab the back of her thighs for leverage and thrust into her. "Oh God!"

Fuck. I knew she'd feel good, but this is better than anything I've ever felt in my life. I slam into her hard and fast over and over again. My fingers dig into her hips, her fingers grab frantically at the sheets. Her eyes are closed but her mouth is parted letting out the sexiest mewls and moans I've ever heard.

"Jared, oh my god. Don't stop. Don't ever stop."

I don't want to stop. I never want to leave her warm wetness. "You feel so fucking good, Zho. So good, I never want to leave."

She wraps her legs around my waist, lifting her hips higher, taking me deeper. Her fingers claw frantically at the sheets searching for anything to hold on to as my fingers trail all over her body. I can't stop touching her.

Over and over again I move my hips into hers, her body taking me all the way to the hilt. Still, it's not enough. I've waited so long for this girl. I swear it'll never be enough.

Pulling out of her, I grab her hip, flipping her onto her stomach. With one arm I reach under her, pulling her belly off the mattress and her perfect ass into the air. My other arm pushes lightly on her back keeping her chest and face pressed into the bed.

For a moment I just stare at the sight in front of me: this sexy girl in heels and thigh highs with her ass in the air begging me to take her. I promised her a red ass and that's what I'm going to give her. Lifting my right hand I smack the right side of her ass hard, the slapping sound echoing through the room.

"Jare…"

"I know, baby," I say as I ease into her again. This time I take my time, slowly entering her sex. Inch by inch I let her body take me. Once I'm all the way in her I pause, reveling in the way she feels – like fucking perfection. Raising my hand again I rub her pinking cheek before slapping it again, this time a little harder.

Zhoe moves her hips forward and back trying desperately to find the friction she needs, watching her slowly ride my cock is a sight to be seen. Once I've had enough of her teasing I rear up grabbing her hips in my hands, slamming into her hard and fast. The only sounds coming from the room are her sweet moans.

Unable to take it anymore, desperately needing release I reach between us with one hand to massage her clit in fast circles, matching the frantic rhythm of our thrusts. With my other hand I give her ass one more good, hard slap sending her over the edge.

"Jared. Jared! Yes!" She screams my name over and over again. I feel her tighten around my cock, her body shaking. I follow behind her, my own orgasm shaking me to my very core.

"Ffuucck! Zhoe!" I've never been one to make noise during sex, but I can't control myself around her. I've never come as hard or as long as I just did.

Best. Sex. Ever.

Unable to hold myself up any longer, I collapse to my side pulling her with me, her back pressed to my chest. I can't stop peppering her neck and back with kisses, she's so soft and sweet.

"Mmm." It's the only thing my mush for brains can think to say at the moment. I can't form a coherent thought, other than *I want to do that again. Soon.*

Finding strength I didn't think I had, I push up from the bed, disappearing into the bathroom. After disposing of the condom, I wet a washcloth with warm water taking it back to Zhoe. She's almost sleeping but I make sure to clean her up anyways.

Throwing the rag onto the floor I climb back into bed with my girl. Placing one last kiss on the back of her neck, I mummer against it. "Sleep, Pretty Girl."

Moments later we're both passed out from exhaustion of the best kind.

***

Waking up I feel lighter, happier, more relaxed. Zhoe and I have been pretty official for a while now, but last night sealed the deal, I think. At least it did for me. I'm never letting this girl go. She's mine. For as long as she'll have me.

I don't care if I sound like a pussy. I want to scream at the top of my lungs so the entire city knows, shit so the entire world knows Zhoe is mine. Mine.

Rolling my head to the side I take in her beautiful features. She's gorgeous all the time, but in sleep she looks like a damn angel. She looks innocent, peaceful. Stunning. My gaze wanders from her full lips parted just slightly in sleep, to her soft neck, to her perfect chest that is still naked from last night's events. Lower still, my eyes linger on her flat stomach, the soft flare of her hips – moving the sheet away I take in the rest of her naked figure.

Unable to resist anymore, I start licking, kissing, sucking my way down her body, until I'm positioned in front of her. My mouth seeking her heat, her sweet honey, her softness. I place several open mouthed kisses on her mound, before taking her clit into my mouth, biting gently.

"Jared." Her sleepy voice is sexy as hell.

"Good morning, beautiful girl." Those are the only words said, after that, the only noises that can be heard are Zhoe's moans and mewls as I bring her to and over the brink with just my mouth. I could wake up to her calling my name every single fucking day and never tire of it.

"So," I ask as I climb back up her body. Placing several soft kisses on her lips. "What did you want to do today?"

She smiles up at me lazily but I see the challenge in her eyes before she can even get the words out. "Oh well, I was thinking..." she pushes on my chest until I'm flat on my back. Climbing up she straddles me, her hands firm on my chest, using it for leverage to rock back and forth on my hard cock. "Why don't we just stay in bed all day?"

Before I have the chance to answer she lowers her face to mine, capturing my lips in a brutal, heated kiss. She lifts her hips just enough to line my dick up with her entrance slowly lowering down on to me.

"Zho. Condom." Somehow I manage to get the words out around her insistent tongue.

"I'm on the pill. I'm clean."

Fuck. She feels so fucking good. I never want to stop. I've never gone bareback with a girl before. Now I know what the hype is all about. It feels so much better. Hotter. "Me too."

"Good," she practically growls before taking over. Using my chest, she pushes her body up slowly, only to slam back down over and over again. I love a girl that knows what she likes and Zhoe definitely does.

I'm not even moving. Zhoe is using my body for her own pleasure. Riding me, taking me exactly the way she needs it. It's the hottest fucking thing ever. Not wanting to miss any of the show she's putting on for me, I place my arms behind my head, raising it just enough that I can see everything.

I give her a little smirk that she returns just as cockily. "Ride me, baby. Take what you need from me."

Part of me feels guilty for not doing anything, not adding to her pleasure. But, really, watching this usually innocent, giving girl be so greedy in bed is such a turn-on. I can't help but take it all in.

The way her head is dipped back, eyes closed in ecstasy. Her breasts that I love so much, bouncing up and down with each thrust. Her hips moving gracefully – up, down, left, right – feeling me fill her over and over again, making sure I hit the right spot. It's a beautiful fucking sight, one I will never *ever* tire of. One I want to burn into my memory forever, for use at a later date when she isn't so willing to ride me until my eyes cross.

Opening her eyes she pins me with her heated blue gaze. "Does that feel good, baby?" Her voice is husky and sexy as fuck. She smirks at me and I know she knows exactly what she's doing to me.

Deciding I've let her have her fun for long enough, I grip her hips tightly before flipping us until she's on her back and I'm hovering over her. "Felt real good, babe. You're fucking sexy when you show me what you want. But, it's my turn."

"Please." Needing no more of an invitation than that I pull my hips back and sink into her. Her eyes slam closed. "More. Harder."

"Yes, ma'am," I answer her demand before giving her exactly what she wants. Over and over again I slam into her, filling her, taking my fill. I feel her tense underneath me before the orgasm takes her over the edge. Her entire body quakes with it, sending me spiraling with her.

I collapse on my side, dragging her body with me. I try tucking her into my side but she apparently has other plans. Swinging her leg over my hips Zhoe climbs back on top of me so she's straddling me.

Looking down on me with a shit-eating grin on her face she says, "See what you've been missing by holding out on me? Don't you wish we'd done this sooner?"

I chuckle, unable to help myself. "You have no idea, Pretty Girl." She laughs lightly before flattening her body against mine, her head on my chest, her arms wrapped around my neck. My arms come up and run a path up and down her spine. Is this what it feels like to be happy? Content? Because, if so, I never want this feeling to go away.

THIRTY

Zhoe

"Ugh," Jared groans in protest underneath me as the alarm on my phone goes off disturbing our mini-morning nap. "Why?"

He finally opens his eyes and I can't help but giggle at him. "Gym time. Let's go big boy, time to show me what you got."

Lifting his hips, he digs his erection into my core to drive his point home. "Pretty sure I showed you several times what I've got last night… and this morning."

"Ha. Ha," I deadpan. "Come on. We have to leave in ten minutes."

We walk hand in hand to the gym laughing and chatting about absolutely nothing. It's easy and comfortable and I never want it to stop. I hate how quickly Jared has immersed himself in my life. I hate how easily I've allowed my life to become more about him than it is about me. I hate it because I've never felt this way about someone before and I'm afraid Jared is going to break my heart someday.

I have no idea why I feel that way there is just this hesitancy from him. I know he's attracted to me, I know he's staked his claim on me, but I don't know if Jared is a future kind of guy. He's had a rough past, a past he hasn't shared very much with me.

"What are you doing this weekend?" I blurt out of nowhere. I know it was a random question and my suspicions are confirmed when Jared looks at me like I've lost my mind.

"Uh, I don't really know. I haven't thought about it. Probably the same thing I always do." He stops walking, stepping in front of me. Grabbing my face he looks at me. "Hanging out with you is the only thing on my agenda this weekend, Pretty Girl."

I can't help but smile up at him. He's so adorable and has this way with words. It doesn't matter if he's being crass or sweet, he always says exactly the right thing to make my heart melt.

"Well, that's good because I want to spend the weekend with you, too." Leaning up on my tiptoes I place a quick kiss on his lips. "The whole weekend. Let's go away. Just you and me."

For a second he doesn't say anything. He just looks down, watching me, studying me. I'm not sure what he's looking for but I work to keep my face passive while I wait for his answer. "What are you up to, Zho?"

"What? Nothing." Shit. How does he read me so well? I really want to get out of town with him, just to spend time with him. No distractions. But, I'm also hoping getting away helps him open up to me a little bit, helps him ease into the next step in our relationship.

"Okay."

"Okay?"

"Yep. Okay. I'll go. I know you're up to something. I can see the wheels spinning in your head but I'm just going to go with it."

"Thanks, baby!" He laughs before catching me, as I jump up wrapping my arms and my legs around him inappropriately.

"You're welcome, crazy girl." We're both laughing our mouths barely touching when we hear someone clear their throat. It's at that moment I remember we're standing in the middle of the sidewalk a block away from the gym.

"Get a room you two. Oh wait, it looks like you already did. Freaking finally." My face blushes beet red as I bury it in Jared's neck trying to hide my embarrassment. Stupid best friends, I swear all they're good for is embarrassing you.

"Don't hide from me now, Pretty Girl." Jared coaxes me out of my hiding spot, gently placing my feet on the ground before turning on Ang. "Hey, Ang. Trust me, it was worth the wait." With that he winks at her, grabs my hand, and drags me behind him into the gym.

Leaving Angelica laughing her ass off as she trails in behind us. "Rico's in the back, Jared." He nods and we follow.

After a kickass workout we all decide to go get some food. Jared and I skipped breakfast, a few things taking precedence over nutrition this morning. As soon as we're seated in the little diner Rico looks over to Jared. "So, Roman. What's the plan for your birthday this weekend?"

"Um, I'm sorry. What?" Jared just smiles at me sheepishly. "Your birthday is this weekend? Why didn't you say anything?"

"I don't know. I don't usually celebrate too much. It's not a big deal, Zho."

"Uh, yes it is."

Rolling his eyes at me Jared turns back to Rico. "Zhoe and I are going out of town next weekend."

"Cool. Where are you guys going?" he asks.

To which Jared defers to me because I never actually told him. "Our lake house," I answer harshly. Jared looks at me, pursing his lips probably wondering what my deal is.

I don't know why I'm pissed and I know I'm overreacting, but I can't seem to help it. It's just another one of those details, however small it is, that he didn't share with me. Once again he didn't open up.

I'm loving being with Jared but great sex, physical chemistry and friendship will only take us so far. We laugh and joke together and I love it. I love how comfortable we are together but if we never open up, never share the hard stuff. How are we supposed to move forward?

Thirty-One
<u>Jared</u>

I know I've been out of the dating game for a while. Actually, I've been out of the dating game forever. I've never had a real relationship before. Sure, I had those high school flings where we called each other boyfriend/girlfriend but I don't think you can classify those as true relationships.

Still, I think I understand women, as much as you can as a man anyways, but whatever the hell I did to piss off Zhoe has me completely fucking lost. I'm pretty sure she's upset that I didn't tell her it was my birthday, but for some reason it feels like that's just the surface reason.

We've been back from breakfast for hours now and we've yet to say a word since we walked in the door. When we got home, I opted for a shower, extending the invitation to Zhoe to join me. She didn't even turn it down. She just glared at me and walked away. Since then she's been cleaning… loudly. I didn't even know you could clean loudly but she's doing it. Every cupboard she opens gets slammed shut, every time she walks by me she gives me a dirty look and sighs. I'm going to lose my ever-loving mind if this shit doesn't stop soon.

"God damn it, Zhoe!"

I snapped. I tried really hard not to, but I just couldn't hold it in any longer. Jumping up from my spot on the couch, I intercept her as she tries to make her way back into the laundry room. Grabbing her by the waist I drag her to the couch and throw her onto it. Climbing on top of her I pin her underneath me.

"Get off of me, Jared. Now." She's looking at me like she wishes she could shoot daggers out of her eyes. If I wasn't so pissed off it might actually be cute.

"No. Tell me what the fuck I did. Stop sulking and pouting."

She tries to fight me off of her again, but I just grab her wrists dragging her arms above her head. "I'm not pouting."

"The whole damn building knows you're pissed, Zho. I'm surprised the cupboard doors haven't fallen off yet." Again she just glares at me. At least she's stopped fighting to get up. Yelling isn't working. Joking isn't working. Time to take a different approach. Leaning down I place several soft kisses on her stiff lips, still she doesn't give in. My stubborn girl.

I keep trailing kisses on her soft skin. Her lips, her cheeks, her nose. I make my way down her neck, kissing that spot behind her ear that always gets to her. Keeping my lips there I whisper against her skin, "Talk to me, baby. What did I do?"

Opening her eyes she looks up at me and I see some of the anger leave her. "I just wish you'd open up to me more. Talk to me."

"We do talk."

"Not about anything important. I didn't even know it was your birthday, Jare. I don't know about your past, your family, how you met Rico. I don't know what you want for your future." She closes her eyes and lets a breath out through her teeth. "All I know about you is that you're sexy and strong and good in bed and can make me laugh. That you like pizza and beer and you don't like sweets. That's it. How are we supposed to move forward in our relationship when we only know the superficial stuff about each other? Do you even want to move forward? I'm going crazy. I don't know anything anymore. I..."

"Shh," I say, showering her face in soft kisses. Once her breathing comes back and her heart slows down, once I know she's calmed a bit, I pull her up to a sitting position with me.

Positioning her on my lap, her legs straddling me I grip her face in my palms. "Look at me, Zhoe." It takes a few seconds but finally she brings her eyes up to meet mine. "You have to understand something. I'm scared. You scare me. I've never had someone in my life to worry about. It was always me against the world. Now I have you to think about, to care about, to protect and it scares the shit out of me."

"I'm scared, too, Jared. I've never felt what you make me feel. I'm scared I'm not enough for you, or maybe that all of this is too much and you're going to leave me. You have the power to completely break me."

Afraid my words aren't going to be enough, I kiss her like I'm never going to kiss her again. I kiss her slowly – taking my time to savor her flavor, the feel of her. I swallow her sighs of pleasure as she sinks into me.

If she thinks I have the power to break her she has no idea the power she has over me. She could destroy me. Eat me alive and spit me out. I'd be nothing without this girl. Pulling back I look deep into her eyes, willing her to understand the conviction of my words. "I love being with you. I can't promise you a future or forever but I don't want this to end. That's all I can give you right now. Tell me now if it's not enough."

"I don't need promises of forever… yet." She flashes me a tiny smirk and I know I've got her back. "But, I do need you to promise you'll try. You'll try to open up to me, talk to me."

"I'll try. For you, Pretty Girl, I'll do damn near anything."

When she graces me with one of her perfect smiles I feel my grip on the ledge slip a little more. It definitely won't be long before I'm pushing off the ledge and falling hard and fast for this gorgeous girl. I'm not strong enough to hold on for much longer.

I promised her I'd try to open up to her and I will, but I'm so fucking scared. When she finds out what I did, that it's my fault Cole is no longer here, I know she's going to bolt. I can't deal with that.

My whole life I've been told I'm nothing but a disappointment, a loser, but Zhoe has never looked at me like that. She believes in me. I'm so fucking terrified of letting her down, letting her go.

Thirty-Two

Zhoe

This last week has been much better, there haven't been any other big declarations of feelings but Jared has opened up a bit more. We talked about our birthdays, when they are for starters. We talked about why Jared doesn't like to celebrate his. I know there is more to this story than he's telling me but like he said, I have to trust that one-day he'll tell me everything I need to know.

He told me he doesn't celebrate because his parents were never coherent enough to remember it was his birthday. They moved around a lot because his parents could never keep a job long enough to pay the rent on a shitty apartment, (his words not mine), for even a few months, let alone an entire school year. This meant he had no friends. No friends, no siblings, and really no parents. My heart hurt for him. I wouldn't want to celebrate my birthday either.

Things are different now, though. Jared has Rico and he has me. I promised myself to make this birthday his best yet. I was nervous about what I had planned. It wasn't anything spectacular but it was probably more than he'd ever had before. I spoke with Rico a little in secret and he informed me the most they ever did was go to the bar for a few drinks to celebrate.

He's never had a birthday cake or gifts and he definitely has never had a party. I'm not going to throw him a party because I know how much he'd hate that, plus this was our weekend getaway… alone.

I did, however, have the cleaning lady decorate the house in blue streamers and balloons. I ordered a cake that should have been delivered by now and I got him a few small gifts. Nothing extravagant. I just wanted to show him that I care about him and want him to be happy. More than that though, I want him to know he's not alone anymore.

"What are you thinking about, Pretty Girl?"

"Just excited to get away for a few days." Then I turn to smirk at him. "I'm excited to get you all to myself for an entire weekend." I flash him a devilish smile so he knows just how much I'm looking forward to it and exactly how I plan to spend it.

"Me too, gorgeous." He reaches over, placing his hand on my knee. I love his little touches, little reassurances. "So, tell me about this house we're going to."

I turn to him with a huge smile on my face my family's lake house is one my favorite places in the world. It's in a tiny town called Sugar Grove; it's about thirty minutes from Hocking Hills State Park.

"It's secluded and peaceful. The little town has all these cute mom and pop shops that I love going to. Oh, and there's a little winery. Or hiking…"

"You really love it up here, huh?" I just nod at him. "Thanks for sharing it with me, Zho."

The rest of the drive is made in relative silence, both of us just relaxing, taking in the view. In the summer months the view is full of rolling hills and lush green forests, today though it's even more breathtaking. The leaves are finally starting to change, painting the scene in rich oranges and reds. It's so pretty and tranquil up here. For the first time in a long time I feel like I can breathe. I can't help the smile that stretches across my face as we pull into the drive.

The driveway itself is a quarter-mile, winding path of gravel, lined on both sides by rich evergreens. At the end of the drive sits a simple log cabin with large bay windows in the front and a bright red door. The porch wraps all the way around the house and is adorned with several Adirondack chairs and a wicker swing. There are flowerbeds that are still blooming somehow in the cool October month. Oh, yeah I love it here.

I jump out of Jared's truck before he even has it in park, closing my eyes, I take a deep breath. Something about this place calms me, grounds me. I don't know how long I stand there like that but eventually Jared rouses me out of my trance. I feel his hands on my hips as he presses my back against his chest.

"Are you okay?" he whispers in my ear.

"Perfect." Turning in his arms I face him planting several soft kisses on his lips. "Sorry, I just love it here, it centers me somehow. I was just having a moment. But, I'm back with you now."

Jared gifts me with his panty-melting grin before taking my bottom lip between his teeth. Leaning up on my toes I deepen the kiss wanting nothing more than to get close to him right now, needing his touch. I want to show him how happy I am to have him here with me, but I can't wait to get him inside to show him his birthday present. "Come on. I want to show you something."

Grabbing our bags in one hand and my hand in his other, we walk up to the front door. I open it and usher him inside. I'm so nervous for him to see what I've done, afraid he won't take it well, but I'm excited, too. As soon as he's all the way in the living room I hear his sharp inhale and I know he's seen the sign.

A huge blue and white banner hangs over the fireplace that reads *Happy Birthday, Jared!* The ceiling is draped in blue streamers and blue balloons are strategically tied to the bar stools at the breakfast bar and on the door handles leading out to the back patio, which is visible from our spot in the entryway.

He still hasn't said anything and I'm starting to freak out. I walk up next to him, wrapping his hand in mine and whisper to him, "Happy birthday, Jare."

"How?"

"The cleaning lady helped. Do you like it?"

Again he doesn't say anything for long seconds. Instead he wraps me in his arms squeezing me to his body. He doesn't speak, he doesn't make a move to kiss me; he just holds me and I hold him back. I wonder to myself if he's ever really been hugged.

"Why?"

I'm taken back by his question; it's a logical question just not one I was prepared for. "Because, baby. You deserve to feel happy on your birthday and because I want you to know you're not alone anymore."

"Thank you." His voice is hoarse, barely more than a whisper. I don't think he's crying, his face is pressed so tightly against my throat I'd feel the tears, but I think I've heard before you can cry without actual tears ever falling from your eyes. Is that what he's doing?

Pulling back I bring his face up to mine. I see so many emotions in his eyes – happiness, confusion, sadness, awe. "Are you okay?" He just nods, his eyes never leaving mine. Deciding to take matters into my own hands I press a few kisses on his full lips, it only takes him a second to catch up.

Picking me up, I wrap my legs around him automatically as he ravages my mouth. He takes a few steps back until I'm pressed against the wall. All I can think is *thank God I wore a dress*. Jared shifts so he's holding me up with one arm, his other hand snakes under my skirt and plays with the hem of my panties, moving them to the side so his long fingers can enter my sex.

Reaching between us, I undo the button on his jeans, lowering the zipper. Again he shifts me, lifts me up higher so I can reach his jeans and boxers, pulling them down enough to free him for me. All the while our lips haven't parted. He's kissing and sucking my mouth like it's providing the air he needs to survive, like I'm what he needs to survive.

As soon as I've freed him, he enters me, filling me until I can't take any more of him. He slams into me several times, hard enough for the picture next to my head to shake, but then he looks up at me. Looks me in the eye and slows his movements.

Sex with Jared has been intense, hard and fast, but so, so satisfying. I would definitely classify what we do as fucking; it's not pretty and it's definitely not sweet. But, this right now, this is different.

Is this what making love feels like?

Jared is holding me, moving in and out of me so slowly like he's memorizing everything he's feeling. His eyes stay locked on mine, even as he lowers his face a bit to meet me for a series of kisses. His eyes never leave mine. His rich brown eyes are telling me so much in this moment; they are swimming with emotions I never thought I'd see from him.

"Zhoe, baby." My name leaves his lips like a prayer. All I can do in response is whimper, too many emotions making it impossible to speak. I can't take it. I try to close my eyes against everything I'm feeling, but of course Jared is having none of that. "Look at me, baby."

Jared thrusts several times, slowly, deeply his eyes searching my soul just as deep. We come together, both of us unusually quiet as we find our release. The only sounds are the two of us whispering the other's name.

I get lost in his eyes; his warm brown eyes that tell me more than sex or words could ever say.

Then it hits me and it hits me hard. I'm falling for this man; I'm spiraling, out of control, free-falling. I just pray he's there to catch me before I hit the ground. Otherwise it's going to hurt like hell.

Thirty-Three
<u>Jared</u>

I still can't believe Zhoe did all of this for me. I could tell she was nervous about my reaction and I'm sure the way I reacted was not at all what she was expecting. I don't even know how to classify what I felt – sadness, love, confusion, and happiness. I felt all of those things simultaneously and had no fucking clue how to process it.

So I just wrapped her in my arms and let her be strong enough for both of us, let her carry my pain and loneliness for just a few minutes. All it took, though, was a few minutes because then her words really sank in – I was no longer alone. *I had Zhoe. I had Zhoe.* Fuck, it feels good to know that, to feel that.

It's an unusually warm day considering the time of year in Ohio but we decided to make the most of it. We ran down to the corner store and picked up a few steaks, potatoes and vegetables and a couple bottles of wine.

When we got back Zhoe had me man the grill while she made the side dishes inside. It was very domesticated, very normal and comfortable. I liked it. Who knew?

So, here we sit on the back patio eating a delicious dinner, drinking great wine and taking in the view.

"What ya thinking about, handsome?" Zhoe breaks me out of my thoughts.

"Just thinking about your surprise earlier. Thank you again, Zho."

She smiles at me sheepishly. "You know, I love celebrating my birthday. It's kind of a big deal. So, you better not forget about it and everything I did here for you. I expect big things, Roman, big things."

I sit there for a second waiting for the panicky feelings to kick in. Her birthday is in August, nearly a year away. This means she's thinking long term about us. Shouldn't that freak me the fuck out? I mean it's a foreign feeling, it makes me slightly uncomfortable, but if I'm being honest I hope and pray that I'm still around a year from now. Zhoe has slowly made her way into my heart and I can't imagine letting her go.

"Don't worry, Pretty Girl. I have a big thing to offer you." I wiggle my eyebrows suggestively at her. It was an awful line and I know it but it did exactly what I wanted it to. Zhoe throws her head back and laughs out loud, and I can't help but join in – it's contagious.

"That was awful!"

"What do you mean, awful? It's the truth. You don't believe me?"

Suddenly she sobers up, pushing her wine glass and plate away from her she looks at me from under her lashes. "Guess you'll just have to prove it."

Challenge accepted. Shoving away from my chair, I lunge at her, ravishing her mouth, feeling her soft curves under my hands. I'll never get enough of this.

I drop to my knees in front of her, gripping her knees in my hands; I slowly part her legs giving me access to the one part of her I physically crave. Thankful she hasn't changed out of her dress, I push it up her thighs a little, placing kisses on her legs along the way.

Once I reach the apex of her thighs, I drag my nose along her already dampening center. "You smell so good, baby. Better than any meal I've ever had." I hear her soft moan as her head falls back on her chair. Not wanting another minute to pass without tasting her, I grip her panties in my hands and drag them down her legs, throwing them behind me, getting lost in the darkness.

I spread her lower lips with my fingers and start ravishing her with little preamble. She's already soaking wet, just as insatiable as I am. I lick each lip, making sure to taste every inch of her before spearing my tongue and letting her fuck my face.

Her hands come down to grip my hair. She pulls so hard it's nearly painful, but I take it, loving that she's this out of control because of me. I lick and suck her clit over and over until she's panting my name.

Not yet satisfied I stand, lowering my own jeans and boxers, my eyes never leaving hers. She licks her lips as she watches me undress. "You're too damn sexy, Stud."

"Stand up, Zho." As always, she listens without hesitating. I grab her hips turning her toward the table; pushing on her back gently I lower her upper body onto the table. So damn sexy – her dress hiked up to her hips, her pussy dripping, eagerly waiting for me to enter her.

Slowly I ease into her, watching in fascination as her body accepts every inch of me. I swear I'll never get enough of this girl. Every time I sink inside her is amazing. It's even better than the last time.

"Jared, you feel so good," Zhoe pants, her face pressed against the table, her hands clutching the side. I lean down taking her lip between my teeth before kissing her senseless.

I feel her knees give out, causing me to press into her harder, deeper to keep her upright. Knowing she's not going to last much longer I drive into her, burying myself to the hilt on each thrust. Zhoe reaches down to massage her clit with her own hand. "Fuck baby. That's so sexy. I want to come with you, work it harder, Zho."

"Hurry, Jared, I'm almost there." Her finger starts working in fast, hard circles as I pump in and out of her. I feel her tighten before she calls out, "Jared."

I follow quickly behind her, her body milking every last drop out of me. I grab her waist as I collapse on the patio ground, bringing her with me.

We lay like that for a long while, wrapped in each other staring at the stars in the sky. I take a deep breath – reveling in the way this girl makes me feel.

Happy. Complete. Loved.

"I wish we could stay like this forever," Zhoe's voice is barely a whisper. It's so quiet I'm not sure she's even speaking to me.

I place a kiss on her forehead, leaving my lips there I mumble against her, "me too, baby. Me too."

Thirty-Four

Jared

After taking Zhoe on the back patio, and then moving back inside to the bed and doing it all over again we're both finally sated. For now. Laying here with Zhoe in my arms I can't help the feeling of contentment that washes over me. This is where I'm supposed to be.

"Hey, Jare?" Zhoe whispers against my chest, her warm breath blowing across my pecs. I tighten my grip on her a little bit, the tone of her voice making me nervous. Whatever she has to ask is going to be hard to answer; I know it.

"Yeah, babe?"

"Tell me about your family." Fuck. I know I promised her I would open up more but I'm afraid she'll run the other way. I gave her the condensed, flowery version the other day when she asked why I never celebrated my birthday but I left the ugly details out.

I'm afraid it'll be the nail in the coffin on what we have. We grew up so differently. She hates that her mom takes anti-depressants and is so high she can't function, but she's never truly seen drug use and abuse – she has no idea how bad it can get.

We've never really talked about where we come from and how different we are. Zhoe comes from money, whereas I'm barely getting by each month. I've never brought it up because I'm afraid one day she'll realize I'm not good enough for her. I can't give her the things she needs, the things she deserves.

But, this? Talking about my loser, druggie parents? That's just another difference between us. Another spotlight on how we come from two different worlds.

"It's okay, if you're not ready. Forget I asked." She places several soft kisses on my chest letting me take this pass if I want to and I want to. I know Zhoe wants me to open up to her but I also know she won't hold it against me if I'm not ready to tell her.

Not even the guys in the NA meeting really know where I come from, we just all pretty much assume we've grown up in shitty homes, surrounded by drugs and alcohol it was almost natural for us to follow that path. So, no one asks.

But, I know I have to tell Zhoe. If not all of it, most of it. Clearing my throat I jump in with two feet and start telling her my story, all the while praying she doesn't run away screaming when I'm finished.

"Well, um. My mother was only seventeen when she had me. She went to my father's house to score some heroine but she didn't have any cash so she paid him with sex."

I pause letting that sink in. I'm painting the ugly picture that is my mother and as badly as I wish I could say just one decent thing about her, I can't. "So, anyways here I am. My father was twenty-five at the time and naturally claimed I wasn't his and didn't want anything to do with me.

"Mom tried to raise me on her own but she was too addicted to her drugs to actually do anything. We bounced from apartment to apartment getting evicted from each one because she chose to use every penny she made or found or stole for drugs."

Zhoe's grip tightens just slightly around my waist. I know she wants to say something but she's silent, encouraging me to continue. After taking several deep breaths I start again.

"My father found us when I was five. For whatever reason he decided he wanted to be a part of my life. To this day I have no fucking clue why, he was decent towards me for a little while, but mostly I was wasted space, wasted money. For a short period of time my parents had their shit together – they worked real jobs, made okay money, at least enough to put food on the table.I'm not stupid, and even back then I knew what was going on. They were still using, still selling but I didn't really care because they managed to hold down jobs while doing it. Which means I had food, clothes, a place to call home. Even if for a short while.

"Like most drug addicts it's hard for them to hold down a job, to be responsible, to live with the rest of society. The *decent* life we had faded into the shitty one I remember so well. I started to rebel; I started getting into a lot of trouble in school, especially in junior high. I started hanging with the kids from our apartment complex, whose parents were typically hanging at our place trying to score drugs. It was natural for us to become friends, if that's what you could call it. Really we were just a bunch of lost kids doing drugs, starting fights, and breaking the law.

"I avoided going home like the plague. My father was so lost in his addiction he couldn't get off the couch unless it was to walk to his bedroom to do another line. Mom was always sick, and looking back I'm pretty sure it was a combination of the drugs and STD's. There was always a parade of guys coming through the house, probably paying her in sex for drugs."

Zhoe gasps when I tell her about the men parading through our home; I'm waiting for her to freak out at any moment. None of this is pretty. It's ugly and gross and dirty. I hate that this innocent, gorgeous girl is being weighed down by my ugly past. "Didn't your father care that she was sleeping with other guys?"

I snort. "Yeah, right. He didn't care about her or me. He really didn't care about himself. As long as her sleeping around brought them drugs, he didn't care. Anyways, in high school I got caught up in some bad shit. I did a stint in juvi, which is where I met Rico. When I got out, my parents were gone. Nowhere to be found. I haven't seen them since."

"Jared, I'm so sorry. Have you tried looking for them?"

"Fuck no. I'm glad they are finally out of my life." It may seem harsh but it's the truth. When I got out I went to where they were living when I left but they weren't there, no one else seemed to know where they went. I turned around and walked right back out of that place and haven't looked back since.

"What did you go to jail for?" Her voice is small, timid. I hate that I put that doubt there. I hate the person I was back then – that I have such a tainted and ugly past. I leave out the part that I knew Cole, and what happened to him, that being with him is what got me busted to begin with. Sort of.

"Drugs. I was selling and using. I was almost eighteen, a month out, so I was lucky they tried me as a minor. It could have been a lot worse." I take in a huge breath, terrified of what's going to happen next. Will she run the other way?

"When's the last time you used?" She reaches for my hand, entwining our fingers, holding on tightly. She seems to know exactly what I need.

"Five years ago. I go to NA meetings on Wednesday nights, that's why I'm never around those nights."

After a long, drawn out pause, she finally says something. "How did you get out of that life? How did you turn into such a wonderful, strong man?" Her voice is so low, so quiet I'm not sure if she's talking more to herself or if she's actually asking me the question. I wouldn't know the answer anyways. I've never thought of myself the way she sees me. I've never considered myself to be strong, and definitely not wonderful.

No, I'm damaged and trash. I'm broken and weak.

It isn't until she moves her head off my chest and looks up at me that I realize she's waiting for an answer. I search her eyes for a long time trying to read her emotions. She's not crying but she looks sad. Her eyes wet with unshed tears. But, she's trying to hold it together, trying to be strong. For me. How did I ever get so lucky to find this amazing girl?

"I found John, or really he found me. Rico and I were living on the streets. Sleeping on park benches, doing side jobs for people to scrounge up change for food. John approached us one day, told us we could work for him but only if we were clean and stayed that way. He was the best thing that's ever happened to me, until I met you, Zho." Zhoe smiles at me, it's soft and sweet and tells me more than words ever could. "Thank you for choosing me, for being here with me."

She's not going to leave me. She's still here, in my arms smiling at me.

"There's nowhere else I'd rather be than in your arms, Jared," she tells me with her mouth pressed lightly against mine. I am so damn lucky. Pulling her head back down to my chest I hold on for dear life. I am never letting this girl go.

Thirty-Five

Zhoe

I'm still reeling from Jared's admission last night. Leaning back against the counter I watch the coffee slowly fill the carafe below as I think of all the things Jared has opened up to me about.

He once told me he was damaged and while that may be true, that is not the word I'd use to describe him. He's strong, determined, amazing. It took so much for him to get out of that life, to make something of himself. It took even more strength to tell me his story.

I knew I was starting to fall for him. I knew the potential was there but last night sealed the deal for me. I love Jared Roman. Holy shit, I love that man. I should be screaming at the top of my lungs, shouting for the entire world to hear but I can't. Jared isn't ready to hear it yet, so I'll hold it in, keep it to myself until he is.

I just hope that someday he is willing, not only to hear those words but to maybe return them. I hope one day Jared can love me back. It would be nice to actually be loved by someone other than my dead brother.

The problem though, I'm realizing, is that I'd stay with him even if he never loved me because I need him to be part of my life that bad because I'm that in love with him.

How did that happen? How did he go from Mr. Sexy-Scary, my one night to do something reckless, to the guy who owns my heart so completely?

"Zho?" Jared calls from down the hall in his sleepy voice. I make my way back to him. He's still in bed half asleep. Leaning against the doorframe I take him in. He's so damn adorable, a word I'm sure has never been used to describe this hard, strong man.

The blanket is barely covering his naked body, leaving that glorious piece of art on display for me to drool over. He's lying on his back; one arm tucked under his head the other lying by his side. His hair is messy from sleep and from the many rounds of delicious sex we had last night. Yummy.

"You called, handsome?" He rolls his head over to the side, looking at me heavy-eyed, giving me a sleepy, super sexy smile that has me wanting to climb back into bed with him and never leave.

"Where'd you go?"

"Just making coffee. Are you okay?"

"A little cold," he smiles at me. "Think you could come warm me up?"

I can't help but laugh at him. "It's a good thing you're sexy because these one-liners of yours are awful."

He just growls at me before flinging the covers off him, diving across the bed, and grabbing me around the waist, bringing me down with him. Before I can even comprehend what's happened I'm flat on my back and Jared is hovering over me with a shit-eating grin on his face. "Warm me up, woman." I don't even have to respond before his lips are on mine.

A morning full of lovemaking and laughter is a good morning. I could definitely get used to this.

***

Several hours later I roll to my side to catch Jared watching me. "What ya thinking about, Stud?"

"You're beautiful, you know that?"

"Thanks. You're not so bad yourself," I reply with a cheeky grin. "I was thinking we could do some hiking today, what do you think?"

Jared smiles, leaning over to place a soft kiss on my forehead. "Sounds good to me."

We stopped by a little diner on the way out of town to pick up sandwiches, chips and drinks for a picnic lunch during our hike. I directed Jared to one of my favorite spots in the park. It's a pretty easy hike, only three miles round trip, but it's gorgeous. It takes us deep into the woods and is surrounded by rocks and cliffs and thick trees.

The top of the hike is my favorite part, though. Once you reach the top it opens completely up, allowing you to see over the hills and the park for miles. If you're quiet you can even hear the waterfall gushing from a few miles away. I used to love coming up here and closing my eyes, lying back on the ground just listening to the sounds of nature. It's peaceful.

"You doing okay back there, rugged?" I call to Jared over my shoulder. We're about halfway through the hike up. I've been leading but only because I know the way.

"Yep, just enjoying the view," Jared calls back. When I turn around, I see his gaze locked on my ass. It's a nice day for October but it's still deep into fall so I've opted to wear a sweatshirt and a pair of long yoga pants... obviously the pants are giving Jared a show.

"You're a perv."

"You shouldn't be so damn sexy." At that I just roll my eyes and continue leading our hike. As soon as we reach the top I stretch my arms out to the side, closing my eyes and take a deep breath. I've forgotten how much I love the outdoors, how much I love coming here.

I feel Jared come up behind me, wrapping me in his arms. If I thought this place brought me peace before, I was wrong. Being here, wrapped up in Jared is peace at its best. "It's beautiful up here," Jared whispers against my hair.

"Mmm." We stand like that for several silent minutes. I love that I don't have to fill the void with meaningless babble with Jared. I love that we are content to just be together. Comfortable in both silence and chatter.

"I want you to know I'm not letting you go, Zhoe." Jared's voice is quiet, serious but full of emotion. "I'm not ready to say those three words, just yet, but, I want you to know I need you in my life and I have no intention of letting you go."

I lean my head onto his shoulder, grabbing onto his arms that are still wrapped around my middle. My eyes close as I try to reign in my emotions. He has no idea what he just said means to me. I want to tell him so badly that I love him. That I love him more than I've ever loved anyone, more than I thought was possible to love another person. But, if he's not ready to say the words he's probably not ready to hear them either. And for now, I'm perfectly content to soak in the way he makes me feel. Perfectly content knowing he cares for me, needs me, wants me.

"Good, because I have no intention of going anywhere." I turn around wrapping my arms around his neck. "I need you too, Jare. You make me so damn happy."

Jared gift's me with one of his panty-dropping grins, the one that lights up his whole face and makes me weak in the knees. "You make me happy, too, Pretty Girl." I don't know if he made the move first or if I did but I've found myself once again wrapped completely around Jared, suspended in his arms as he kisses all rational thought out of me.

***

"What are you doing for Thanksgiving?" After Jared's big revelation we found a semi-secluded spot away from the trail but still out in the open, we spread out a blanket and enjoyed our packed lunch. Since then we've been cuddled up next to each other dozing in and out, watching the clouds move and transform, occasionally pointing out shapes– it was peaceful and easy and even a little cheesy, but it's been perfect.

Rolling his head to the side he looks at me from his spot on the ground. "Uh, nothing. Rico and I usually spend it on the couch drinking beer, eating leftover pizza and watching football."

I look up to the sky taking a moment to find the courage to invite him to our family's dinner. I have no idea how he's going to react. We've been together for a couple of months now, and in my mind things are pretty serious, but that doesn't mean he's ready to meet the parents. "Come with me to my parents?"

He clears his throat a few times, something I've noticed he does when he's unsure about something. Shit. I pushed too far this time. "Sure."

My head snaps up to look at him. "Sure?"

He smiles down at me, placing a gentle kiss on my temple. "Yes, Pretty Girl. Sure. I'll go to your parents with you. It's probably about time I meet them anyways."

"Thanks, Jare. That means a lot to me that you'll go."

"So tell me what to expect." I can't believe how calm he's being. He's taking all of this in stride and truthfully it's rather shocking. For someone that has never done relationships before, and for someone that has probably never seen a healthy relationship, he is a damn good boyfriend.

"It's awful." I look up at him with a grin on my face. My tone is joking but I am so serious. Holidays around my family are always awful. Especially since Cole died.

"Great, can't wait," Jared deadpans.

"I'm just being honest. Our housekeeper, Ms. Taylor is amazing. She is hilarious and sweet and kind. She was a mother figure to me even before my own mother checked out. She's the only reason I still go to holidays."

"What about your parents? What will they be like?"

"Daddy won't come out of his office until it's time to eat and he'll go right back to working as soon as dinner is over. Mom will lie on the couch like the zombie she is – she probably won't eat. She'll just sit at the table staring into space. It's a blast."

"I'm sorry, Zho."

"No big deal. It is what it is, you know? It wasn't always that way. Before Cole died we were a family, a real family. Sure, Daddy pretty much told Cole and I what our dreams were going to be, what we were going to do after high school and college, but, other than that, things were good. There was laughter and family dinners and vacations.

"Once we lost Cole, we lost everything. Everything changed that day and we've never gotten it back. Part of me hates it. Part of me wanted to scream at them that they still have another child that needed them. But, I know they are hurting and trying to get over it the only way they know how."

Jared pulls me into his arms, wrapping me tightly in his strength and comfort. "And what about you, Pretty Girl? How do you cope?" he asks quietly.

"I live. Cole wouldn't have wanted my life to stop because he's no longer here. He would've wanted me to enjoy life, celebrate it. So, that's what I do. Some days are hard. Some days I want to curl up and cry and grieve and sometimes I do, but mostly I smile and remember all the good times I had with him."

"You, Zhoe Dawson, are the strongest girl I know." Before I can respond Jared covers my lips with his own. Kissing me sweetly, lovingly. I soak it all in. For five years it's really just been Ang and me. She tells me I'm strong and she's proud of me all the time, but for some reason it means so much more coming from Jared.

Maybe it's because of all he's dealt with in his life. Maybe it's because I want to be the woman he's proud to call his. Maybe I have daddy issues and I need a man's approval – though I doubt that's it. Maybe it just feels good to be appreciated and understood by someone other than family, because Ang is family in every sense of the word.

Thirty-Six

Jared

For years I've lived with the guilt of Cole's death. I've dealt with those feelings; I've learned to live with the guilt – after all, it's the least I deserve.

But, now I feel like I'm drowning in it. Sitting here holding Zhoe in my arms her pain radiating off of her breaks my fucking heart.

Cole and I hadn't been friends long. We met at a party one night and truthfully I thought Cole was just a typical rich kid trying to rebel against his parents. He wasn't into the hard stuff like the rest of us. He stuck to drinking and pot mostly, but one night we were all higher than a fucking kite and Cole opened up to us about his asshole father.

An asshole father was something I could definitely relate to. It didn't take long for us to become fast friends, as corny as it is we become each other's confidants. We confided in each other our fears, our anger – things we couldn't talk about with anyone else we talked about together.

That fateful night I tried to score some coke from my usual dealer but he was out. He passed me on to a friend of a friend. Cole went with me. Neither one of us should have been there, but Cole especially. We met up with the guy in a sketchy neighborhood, in a back alleyway. Hindsight tells me I should have turned around and walked away then, but I was too worried about getting my next fix.

When the guy tried to charge me double what my usual dealer did, I raised my voice. One of his little goons pulled out a knife stabbing me in the back with it, before either of us could move to do anything, the dealer pulled out a gun and pointed it at my face. Being the coward I was I turned and ran.

Realizing I could no longer hear Cole behind me, I turned and saw the one thing I'll never be able to erase from my memory. Forever the image of Cole, face down on the ground with a gun pressed into the back of his head will haunt me.

Before I could react, the guy pulled the trigger and shot Cole right in front of me, the echo of the shot drowning out my own pleas for help, for him to shoot me instead. It didn't matter. I couldn't stop it from happening and I couldn't bring Cole back.

As much as I wished it had been me that day, even in the heat of the moment, I wished it were me he shot instead, my fight or flight instincts kicked in. I ran until I could run no more, until the tears in my eyes were blinding me. I just killed one of my best friends.

I was several blocks away when the police caught up to me. I had the coke on me, because instead of trying to grab Cole, I grabbed the coke from the guy's hand like the true junkie I was. I was arrested for possession and questioned until my face was blue about Cole. I denied it all, telling him I had no idea who he was or what he was doing back there.

Every single fucking day I've had to live with the regret, the guilt. If I could go back in time and change everything about that day I would. Part of me wishes I'd never met Cole. He was so much better off without me. He deserves to be here, soaking up his sister's love. Not me. I'm nothing. Why was I the one to survive that day?

I knew Cole had a sister and a family, but their feelings were always too far back for me to think about them. All I could focus on was Cole – his death, his life and my own feelings – the guilt, the desire to give up, the desire to move on.

I destroyed this beautiful girl's life. She had a brother she relied on and loved and I took that from her. Not the drug dealer, or his goons, not the gun or the bullet. Me. I took Cole's life. I'm responsible for years of pain for Zhoe and her family.

"Jared? Did you hear me?" Zhoe's sweet voice breaks me out of my thoughts. Realizing I'm squeezing her to me tightly I focus on loosening my hold on her.

Shaking my head I answer her. "No, sorry, baby. What did you say?"

"I asked if you were okay?"

I try to smile but it comes out more like a grimace, "Yeah. Fine."

Zhoe rolls onto her side and stares at the side of my face for a long while. I'm too much of a chicken shit to look at her, afraid of what she'll see in my eyes. I hear her let out a long sigh. "Okay, don't take this the wrong way, but every time I bring up Cole you get all cagey and distant."

I stop breathing. Like literally, I stop fucking breathing, my heart feels like it's going to explode out of my chest. This is it. This is the moment I tell her my deepest, darkest secret. "I just don't deal with death well. Sorry." Fuck. I'm such a goddamn coward.

"I'm sorry I make you uncomfortable. I just want you to know about me, about my life. But, I won't talk about him anymore," Zhoe's voice is strong, determined. I'm seriously an asshole. She's trying to protect me and my feelings, when really my feelings don't matter.

"You can talk to me about anything, everything. I want you to." I take a deep cleansing breath before rolling onto my side and looking into her bright blue eyes. "Zhoe, I have to tell you something."

I have no idea what look I'm wearing but whatever it is must be serious. Zhoe slides closer to me, her hand gripping mine tightly. Leaning forward I press my lips against her forehead, leaving them there for a minute – soaking in her scent, her warmth, her strength.

"Jare?"

As if God heard my undeserved prayer to prolong this moment, my time with Zhoe, the sky opens up. Rain beats down on us relentlessly as Zhoe screams and jumps to her feet. Quickly we gather our things and race down the path back to our car.

The almost conversation forgotten – by Zhoe anyways. For now.

Thirty-Seven

Zhoe

Ugh, I am so dreading this damn dinner. Trying to prolong the inevitable as long as possible I take the long route to my parents' house; which really only adds an extra five minutes to the commute.

Daddy called me this morning asking me to come to his house for dinner He wanted to talk to me about something. I've done a pretty good job of avoiding my lovely parents the last several months, only talking via text and email when necessary.

I've tried desperately to live in the fairy tale world with Jared. It's been a few weeks since our impromptu weekend getaway and things have been amazing. I live for my nights with him – the nights we stay up late ignoring the rest of the world, wrapped up in each other. Wrapped in every sense of the word – wrapped around each other's usually naked bodies, and wrapped up in every word that spills from the other's mouth.

We've been talking more – we have real, deep, intense conversations. The only flaw, the only crack in our relationship is Jared's aversion to talk about Cole, and death. He's opened up to me about his family, but he's never spoken of death. As far as I know he's not experienced the heartbreaking, gut-wrenching pain of loss.

Yet he always shuts down when it's brought up. Somehow I have to find a way to bring it out of him, find out what's eating him and get him to open up to me even more.

Other than that, Jared seems happier, lighter even. Whenever I talk to him about my father, or my future, he's always supportive and understanding of the choices I've made. But, he always encourages me to pursue my dreams and to stop living for my parents, and even for Cole, and start living for myself.

This is one of the reasons I've been avoiding my family – my father in particular. I've decided I'm not going to finish business school. I'm going to switch my major next semester and somehow I have to find a way to tell him.

I know Daddy isn't going to react well; he's going to threaten me and try to manipulate me into staying in business and following through with the plans as they've been set for years. I had planned on having Jared with me when I had this talk with my parents. I need his strength, his encouragement, but, with Daddy's impromptu phone call it's looking like it's me against them. Again.

I open the large front door and immediately feel like I can't breathe. Funny how walking into this giant home can feel so suffocating. That is, until Ms. Taylor greets me at the door. "Zhoe, baby! I've missed you, darling. You look so good."

I can't help the giant smile that moves across my face. This woman has been a mother figure in my life for as long as I can remember. "You look good, too, Ms. Taylor." Ms. Taylor is an older, black lady. She is short, but stocky and is totally rocking a full head of grey hair.

She takes another moment to inspect me. "You're glowing, darling. Tell me, what's his name?'

"What?" How the hell did she do that? I can't look happy without having a man in my life? I voice that thought to her, which causes her to bust out laughing.

"Well, of course you can. But, now you've just reaffirmed my suspicions. So, now tell me everything!"

She turns and starts walking back toward the kitchen, leaving me to trail behind her. We walk down the sterile hallway, with its bare white walls. We've never had pictures of us on the walls; mother always said it was tacky. I follow Ms. Taylor into the large, open kitchen. This has always been my favorite room in the house.

I take a seat at the breakfast bar so she can continue cooking and I don't get in her way. I spent a majority of my life in this exact position – her cooking and me sitting here telling her all about my life.

My mother could never be bothered with me for longer than five minutes; even then she only cared about my image and whether I was upholding the family name properly. She never cared about me, or what was going on in my life. Not like Ms. Taylor did anyways.

"Well, his name is Jared and oh my gosh... he's amazing Ms. Taylor!"

"How'd you meet this Jared?" I must blush at her question remembering first the night I stalked him with my eyes, and then the night we actually spoke and I brought him home. "Miss Zhoe, are you blushing? My goodness, I must meet this man. I've never known you to blush."

"He says that all the time. Apparently my blush is cute... I think he purposely says and does things to make blush." I laugh. Before I met Jared I wouldn't have guessed I even had a shy bone in my body. He makes me feel so sure, so confident and sexy; yet so vulnerable and shy. I don't understand it, but I wouldn't trade the way he makes me feel for anything in the world.

"I met him at the bar. I know, not the best place to meet people, but whatever. He's so great. He's this big, huge, muscular man – he's completely covered in tattoos. He looks so hard on the outside but he has the best heart, Ms. Taylor. He makes me feel feminine and special, but strong and independent at the same time." I stop my disgusting rant about how perfect he is to smile huge at my surrogate mother, "I love him, Ms. Taylor."

She looks over at me with a warm smile. "I can tell, sweetie. I hope he knows how lucky he is to have you."

I don't have time to respond to that comment because my mother choses that moment to make her appearance. "Oh yes, who wouldn't be lucky to have you, *Princess*?" She scoffs before pulling a bottled wine cooler out of the fridge, making her way to the dining room. "Is dinner nearly ready, Ms. Taylor? I'd like to get this night over with as soon as possible."

"Yes, ma'am. It will be ready in just a few minutes." She turns back to me as soon as my mother is out of the room. "You better get in there. Give me a call and we'll get together to talk more about this man-hunk you've got yourself."

"He's actually coming to Thanksgiving, so you can meet him then. Love you."

"Love you, too sweet girl."

Reluctantly, I hop off the barstool and trudge into the formal dining room. Daddy is seated at the head of the table as usual with my mother sitting to his right.

"Daddy," I say before placing a kiss on his cheek and taking my usual seat. My seat is to Daddy's left, which means I'm privy to mother's nasty looks all night. Great.

"Oh, Zhoe. Thank you for joining us tonight." Ugh, this why I hate this family. Why is he acting like I'm some client he invited to a business dinner? This was my home, damn it. I should be able to come here for dinner whenever I want without it being a big deal. Of course, I would never do that because I hate it here but it's the point.

"You wanted to talk to me about something?" I ask trying to get this out of the way as soon as possible.

"Oh, yes. I wanted to let you know I have an opening at the office for a sales intern. I've told Barbara in HR you would be taking that position. It starts January 1. So, you'll have to schedule night classes for next semester, but it'll look great on your resume should you decide to work somewhere other than my company, though why you'd do that is beyond me." Finally, he stops talking long enough to take a sip of his wine.

I am so over him telling me how to live my life. I'm so over being told what to do all the time. I'm an adult damn it. I get to make my own choices. "Daddy, no. I'm not taking the internship. I'm changing my major next semester. I don't want to be in business. I don't want to work for you. I want my own life."

Mother chuckles into her bottle like the classy bitch she is. "You are so ungrateful."

"That's rich coming from you, Mother." This from my mother who hasn't worked a day in the last twenty years, since she's been with my father. My mother who can't appreciate the fact that she has another child that is still living, still breathing. How dare she tell me I'm ungrateful? "Besides, how is me standing up for myself, and doing what I want being ungrateful? Life is short. I want to do something that makes me happy."

"Enough," Daddy booms. "This is not up for discussion. If you want to live in that nice apartment and you want to have your schooling paid for you will continue to go to school for business."

Fuck this. I'm done with this family. "Fine, take my apartment and my tuition money away. I'll be just fine. I'm not working for you, and I'm changing my major – end of discussion." With those final words I stand from the table, walking away exuding a calm I so do not feel.

Before I can reach the front door Ms. Taylor stops me, wrapping me in her arms. "I'm sorry, sweet girl. Don't worry about next week sweetie; I'll meet your man another time."

Pulling back I look her in the eyes, trying to force a smile. "I'll be here. For you, Ms. Taylor." With a quick kiss on her cheek I pull away, desperately needing the peace and solitude of my car.

The tears start falling seconds after I close my car door. Who the hell do they think they are? You'd think they'd want their only child left to be happy, you'd think they'd understand the concept of life is short.

Needing something to make me happy, to calm me down, to comfort me I call Jared. He answers after just two rings. "Hey, baby. I was just thinking about you."

Amazing how ten minutes with my family is enough to bring me to tears and ten seconds on the phone with Jared is enough to bring a smile to my face. "Hey, Stud. What are you up to?"

I tried to reign in the tears, but he must have been able to hear the wavering in my voice. "What's the matter? Are you crying?"

"Yeah, but I'm fine. Just leaving my parents, we had a wonderful family dinner."

"I'm leaving my NA meeting downtown. I'll be at your place in twenty minutes," he says. Damn, this man makes me deliriously happy. I didn't even have to ask and he already knew I needed him.

"You don't have to do that. I'm fine now. I just needed a minute to calm down and you did that. Thanks for making me smile."

"I'll be there in twenty, Zho." He hangs up before I can say anything else. What's with the men in my life telling me when conversations are over? He's lucky I'm happy with the way this particular one ended.

Thirty-Eight
Zhoe

Taking my anger out on my clothes. I rip my dress over my head throwing it across the room. My shoes were lost somewhere between the front door and the stairs. Finding comfort in a t-shirt Jared left here last weekend I take a deep breath as I plop down onto my bed.

I'm still lying like that, in the middle of my bed with my arms crossed over my eyes in nothing but Jared's shirt when he walks into my room. "Baby?" Uncrossing my arms I roll my head to the side to look at him. "You have three choices…" He ticks them off his fingers to emphasize his point. "Ben and Jerry's, beer or me. Which would you rather have first?"

He's standing in my bedroom door wearing jeans and a long-sleeved Henley shirt that clings to his muscles exquisitely, holding up a grocery bag full of the best things in the world. "Um, all of the above?"

He just laughs, pushing off the door making his way to me. He sits on the bed at the same time he pulls the beer from the bag, opening a bottle he hands it to me. Wasting no time I take a giant swig of it, in the most unlady like way, downing nearly half in one gulp. "Want to talk about it?"

"Not 'til I get some sugar in me, hand it over." I stick my hand out in a grabby motion until he finally places the pint of heaven in my hand. Looking at the label I feel even more of the irritation leaving my body, he picked up Chocolate Fudge Brownie – my favorite. Oh, and he even remembered to grab a spoon from the kitchen on his way up. "You're a lifesaver. Thanks, baby."

"You're welcome. Sorry tonight was so shitty."

Lifting one shoulder in a shrug, I try to brush it off like it doesn't bother me. "Eh, it was nothing short of typical in that house."

"What happened?" he asks, looking at me like he's afraid I'm going to burst into tears all over again.

"I told him I wasn't going to stay with business after this semester."

Jared moves so he's leaning back against the headboard. Lifting me he places me between his legs so my back is against his chest. "What did he have to say about that?"

Mimicking my father's voice as best I can I recount both his view on the argument, as well as my own parting words. I take a huge bite of ice cream, leaning back against Jared and let out a huge sigh. "It's not worth fighting about. They'll never see things from my point of view. I just need to get a job so I can afford a place on my own, and I can do what I want without them having their hands in everything. You know?'

"You can do it, you're strong and determined. I'll help you with whatever you need."

Tilting my head I look back at him. "Thanks. Thanks for being here, too. Want to see how much I appreciate you?"

"Mmm, I like the sound of that," he says, trailing kisses down my neck.

"Perv." I bring a spoonful of ice cream up to his mouth. "This is how much I appreciate you." He just laughs before taking the bite. "I never share my ice cream, just so you know."

"I'm honored you shared it with me then."

How did I ever get by without him? He's managed to make me relax, make me forget about my fight with my parents, and made me feel good about my decisions to branch out without even really trying. Oh, and he managed to get me to share my ice cream. Is this man God?

"How was your meeting tonight, by the way?" I ask trying to change the subject.

"Good." That's all he offers, he never talks about them much and I don't ask because I don't want to pry. That's his thing, his way of dealing with his past and I don't want to intrude or invade.

"You know you can always talk to me about that part of your past or whatever if you ever need to. I'm here."

He places a kiss on my temple. "I know, Zho. I'm sorry I don't let you in that part of my life. It's hard for me. One day I will, just be patient with me, okay?"

"Okay."

"Now give me more ice cream, woman." We both laugh as I give him the smallest bite possible. We spend the rest of the night laughing, and talking about absolutely nothing and sharing a pint of ice cream. Perfection.

Thirty-Nine
Zhoe

Angelica: I need a girl's night ASAP. Tonight?
Me: I was just about to ask you the same thing.
Angelica: Your place?
Me: Sounds good. I'll pick up food, you bring wine. See you tonight.
Angelica: Deal. Love you bitch.
Me: Love you, too, whore.

I'm still chuckling at my exchange with Ang when my phone rings. I look down my smile growing on my face as Jared's name appears on the screen.

"Hello?"

"Hey, gorgeous. What are you doing?"

"Sitting at a coffee shop on campus. Trying to get some studying done. What are you doing?"

"On my lunch break." He pauses for a minute and I can hear him talking to someone in the background. "Sorry about that. What are your plans for tonight?"

"Actually, Ang just texted me and she wants to do a girls night. Is that okay with you?"

"Perfect. Rico and I were thinking about going out for a beer anyways. So," he starts his voice dropping a few levels, "what exactly happens on girl's nights? Is it like the movies with pillow fights and make out sessions?"

I can't help but crack up at his ridiculousness, drawing the attention of several people. "You're stupid. No. We'll order fatty foods, and drink a bottle of wine, that we'll cry into as we're watching chick-flicks."

I hear him make a disgusting sound on the other end of the line. "Sounds awful."

"Oh yeah? And what exactly happens on boy's night out?"

"Beer. Arm wrestling. A lot of grunting and growling, trying to prove which one of us is more man than the other." I can hear the laughter in his voice and I can't help the smile on my face. He's so lame sometimes. But I love it.

"And you thought my night sounded awful."

"Alright, Pretty Girl I've gotta get going. Have fun tonight."

"Jare?"

"Yeah, baby?"

"Don't let me down tonight. Show those boys what a real man looks like." I hang up to the sound of his deep, husky laugh. That man, I swear.

I've resigned myself to the fact that I'm not going to get anymore studying done for the day so I pack up and head out. I picked up a large pizza after stopping by the grocery store to pick up ice cream, chocolate and a few other junk foods to munch on throughout the night. I don't understand how Jared could think girl's night sounds awful it's pretty much the best thing ever.

I love having an excuse to pig out and gossip. I also love spending time with just Ang. Ever since Jared and I got serious I've kind of put her on the backburner, something I've been feeling guilty about as of late. I've always hated those girls that drop their lives when they have a new boyfriend. I've always said I would never be that girl.

I feel like a hypocrite because that's exactly what I've done. It's just so damn hard not to get wrapped up in Jared. I never want to leave his arms, or his bed. I love just being with him – it doesn't matter what we're doing.

"Zhoe?"

"I'm in the kitchen." I turn just as Angelica bounds in. She's wearing a loose fitting, off the shoulder sweatshirt and yoga pants. I'm in a similar outfit – standard for girl's night. "Hi, friend." I wrap her up in a tight hug.

"Missed your face, bitch. Where've you been all my life?" She gives me a pouty face I can't help but laugh at.

"Sorry. I've been a little preoccupied. I didn't mean to be a shitty friend."

She just rolls her eyes at me. "You're forgiven, only if you dish. What's new with you and Jared?" I have to think about that. I really haven't spoken with Ang since we got back from our weekend getaway.

I reach into the cupboard grabbing a couple wine glasses and the corkscrew as Ang grabs napkins and the pizza box; we head into the living room. "Um," I pause unsure where to start and exactly what I want to share. She's my best friend and all but I'm not one to kiss and tell. "Things are good. He's been opening up more, and he's always so damn supportive and loving and kind."

"You seem happy."

I smile at my friend. "I am happy, Ang. He's amazing. I know he seems so dark and scary and hard on the outside, which by the way is so damn sexy but on the inside." I stop failing at finding a word to describe him. Jared is so complex one word is not enough to describe him. Amazing comes close be even that doesn't feel like enough.

"You love him, don't you?" Angelica asks with a huge smirk on her face. I just nod at her, with a dopey smile on my face – the same smile I seem to be wearing constantly these days. "Have you told him?"

"Not yet. I will soon, I just don't think he's ready to hear it yet." We're quiet for a few minutes as we eat our dinner and sip from our wine glasses. I can tell something is off with Ang but I'm not sure how to broach the subject. She loves being all up in my business but she's a closed book when it comes to her life, so I have to tread lightly to get any information out of her. "What about you? What's new?"

She scoffs taking a giant swig of her wine before reaching for the bottle to refill her glass. "Absolutely nothing."

"What about Rico? What's going on with that?"

"Eh, nothing really. I think we're friends… with benefits," she laughs and I can't help but join along. Leave it to her to find herself in that situation. "Which is fine, we're better off that way. Neither one of is capable of having a relationship so at least we have that understanding up front. Less messy."

"How's the sex?" I ask even though I don't really care. I just know she needs to switch to a lighter subject, a subject she's more comfortable with.

She looks over at me sheepishly; though the look lasts only seconds as she starts animatedly telling me detailed descriptions of their sex life. "A-maz-ing. He can go for hours, seriously. We're up to three orgasms in one night." I laugh at her description, but damn... three times? Really?

Ang gets a serious look on her face all of a sudden, which puts me on guard; she's never serious about anything. "Rico is great, Zho. He's funny and cute and so damn good in bed. But, he's broken, you know?" I just nod at her, I do know. Jared is kind of broken, too. But, so am I, so who am I to judge? "I think we're better off as friends."

"Okay, so be friends. I know he doesn't have many and maybe you being in his life is what he needs to fix himself a little."

She looks over at me and gives me a half smile. "Yeah, maybe. But, I want what you have. I want my happily ever after." She downs the rest of her wine. Good thing she brought several bottles as we've almost polished off the first one already. "I've never wanted that, you know? But, when I hear about you and Jared it makes me want someone else to lean on. Someone else to share things with."

"I don't know if what Jared and I have is happily ever after. We have problems, too. We're just trying to work through them. He's worth it."

"Yeah, but how did you know he's worth it?"

"I don't know, Ang. I just knew, I guess. He makes me feel things I've never felt before, he makes me happy – disgustingly happy."

She laughs. "You two are disgusting sometimes." I stick my tongue out at her and we fall over laughing. Wine... it makes everything ten times funnier. "I know Rico isn't the right guy for me, but I was secretly hoping he would be."

"You'll find him, Ang. You're stunning, and you're smart and funny. Any guy would be lucky to have your bitchy-ass."

She leans over smacking me on my arm. "And you say I'm the bitch. I'm not sure if I'm ready to give up my man-eating ways, but maybe sometime in the near future. Especially since I'm starting to lose my touch."

"Losing your touch? Don't tell me someone turned you down." I mock gasp at her. Angelica has never had a problem getting men, any man, to fall over their feet to get to her. I was joking but I'm pretty sure she's never heard the word no before.

She rolls her eyes at my antics. "There's this guy in my class and ohmigod he's so sexy. He's like nerdy GQ. But, he doesn't even notice me."

"Well, have you talked to him?" I have to laugh a little at the situation, every guy notices Angelica.

"Yeah, we met last year and have actually had a few classes together."

"Um, why am I just now hearing about this guy?"

She looks a little embarrassed. "Because he turns me down. Every single time. He's always pissing me off on purpose, he calls me Duchess and makes fun of my money, and he's always correcting me when I'm wrong." She growls and throws her body back into the couch. "He drives me fucking crazy. When we first met, he seemed interested, but ever since that night he's been nothing but a douche. Whenever I try to flirt with him he shuts me down before I can even turn on the charm."

I bust out laughing at my friend. This guy is so flirting with her, it may not be in the blatantly obvious way she's used to but he's definitely flirting. "Maybe tone down the flirting and just try conversation. Now tell me what he looks like, nerdy GQ is not cutting it for my imagination."

She tips her head back and closes her eyes. "Mmm, seriously Zho. He's tall and muscular, but not like Jared, he's leaner. His blonde hair is always messy like he just rolled out of bed, his eyes are brighter blue than yours but he wears these dorky black rimmed glasses and all I can think about is doing him in nothing but his sexy, nerdy glasses."

"Yum!" We laugh again. "Seriously, Ang. Don't give up on him. He sounds too sexy to walk away from."

"Seriously, the only way his face could get any better looking, is if I was sitting on it," she says this with a completely serious look on her face but I can't help but die laughing.

"Oh my god, I can't believe you just said that!" We fall into a fit of laugher.

For the next several hours we exchange sexcapades stories, laugh and get drunk off our asses on wine. Eventually we pass out on my large sectional, still wearing the same clothes, our wine bottles, pizza box and ice cream containers left discarded on my coffee table. I love girl's night.

Forty

Jared

Last night was definitely needed. It was nice spending time with Rico, drinking and blowing off steam like we used to do. I didn't realize how much time Zhoe and I had been spending together until I saw Rico again and felt like it had been forever since I'd last seen him.

As much as I needed last night and my boys, I needed Zhoe more. I slept for shit not having her next to me, and I woke up with the worst case of blue-balls ever.

I texted her when I woke up to see if she was awake yet, or if Angelica had gone home so that I could come over, but I hadn't heard back from her. Deciding to surprise her anyways, I got up, got dressed and ran to the grocery store to pick up stuff for French toast and bacon.

I figured even if Ang was still there I could win a few bonus points for showing up with breakfast. Zhoe had given me a key to her place a few weeks ago, after she left the door unlocked for me. My protective instincts took over, demanding she never leave the door unlocked like that again when she's home alone. Her response was to get me a key. Stubborn girl.

Using her stubbornness to my advantage, I let myself into her place as quietly as possible. Setting the groceries in the kitchen I make my way into the living room, hoping Angelica at least slept in the guest room and I can get Zhoe to myself for a few minutes.

I have to swallow a laugh as I reach the living room. Both girls are passed on the couch, Zhoe's couch is a large L-shaped sectional, each girl has taken up one side their heads nearly touching in the middle. Neither of them have pillows or blankets and are still fully dressed in yoga pants and sweatshirts. Zhoe's leg is partially hanging off the couch, and Angelica is letting out a cute snore.

The coffee table is completely covered in trash. There's an empty pizza box, and not one, but three empty wine bottles. Two Ben & Jerry's pints are nearly empty, the remaining ice creaming melting onto the table.

I just shake my head at the scene and girl's thought guys were messy. This is disgusting, but so damn cute. Knowing they are both going to have hangovers from hell and aren't likely to wake up anytime soon I quietly pick up their mess, replacing it with two glasses of ice water and some aspirin.

I have coffee brewing in the coffee pot, bacon sizzling on the stove and am flipping my last few pieces of French toast when the girls finally show signs of life.

"Oh my god. What is that smell? I need it in my belly now," this from Ang in a scratchy, sleepy voice. I peek around the corner so I can see them but they can't see me, Zhoe still hasn't budged I'm pretty sure she's still out. "Zhoe!" Angelica reaches out, giving her a rough shake. "Wake your lazy ass up and feed me."

"Go away, whore. Feed yourself," Zhoe mumbles back. I can't hold my laughter back any longer.

Zhoe is the first to notice me She's wearing the cutest, sleepy grin on her face that makes me smile. But, Angelica is the first to speak. "You cooked?"

"Yeah, there's coffee, French toast and bacon. You want some?"

"Obviously." I chuckle at her, glancing back at Zhoe sending her a wink as I head back to the kitchen to dish up their breakfast.

I can hear them mumbling excitedly back and forth to each other but I can't hear what they're saying. I plate up a few pieces of the toast and bacon and a cup of coffee for each of them, carrying them into the living room.

After I set the plates on the coffee table I lean over place a few soft kisses on Zhoe's forehead. "Morning, Pretty Girl."

"Morning, handsome. Thank you for breakfast." I take a seat next to her leaning back into the couch. "You're not eating?"
"Nah, I'm good."

"What did you do wrong?" Angelica asks around a mouthful of food.

"What are you talking about?"

She glares at me for a long second before taking another bite of her food. "This," she gestures to their plates, "doesn't happen unless you did something wrong."

"A guy can't do something nice for his girlfriend and her friend unless he did something wrong?"

"Right."

I glance over at Zhoe who is trying not to laugh at the ridiculousness of the situation. "You caught me," I say. "I messed up big time." I watch as Zhoe's face drops, she looks genuinely concerned at what I may have done.

"Ah-ha. I knew it. What did you do, asshole?"

Still looking at my girl I answer as seriously as I can. "I let my girl sleep somewhere other than my arms last night."

Zhoe busts out laughing at the same time Angelica makes gagging sounds. "You two are disgustingly cute." She stands up and starts to head upstairs. "Excuse me while I go lose my breakfast."

Both Zhoe and I laugh at her as she goes. Until Zhoe sets her fork down, climbing onto my lap. My laughter dies immediately – that case of blue-balls I had this morning is back and it's fucking painful.

"That was an awful line, Stud," she says against my lips. "But, the breakfast made up for it."

I grab her head in my hands deepening the kiss for a few beats, before pulling back to look into her eyes, "it wasn't a line. I missed you last night, Zho."

"I missed you, too. She'll leave soon and I'll show you just how much."

Growling at her promise I kiss her until Angelica comes barging down the stairs. "Seriously? I'm leaving. See you at the gym, love birds." We don't even acknowledge her; completely lost in each other, in the kiss. Damn I missed this girl last night.

***

"Wake up, baby."

"No, go away," Zhoe swats at my hand as it creeps up her body. I can't help but laugh – it doesn't matter what time of day it is if Zhoe is sleeping she does not like to be woken up.

"Come on, Zho. We told Ang and Rico we'd meet them at the gym this afternoon."

"Ang won't be there. She's still hung-over," rolling onto her side she buries her face in my shoulder. "I am too. Let's just sleep."

"Nope. Get up. A workout will make you feel better." After a few minutes of prodding she finally gets up but not before shooting daggers at me.

We stumble into the gym for their afternoon kickboxing class and find Ang and Rico waiting for us near the back of the class. Ang makes her way over to Zhoe as soon as we get through the doors. With a kiss on her forehead I walk away to leave the two of them bitch about being hung-over alone.

"Sup," Rico and I share a handshake. "Damn," Rico lets out a low whistle of approval.

Jerking my head in the direction he's looking I spot what's caught his attention. A redheaded bombshell is making her way towards us wearing a sexy smirk. "Excuse me," she says as she slides in between Rico and me placing a hand on each of our arms. "I needed to break you two up. Too much sexiness in one place."

Rolling my eyes at her I shrug my arm away from her grasp. This one is all Rico. She's hot but she has nothing on my petite, curvy, brunette. Zhoe is the only girl getting it up these days.

FORTY-ONE
Zhoe

Jared and I have come here a few times together but we always workout separately. I'm not sure why. It's just this unspoken rule we have. Plus, I think if I had to watch him beat the shit out of a punching bag, dripping in sweat for an hour I'd be too distracted to get in a good workout.

I start throwing a few soft punches at the bag to warm up when I hear Angelica's voice. "Uh, Zhoe?" I just turn to her, lifting one eyebrow in question. "Who's that girl?" She points to the back of the room.

I turn to see Jared leaning against the wall, Rico next to him and some bimbo sandwiched between the two. The girl is fucking gorgeous. She's tall and thin – built just like Angelica – she has long red hair, big boobs and perfect ass. Her perfect body is pressed snugly up against Jared's perfect body. Her breasts are lying against his arm; her arm is running a path along his bicep, tracing his tattoos.

For his part Jared is leaning against the wall as casually as possible, like nothing strange is happening. He's wearing a polite smile, and is engaging in conversation with her. Apparently, Jared decided to bring his fucking manners today. Why the hell isn't he telling her to buzz off?

I don't move and I don't take my eyes off them as I process the emotions flying through me. The first thing I feel is envy, then self-consciousness, and then jealousy and anger. I focus on the jealousy and anger. I take one step in their direction, when the instructor calls attention to us, stopping me. I don't know what I was going to do, but I was definitely going to do something. Say something.

"Okay, class. Grab a bag and let's get started."

"Take it out on the bag," Angelica instructs me. "We'll figure it out later."

Take it out on the bag is exactly what I do. I beat the shit out of that thing. The bag shifts back and forth throughout the hour-long class. One punch, it's Jared's face I'm beating in. The next kick is the hoe bag's pretty face. By the end of the class I'm panting hard, dripping in sweat, my hands feel bruised and I'm still fucking pissed.

I turn as soon as the last punch is thrown seeking him out. I find him instantly. He's taking a swig out of his water bottle and drying his face with his towel. I start walking in his direction ready to tell him where to go when she walks up to him again. I stop my pursuit hoping to overhear what she has to say.

"Hey, sexy," her voice is low and seductive, not that Jared needed any clues as to what she wanted. Her body language was pretty damn clear. "I only live about a block from here if you need a little extra workout." She gives him a wink, which for whatever reason seals the deal for me.

Without a word I turn and head out of the gym. My only thought is that I need to get out of there. I don't care that I left Ang without saying goodbye. I don't care that I'm Jared's ride… it's glaringly obvious he has another offer to be ridden with me out of the way.

Planning on going to the grocery store after the gym, we decided to take my car and I'm so grateful for the option for a quick getaway. The drive to my apartment lasts less than five minutes; in those five minutes my phone has gone off at least ten times. Some of the missed calls are from Angelica, but most are from Jared. I've ignored all of them.

I slam and lock the door behind me as soon as I get home. Though, little good it'll do me if Jared decides to follow me here since I stupidly gave him a key.

Stripping my gym clothes off on the way, I'm completely naked by the time I make it to my bathroom. I turn the water on hot, as I let the water wash over me, I can feel some of the tension leave my shoulders. Then I remember why I stormed out of the gym like a crazy person to begin with.

Asshole.

I grab the shampoo off the shelf and start aggressively washing my hair. "Fucking idiot," I mumble to myself. I'm rinsing my hair a few minutes later when the shower curtain flies open revealing a pissed off Jared. *Well fuck you buddy I'm the one that gets to be mad right now, not you.*

Jared strips out of his sweaty workout clothes quickly and for just one second I'm transfixed on his bulging muscles as they flex with every movement.

It's not until he starts stepping into the shower with me that I snap out of it. "What the hell are you doing? Get out."

"You don't want me, Pretty Girl?"

"Wasn't that clear when I left your stupid ass at the gym?" I'm drawn to the erection he's proudly sporting; apparently the feeling is not mutual.

I start to doubt us; I doubt me, and my body – whether or not I'm enough for him. Who is he hard for? Is he hard for me because I'm naked in the shower with him? Or is he hard because he got to watch that bimbo's perfect ass workout for the last hour? I turn my back on him needing a minute to get my thoughts and emotions under control.

Of course, he won't let me block him out, wrapping me in his arms from behind, effectively halting any chance at getting away. "What happened back there?" His voice is soft and low in my ear. This is his newest defense mechanism. He's learned if I'm pissed off, him yelling and fighting with me isn't going to work, laughing it off definitely isn't going to work. So, he's taken to distracting me with his lips, his body and his sweet words. Not this time. I'm too hurt, too pissed off.

I struggle against his hold. "Let me go, Jared," I bite out between clenched teeth. I don't stop struggling until he releases me. I don't make it far, though. Before I know what's happening, he spins me until my back is against the wall, and my arms are pinned in one of his hands above my head. He grips my chin between his thumb and forefinger forcing me to look at him.

Up until this point I've been angry – with myself for doubting what we have, for not trusting him and for not confronting him and Malibu Barbie. I've been angry with him for talking and flirting with her, and for not understanding why I'm upset. If I'm being honest, I was a little jealous, too.

"Talk to me, baby." Jared's breath is hot on my neck as he whispers in my ear, placing soft kisses on my skin.

"She was really pretty. A little slutty, but still pretty."

"You're jealous? That's what this is?" He laughs. He fucking laughs and just like that the anger is back. I writhe against his hold, desperate to get a hand free so I can punch him in his stupid smiling mouth.

"Let my hands go so I can punch you in your stupid, smug face."

Jared doesn't give me an inch, instead he pins my hips against the wall, his hard erection hitting me between my thighs. "You feel that, baby? That's yours; it's only for you. Your body is the only one I want under me, on top of me, anyway you want to give it to me."

Finally freeing a hand I cup his jaw in my palm. Biting my lip in the way I know drives him crazy I lean forward ghosting my lips across his, teasing. "For me?"

"Yours."

My hand slides down his perfect abs until I reach his impressive cock; gripping it tightly I run my hands up and down his length a few times. Letting him go I place my palms flat on his chest shoving him back away from me with all the force I can muster. "Keep it away from other girls then." Quickly I jump out of the shower before he can stop me, calling over my shoulder on my way out of the room, "Oh and Jare? I'll chop it off if you think about her while getting yourself off. Got it?"

"You are cruel woman. Fucking cruel."

That'll teach him to flirt, or be flirted with by some bimbo in front of me. Eyes on me or you'll get a massive case of blue-balls.

Forty-Two

Jared

I knew Zhoe had a confident side, I knew she had a shy side, but I would have never guessed she had a jealous side. It was adorable, and terrifying at the same time. It was not adorable the way she left me hanging though, I had blue balls for days.

Seeing her jealous showed me how much she really cares about me. It made me question what I'm doing here, if I can be the guy she needs or if I can let her go.

Walking up to her front door I steal myself for a minute or two. On my drive over, I was panicking about meeting her parents. I've never done that before. I've never had a girl in my life I cared enough about to take that next step. But, standing here now, I realize there is nothing I won't do for this girl.

I may not be ready to tell her I love her, I may not be quite ready to take that giant leap of faith, but I am ready to tell her how much she means to me. How much I need her in my life. I'm ready to admit to both myself and to Zhoe that I don't want to live without her. I can't live without her.

I am slowly falling for this girl. She makes me feel things I haven't felt in a long time. Shit, some things I've never felt before. I can see it in her eyes that she loves me. I know it without a doubt that I own her heart. I'm not saying that to be cocky or arrogant, because honestly? It scares the shit out of me.

My heart, and my soul are broken, shattered, tattered, useless. Zhoe's heart? Zhoe's soul? Beautiful. The most beautiful things I've ever seen, ever touched. She deserves so much more than what I can ever give her. She deserves someone that will give her a whole, strong heart in return for her own. But, the thing about Zhoe is she doesn't care if I ever give her my heart, as long as I hold hers she's okay with that.

That thought is sobering. I vow to myself right then and there to never let her heart go. I'll cherish it. Protect it. Appreciate it. I'll never let it fall, never let it break. Her heart is the most beautiful gift anyone has ever given to me and I plan to honor that gift with my whole being.

The doorbell echoes through her place, but I'm only left waiting for a few seconds before she opens the door to me. My mouth goes dry. I've seen Zhoe is sweats, in skimpy dresses, in jeans and in nothing but sexy-ass lingerie - it doesn't matter what she's wearing, she is the most stunning girl I've ever seen.

She's wearing a cream sweater that lands just past her luscious ass; it hugs her curves in all the right places. She's paired it with brown leggings and knee-high brown boots. Her hair is down in soft waves and as usual she has little make-up on. How this girl can manage to look sweet and innocent, and sexy as sin at the same time boggles my mind.

"Happy Thanksgiving, Pretty Girl. You look gorgeous," I take her in my arms planting soft kisses on her lips, forehead and cheeks. She flushes slightly before grabbing me by the tie and dragging me into her place.

I had no clue what to wear and Zhoe was absolutely no help, telling me it didn't matter what I wore since she was just going to tear it off of me by the end of the night anyways. She had a point there, and I couldn't help but laugh at her eagerness. In the end, I decided on a pair of black dress slacks, and a black and white checkered button up with a plain black tie.

"You look so fucking sexy." She's still dragging me through the house by my tie. "I'm going to call Daddy and tell him we can't make it."

"What? Why?"

She looks at me from under her lashes, flashing me her come-hither smile. "Look at you, Stud." She drags her eyes up and down my body blatantly checking me out as if to prove her point. "I want to tear these sexy clothes off you, fuck you on the couch, and redress you just so I can watch you strip for me all over again."

Throwing my head back, I laugh my ass off at this girl. Every time she opens her mouth something unexpected comes out of it. Life will never be dull as long as Zhoe's in it. "Baby, I'd love nothing more than for you to do that. But, here's the thing. On the way over here I realized something…"

"Hmm? What's that?"

"I realized I need your parents to like me." She doesn't answer right away, too distracted with my belt to pay attention. "I need you in my life, Zho. For a long time."

She stops moving. Stops whatever she was trying to do with my belt buckle and looks at me. Her eyes are wet with unshed tears. "You what?"

With her face between my palms I handle it like it's her heart – delicately, carefully. "I need you, Pretty Girl. I can't live without you. I'm falling for you. Hard. I can't imagine my life without you. When I look into my future I see you. Is that enough for you right now?"

Her head starts bobbing up and down, tears spilling down her cheeks landing on my hands. I try to wipe them away but they are falling faster than I can remove them. Wordless, Zhoe jumps up wrapping herself around me, squeezing me in a death grip.

"It's more than enough, Jare. I need you, too, so much." Then her lips are on me. She's not sweet like I expected her to be. She's kissing me like I'm the air she needs to breathe, like I'm her lifeline and I relish in the moment. I never thought I'd have this. I always thought I was too broken to be able to save someone else but for her I can do this. I'll be whatever she needs me to be. For as long as she needs me.

Pulling away from her kiss, I lean back enough to look into her eyes. "No more tears, gorgeous."

"Not even happy ones?"

I just smile at her, scattering a few kisses on her face before putting her back down on the ground. She takes a step back and smiles up at me, a smile that I swear lights up the whole damn room.

"So, as sexy as you look in this outfit, I need to make a few changes. I know you want to impress my parents but I want you to do it as you, not who you think they want you to be."

She grabs my tie again, this time loosening it enough that she can pull it over my head. Moving to my shirt buttons she undoes the top three so my white T-shirt is visible. Finally, she removes the cuff links from my shirtsleeves, unbuttons them and rolls them halfway up my forearms. Already I feel more comfortable, more myself. I don't know how she knew I needed this but it makes facing her parents that much easier, knowing she's proud enough of who I am to take me as is.

"Much better," she smiles up at me. "Let's go get this over with sexy. The sooner we go, the sooner I can get you home and naked."

Grabbing her hand I practically drag her behind me out the door, all the while she's laughing her very loud, very contagious laugh. "You don't have to tell me twice, sweetheart."

Forty-Three
<u>Jared</u>

Obviously, I knew Zhoe and I came from two different worlds. The money, the differences have never really been brought up in our relationship because they've never been an issue. But, pulling onto her parent's estate, because that's what it is - a fucking estate - our differences become blatantly obvious.

Until I went to juvi I'd never been able to rely on having a bed to sleep in. My next meal was never a guarantee and more often than not I went without food for days at a time. Whereas Zhoe has never had to worry about those things - in fact, she's never wanted for anything. She lives in a brand new apartment, drives a car that cost more money than I've ever made in my life and grew up in a fucking mansion.

When we first pulled up, we had to speak to a guard at the front gate, Zhoe had to give her full name – as in first, middle and last – before they opened the gates and let us in. The drive felt like it went on forever. It was lined on both sides by beautiful flowerbeds, and adorned with mini lanterns before finally coming to a stop in front of the house.

The house itself is like a replica of the White House; I'm sure it's smaller but not by much. White pillars run the length of the front, ten windows between the first and second floor interrupt the siding. There is even a fountain, a goddamn fountain, in the front lawn.

Zhoe reaches over and grabs my thigh, giving it a squeeze before getting out of the truck. I snort to myself. I bet the hired help has nicer cars than my piece of shit Chevy. I've never been ashamed of myself, but I feel completely lost and out of place here. I have no idea what look I'm wearing on my face but whatever it is has Zhoe coming over to attempt to calm my nerves.

Coming to a stop directly in front of me she grabs both of my hands in her own. "Look at me, baby." Tipping my chin down I look into her bright blue eyes. Neither one of us says anything for several moments. We just stand there staring at each other. Looking at my girl grounds me, and eventually my nerves start to disappear, my heartbeat slowing to a normal pace.

This is why I'm here. For Zhoe. Reaching up I tuck a stray piece of hair behind her ear, and even that helps settle me. "Zho, I can't give you this life. I'll never be able to give this to you."

"I don't want this life. I hate this life. I want you, that's it. Just you." Thank fuck for that. I needed her to know that this life isn't something I've ever aspired to. As long as I'm alive and healthy and relatively happy that's all I need. Well, all that and Zhoe. It's nice to hear her say she doesn't want this life. Deep down I think I knew that, but I just needed that reassurance.

Fuck. I sound like a pussy. What kind of man needs reassurance from his woman? Isn't it my job to make her feel secure, not the other way around?

"Miss Zhoe?" We both turn at the sound of her name being called. Zhoe's face lights up into a bright smile at the woman standing on the stairs.

With a light kiss and a wink Zhoe starts toward the front door and the woman dressed in all black, dragging me behind her. I give her credit though, she never lets go of my hand as if sensing I need her touch.

"Ms. Taylor!" Zhoe exclaims, wrapping the woman in an awkward one-armed hug since she still has a firm grip on my hand.

"Hi, darling. This striking young fellow must be Jared?" Her smile is infectious and I can't help but smile back at her. I'm also a little shocked that she seems to know about me. Zhoe must be talking about me. The thought has my smile to widening.

"Yes," Zhoe leans into me, "this is my boyfriend, Jared. Jared this is Ms. Taylor. She is our housekeeper slash nanny. She pretty much raised me."

Zhoe has only spoken of her parents a handful of times but each time has been with a tone of distain and disgust. Whenever Ms. Taylor was brought up, however, she seemed happy. This is a woman Zhoe obviously cares about. Instinct tells me it's more important for me to impress Ms. Taylor than it is Zhoe's parents.

"It's nice to meet you, Ms. Taylor." I smile warmly at her, kind of hard not to, and stick my hand out in a gesture of greeting.

Ms. Taylor rolls her eyes at me before knocking my hand away and going in for a hug. I have to drop Zhoe's hand in order to hug the old woman back. She hugs me for longer than I would think is polite in a situation like this, but it's not uncomfortable. I can see why Zhoe likes her so much. She has a way of making you feel special, cared for. I'm glad to see my girl had someone like that to look after her, since her parents were too selfish to do it.

"Well, Jared. You are a handsome young man, aren't you? You take care of my girl, you hear me? It's not her father you should be worried about if you break her heart, it's me." She glares up at me and while I'm sure she's deadly serious it's hard to take her seriously when she's so tiny.

Of course, I don't voice that. I just nod my head and respond, "yes, ma'am. I don't intend on hurting her. She's too important to me." I glance down to find Zhoe looking up at me with a huge grin on her face. It's so damn pretty it makes my heart hurt. I make a mental note to say more sappy shit to her if it gets her to look up at me like that more often.

"Good answer, boy. Well, let's move this party inside shall we?" Zhoe snorts in response and Ms. Taylor throws her head back in laughter in a very Zhoe-like fashion. "What? You wouldn't classify your mother's impression of the walking-dead a party?"

I follow behind both of them, giving myself a moment to freak out. I can't believe I'm going to meet Zhoe's – and Cole's – parents. Zhoe has brought up Cole a few times now and every time I've panicked. I want to tell her, to apologize but I'm afraid she'll leave me. I know one day she'll find out, it's inevitable, but I want to be selfish for a little while longer.

Forty-Four

Zhoe

Honestly, Ms. Taylor was more of parental figure in my life than either of my parents. She raised Cole and me – she helped with homework, she cooked and cleaned up after us, and she helped me with boy problems. To this day she'd be the first person I'd call, after Ang of course, if I needed advice or help with anything.

I'm glad to see Jared get her seal of approval. I don't know if it was instinctual or if he just knows me that well, but he seemed to sense her approval is more important to me than Mother and Daddy's – and he's right.

I know the money, or lack thereof, is going to be an issue with Daddy. I was surprised to see it was such an issue with Jared when we pulled up to the house. But, like I told Jared, I hate this life. I hate what money and the power that comes with it, does to people. I'd much rather have to take public transportation every day and live in a shitty apartment as long as I had Jared's love. Jared might not understand that, or someone that comes from the life he did, but I've seen what money does. I've seen this life and I want out.

We walk through the large, ostentatious foyer and make our way down the long hallway that leads to Daddy's office. Turning to Jared I place my hands on his chest, hoping he can see in my eyes the words I'm too afraid to say. Hoping that little encouragement is enough to help him find the strength to walk into Daddy's office with his head held high. I'm not ashamed of him, or of where he comes from, but I think deep down Jared is.

"Ready, Stud?"

He smiles at me before placing a sweet kiss on my forehead. "Ready, Pretty Girl."

Together, we make our way into Daddy's office. I knock once before opening the door. As always, I find him behind his large mahogany desk, glasses on with his face practically pressed up against the computer screen.

Daddy is a large man, at about 6'3" and easily over 250 pounds. At one point he was probably more muscle than fat, but for as long as I can remember it's been opposite. It's not his size that's intimidating, though, it's his demeanor. He's cool, aloof, and pompous – he's everything I'm not.

I clear my throat to let him know I'm there, otherwise he'll never acknowledge me. "Hi, Daddy."

"Princess," he says without even looking up.

Groaning, I roll my eyes and look at Jared. He's trying to hold back a smile, he knows how much I hate that nickname, as a matter of fact, so does Daddy. "Daddy, I want to introduce you to someone."

Finally he lifts his head to look at us. I swear every time I see him he looks tired, older. It's only been a week since I've last seen him, but he looks to have aged about ten years since then. The wrinkles around his eyes and mouth are more pronounced, his hair is greyer. He glances at me for a second before turning to the man standing next to me. Through narrowed eyes he focuses on the tattoos on Jared's arms peeking out of his shirtsleeves.

"This is Jared Roman, my boyfriend. Jared this is my father, William Dawson."

Jared lets go of my hand and reaches it towards my father. I'm happy to see he's standing tall; his shoulders squared, and is making direct eye contact. This is the Jared I know – strong, confident, and sexy as fuck. "Mr. Dawson, it's a pleasure to meet you, sir."

Daddy doesn't stand, doesn't smile; he *does* return Jared's handshake, never taking his eyes off of him. "Jared Roman. That name sounds familiar. Do I know you from somewhere, boy?"

"Uh, no sir. I don't believe we've met before."

Daddy just grunts, "Are you the reason business school and working for my company are no longer good enough for Zhoe?"

"Daddy!" I hate how condescending he's being. Jared was perfectly polite and Daddy has to go and ruin it, making sure to knock Jared down a few steps in the process. So typical. This is exactly what I meant when I said I know what this life does to people – it does this. It makes them selfish, arrogant, cold. I've never wanted out so much in my life. "That's enough. Jared has nothing to do with my decision, other than he supports me. I decided I didn't want that life. That's your dream, not mine."

"I don't believe I was talking to you, Zhoe. I asked Mr. Roman a question, not you." He looks at me over the rim of his glasses before turning his glare on Jared.

Jared stands taller, throwing his shoulders back as he squeezes my hand and looks my father in his eyes. "No, sir. I didn't make the decision for her, but as she said I support her decision 100 percent. Life is short. I believe you should live it the way you want to. Not the way you were told."

I just stare at him in disbelief. He just stood up to my father for me. He told me before we left how important it was that my parents like him. He has to know he just guaranteed it that they will not. Especially Daddy. But damn it, that was sexy and so amazing.

Daddy snorts, his focus back on his computer. "Get out of my office. I'll see you for dinner."

Dismissed. I turn and make my way out of his office, Jared hot on my heels.

Once we're in the living room, and out of earshot of Daddy's office I turn to him. "Sorry about that. As much as I'd like to say that was unusual, I can't. That's how he always is. A pompous jerk."

"Zhoe, it's okay. It wasn't that bad. If you were my daughter I'd be the same way. No one's good enough for you baby, especially me."

"But you are good enough for me, Jare. Besides, he doesn't care about me, he cares about his name and image. Not my happiness."

In true Jared fashion, he pulls me into his chest giving me the comfort I need in that moment. "Are you happy, baby?"

"Deliriously." I smile against his warm, hard chest. "Thank you for defending me and supporting me back there.'

"Always, Pretty Girl."

Forty-Five

Jared

I had a bit of a panic attack in her father's office. Not because of his asshole words, and his arrogant attitude but because I was picked up by the police a few blocks away from where Cole was shot. I don't think they ever really mentioned in the media the possibility of me being at the scene of the crime, but then again I was locked up in juvenile so they could have and I'd never know it.

I hate that day. I hate my role in it, my memories and that I'm still alive when Cole isn't. I hate that I'm so fucking terrified of Zhoe finding out from someone other than me I've become a paranoid wreck.

I'm still holding Zhoe against my chest. Her arms are wrapped around my waist when her father comes barreling down the hall towards me, his face red, taut with anger. "You son of a bitch!" Her father may be an asshole, but I doubt he'd hurt his own daughter. Instinct takes over anyways, as I push Zhoe behind me to protect her from whatever is about to go down.

As soon as he's close enough he reaches around me grabbing Zhoe by her upper arm dragging her behind him instead. "Oh, hell no. You don't get the right to protect my daughter, asshole."

She's been quiet up until this point, confused I'm sure, but Zhoe isn't about to let someone tell her what to do. "Daddy! What the hell is your problem?" she screams at him, moving from behind him to stand next to me again. Her eyes are shooting daggers at him.

I fall even more in love with this girl right then. The girl I'm about to lose in a few seconds, because no one has ever had my back the way she does. It doesn't matter though. He's figured it out. He knows I was there that night. I don't know how he knows but he does and as soon as he tells her she'll be gone. Just like everyone else. Just like I deserve.

"You're defending him? How dare you disrespect your brother's memory like that!"

"What the fuck are you talking about? What does Jared have to do with Cole?" Zhoe asks moving closer to my side, almost stepping in front of me to face her father head on.

Taking a few steps forward until he's in my face he seethes at me, I can feel his anger rolling off of him in waves. "Your boyfriend was with Cole the night he died. He was there. He left him there to die. Alone."

Zhoe whips her head at me. I can see the war she's battling internally. Her eyes look sad and hurt, broken, but her posture tells me she doesn't want to believe him. I don't want to tell her, I don't want to lose her but I don't have a choice.

Reaching for her, I grab her hand in my own, intertwining our fingers. It's not enough. I need to hold her and kiss her, to feel her skin, but I know this is all I get. This is the last time Zhoe will ever let me touch her, once she knows the truth she'll bolt.

"Jare?" My name is barely a whisper. Her eyes are wet; her tears falling uncontrollably down her cheeks.

"I'm so sorry, baby. I didn't know how to tell you. But, you have to know every single day I've wished it was me that died, not him. I'm so, so sorry."

Before anyone can say anything else, she turns and runs through the house. I don't react for a moment until I hear the front door slam shut. I know I deserve for her to walk away from me, but I can't. I'm too selfish to let her go. I don't know who I am without her.

"You leave my daughter alone, you fucking piece of shit." Her father is following behind me, as I run after Zhoe. I want to scream at him that I can't let her go, I love her too much, but I haven't even told Zhoe yet and she should be the first person to hear those words.

I burst through the door almost running over Zhoe in the process. She's sitting on the front steps her legs pulled up to her chest, arms wrapped around them tightly. Her hair is acting as a veil so I can't see her face but I can hear the sobs as they rack through her body.

Leaning down I go to reach out for her, before I can even lay a finger on her, her father comes barreling out of the door plowing into me. He tackles me to the ground all the while screaming at me, telling me what a worthless piece of shit I am.

As if I didn't already know that.

I take it though. I take his anger and his pain because I deserve it. I lie on the ground while he just batters me in the face, the chest, and the ribs over and over again. He beats me and I take it. Closing my eyes, I will God, if he even exists, to take me right now. I want to die. I should've died a long time ago. Why not now?

In the back of my mind I think I hear Zhoe screaming for us to stop. She sounds sad and scared but every time I try to get up her father knocks me back down. I know I can take him, but I don't want to hurt him. I don't want to hurt Zhoe… I've hurt her enough as is.

Forty-Six

Zhoe

"You son of a bitch!" Daddy is screaming at him. Pummeling him with his fists. "You ruined us. It should've been you!"

I'm standing here screaming, tears running down my cheeks. I don't know what to do. I keep yelling for them to stop but they won't listen.

Just when I think Daddy is going to kill him, Jared jumps up and starts hitting Daddy back. Something must have snapped in him, something made him react because up until this moment he was just standing there letting Daddy pummel him. He wasn't hitting back; he wasn't even trying to block Daddy's punches. He was just taking it.

He could easily take Daddy. He's so strong and huge and he trains all the time. It would be easy for him to knock him to the ground. But, he didn't, he just took it, probably believing he deserves what's happening to him. Until just now. Now he stands up and hits back. Fights back.

One punch is all it takes and there is blood everywhere. I don't know whose blood it is. I don't know who is hurting worse. All I know is they are going to kill each other.

"STOP!" I'm screaming at the top of my lungs. But it doesn't matter. They are rolling around in the grass of our front yard, each of them trying to get an edge on the other. If it weren't the scariest moment of my life it might actually be humorous watching two grown men roll around like they are little kids wrestling.

"Oh. My. God. Please! Stop!"

Again it's as if I don't even exist. I'm so scared but I don't know who for. Someone is going to die. If I don't get them to stop they won't until one of them is dead. I try again, this time running towards them. I touch Jared's shoulder hoping my presence will calm him enough for him to gain some sort of composure; it's always worked before.

"Baby. Please, please stop!" Nothing. "You're going to kill him. Stop!" This time he pauses long enough to look at me. I'm not sure what he sees in my face but whatever it is makes him stop dead in his tracks. He stands up and takes a few steps back from Daddy.

I let out a sigh of relief, but it's short lived. As soon as I start to go to him, Daddy gets up from his spot on the lawn and charges. Daddy hits him so hard his back hits the fountain that sits in the middle of our circle drive, cracking it along one side.

I'm so shocked I don't move for a moment. This is a side of Daddy I've never seen before. He looks evil, I'm not sure he's ever going to stop. I take off at a sprint towards Jared's truck. Opening the driver side door I lean over and reach under the passenger seat pulling my gun out of my purse, hoping only to get their attention, to get control of the situation.

I try reasoning one more time; hoping I don't have to fall back on my last resort, "Stop! Fucking stop. You're going to kill each other!"

Jared turns his head to look at me and I feel like my world stops. He's gushing blood from a cut on the back of his head, his eyes are swollen, his lip is busted open and he's lying limp on the ground propped up against the fountain. It's in that moment that I know I can't live without him.

I raise my arm in the air and shoot one shot straight up. The sound of a gunshot is enough to give Daddy pause as he turns to look at me, shock written all over his face. "Zhoe! Where did you get that gun? Did this scumbag give it to you? Is it his?"

I ignore him and his hateful words rushing over to Jared before he has time to turn his attention back to the beating he was so thoroughly doling out. I place one of his arms around my shoulder and wrap one of mine around his back pulling him up to his feet with all of my strength. "Come on, baby. I got you. Let's go home."

He doesn't say anything, just hobbles along, letting me drag him to the car. All the while Daddy is screaming at my back. "Zhoe. Get back here. Don't you dare leave with him." Still, I ignore him.

As soon as I have Jared tucked safely into my passenger seat and the gun tucked back under his seat, I walk around the front of the car to the driver side and as I reach for the handle, I feel Daddy's hand come down on top of mine. Looking through the window I see Jared reach for his seatbelt. I know he's getting ready to come out and save me. How pathetic I have to be saved from my own father. I shake my head just slightly, just enough to let Jared know I don't need him – I can handle my father on my own.

"If you leave with him I'll cut you off. You'll have nowhere to go. Do you hear me?" His voice his calm, eerily calm. His words would hurt less if he were screaming, if he was still worked up from the events of the day. But, instead he sounds calm like disowning me and cutting me off is normal, natural. Turning as fast as I can, I rip my hand out of his grip before quickly slapping him across the face.

"I'm leaving with him and you're not going to stop me," I spit out through clenched teeth. I don't know what I'm feeling or thinking anymore. But I know without a doubt that I can't live without Jared and so I'm taking him home with me.

I turn my back on my father, my home and everything I've ever known. As soon as I'm in the car, Jared's bloodied hand reaches up to brush the lingering tears from my cheeks, and I know this is where I'm supposed to be.

Forty-Seven
Zhoe

"Can you walk?" I ask Jared when we pull up in front of my apartment. He just nods. He looks so bad, I really think he should go to the hospital but I'm sure he won't let me take him there.

I haven't been able to stop crying. I'm not really sure what I'm crying for. The crazy person that took over my father's body, the loss of my family, or seeing Jared so hurt; or maybe it was watching Jared give up because he thought he deserved it, finally realizing I'm in love with this man, or knowing he was with Cole in the last moments of his life. I don't really know which is the main cause of my tears, but I'm pretty sure it's a combination of all of them.

It's in this moment I realize why Jared was always so distant and cold whenever Cole would get brought up. He was hiding this secret from me; he was keeping it to himself. But, why?

Jared never said a word, never hushed me, and never promised it would all be okay. But, he never stopped touching me. He never stopped reassuring me that he was there with just his touch. Most of the ride was spent with his hand squeezing the life out of mine, like he was afraid to let me go. Occasionally he'd reach over and wipe away a tear or two, or brush my hair out of my face. Sometimes he would lift our joined hands and place a few soft kisses on mine.

Once we were in the house I guided him upstairs to my bathroom, setting him on the closed toilet seat. I rushed to the linen closet to grab several towels and washcloths. In the light I examine him and another bout of tears start. He's so battered and bruised and bloodied that I don't know where to start.

"Shh, stop crying, Pretty Girl. I'm okay," Jared says wiping away the endless stream of tears running down my face. "Shh."

"Where does it hurt the worst?" I ask him through my tears. Once I remove his shirt and see the cuts and bruises on his chest and sides, I start to panic. I have no idea where to start. It feels like every part of him is injured and bleeding. My hands are shaking, my breathing rapid. "Baby. We should really take you to the hospital."

"No hospital. It's just a few cuts and bruises." Grabbing the wet washcloth from my hand, he starts rubbing it along his eyebrows and cheeks, wincing a few times in the process. I wet another one and start on the cut on the back of his head. It's bleeding more than I'd like but it's not as bad as I originally thought.

"Why do you have a gun, Zhoe?" Jared asks quietly. Unlike my father, he doesn't sound upset or disgusted that I have a weapon, just curious.

"I got my concealed carry license after Cole died. I practice a few times a year with it." End of discussion. Jared doesn't ask any more questions, he doesn't pry or condone. He just lets it go.

It feels like an eternity before I can see his handsome face again. I gently grab his cheeks between my palms and just stare at him, mentally taking inventory to make sure nothing is too damaged. His cheeks and eyes are starting to swell where I'm sure a few ugly bruises will appear by morning but otherwise he looks okay. Okay as one can in this situation, I suppose.

I can still see my man under all of the ugliness. I see the man I fell in love with, the man I know now I can't live without. "I'm so sorry, Pretty Girl. I'm so, so sorry for everything."

"Shh. It's okay. You're okay and I'm okay and that's all that matters." I place a few soft kisses on his forehead just to reassure myself that he's still there, still here with me. As soon as I pull away, his hands come up to grip my waist, pulling me into him as he places his forehead against my belly.

"It's not okay. You deserve so much better than me." His voice is so low, it's like he's talking to himself. He's whispering things that sound like goodbye and he's holding me so tightly like he's afraid to let me go but he knows he has to. I'm afraid of where his thoughts are headed. He can't leave me now, not after everything we've gone through. But, it feels like that's what he's doing.

"Why didn't you tell me, Jared? Why didn't you tell me about Cole?"

Still talking into my stomach he mumbles with tears in his voice. "I was scared. I knew you'd run from me if I told you and I didn't want to lose you." The words come out slowly, his voice quivering with each syllable.

Gripping his cheeks in my hands I tilt his head back so I can look in his eyes, or rather he into mine. He needs to know how much I mean what I'm about to say. "I don't blame you Jared. I can't walk away from you; I need you too damn much. I'm not going anywhere."

He stares up at me for a long time without saying anything. I'm usually so good at reading his expression, understanding his feelings just from the look in his eyes but right now I have no idea what he's thinking. "You should walk away from me, Zhoe. I'm toxic," his voice sounds tortured.

"Stop saying stuff like that. You're perfect for me. We're perfect together. It's all going to be okay."

He pushes me away from him and stands up quickly. I move back a few steps to lean against the wall, shrinking back from the anger radiating off him. I know he's not angry with me, but after seeing what he can do when he's angry it's instinct to back away from him.

"How can you say that? I'm not good enough for you, damn it! I never will be!" He starts pacing, pulling at his hair, his breath coming in harsh pants. He punches the wall once before turning his attention back to me. "What do I have to offer you? Huh? I have no money. I didn't go to school. I can't give you the life you deserve."

He comes to stand inches from my face, running the back of one finger from my temple to my jaw. It's soft and sweet and so at odds with the man that was screaming at me only seconds ago. "You're too damn good for me."

He starts to back away but I can't let him leave me. I can't let him walk out of my life so I start yelling back. "Why? Why am I too good for you? I don't care about your money or status or education; that's not who you are."

I walk up to him and much like he did to me, I gently touch his face, placing my palm flat on his cheek. Showing him through my touch how much he means to me. "Who you are is the guy that pretends to watch chick flicks with me because you know they're my favorite. You're the guy that brings me my favorite ice cream when I've had a bad day. You're the guy that holds me close at night and leaves me sweet notes in the morning. You're the guy that makes me feel sexy and wanted and loved. You're the guy that makes me happier than I've ever been, happier than I ever thought I could be."

Pressing my body into his I bring his face down to mine and whisper against his lips. "That's the guy you are. Those are the things that make you, you. And that guy? That guy is plenty good enough for me."

Before he has the chance to respond, I place soft, gentle kisses against his lips. I want him to feel me, to feel how much I love him and need him. It takes only a few seconds and before long I find myself in my favorite place in the world: wrapped in Jared's arms, getting kissed senseless.

Forty-Eight

Jared

There is nowhere else in the world that I'd rather be than right here – holding Zhoe in my arms. The only thing that could make this moment better is if it could last, if I didn't have to leave her. It was so easy to picture forever with her, so easy to fall in love with this sweet, confident, shy girl that I forgot for a moment who I was.

I forgot I was the one responsible for all of her pain. I forgot I was a poor, nobody with a sordid past and no family. I forgot for a moment that I'm not good enough for her. For just one moment I forgot that I'm not the kind of guy a girl like Zhoe falls in love with. But I'm a selfish bastard and so I hold her, and kiss her, and pretend like I am. I pretend like I'm the guy she spoke of; the guy that deserves a girl like her. I squeeze her a little closer to me, my lips kissing her head repeatedly, whispering reassurances. "Shh, baby. Please stop crying. I'm here. I'm right here."

"Don't leave me, Jared." She looks up at me with tear filled eyes, I'm still not sure if they're sad tears or tears of relief because I stopped yelling at her. She seems to think I believed her words of affirmation, believed that I'm good enough for her and for a moment I did.

But, the funny thing about time is she's a whore - she fucks everyone. Always going by too fast in the good times and too slow in the bad. Every single moment with Zhoe has flown by, every second we've laughed together and played together; it was all over with in the blink of an eye. So that moment where I believed her was fleeting. Still, it was one of the best moments of my life.

I could picture a future with her. A future where I was enough for her, where I could provide for her and make her happy. I could erase her tears and only make her smile. I saw us growing old together and starting a family together. It was so easy to believe I could have that, but then life came crashing down on us.

"I need you, Jared. So damn much."

Looking down into her big blue eyes I see several things - I see determination, pain and fear, lust and something that looks almost like love; but that can't be. Zhoe can't love a guy like me, especially after everything she learned tonight. After she learned I took Cole to that place, I left him there to die, alone and scared. I did that. How could she love a guy like me?

"Jared," Zhoe whispers, leaning up on her toes placing her lips on mine gently. "Make love to me. I need to feel something good, I need to forget about this horrible day. Help me do that. Please?"

Leaning down I scoop her into my arms, one arm behind her back the other holding both of her legs. She wraps her arms around my neck, tucking her face into my neckline, placing gentle kisses all over it.

Setting her down on her bed I lean over her, kissing her softly, trying to convey my feelings through touch – trying to show her with my lips how much I love her. I'll deal with the guilt of making love to her with the intentions of walking out that door, later. Yes, I'll deal with that guilt much later. After I take just one more moment with Zhoe.

I pull her shirt over her head before removing her bra slowly, kissing each inch of skin as it's exposed to my greedy mouth. Kissing my way down her belly. I make my way to the waistband of her pants. I place kisses along it before sliding them slowly down her legs. Again I kiss each soft, creamy piece of her skin as it's uncovered. Once I have her jeans off, I remove her panties and stand back up looking down at her.

"You are so beautiful, Zhoe." She sits up on her knees and moves toward me. Reaching out she lowers my jeans and boxers. Flattening her palms she runs them over my shoulders, down my arms and across my chest to my stomach as she's done so many times but this time feels different. This time feels like she's cataloging every detail to memory. I recognize what she's doing because I'm doing the same thing.

I never want to forget the way her lips feel against mine, the way her breath always smells like mint, or the way her hair always smells like vanilla. I never want to forget the softness, the smoothness of her skin. I especially never want to forget the way she pants my name when she comes, the way her big, blue eyes look at me like I'm the best thing that's ever happened to her, the way she laughs and blushes. I want to remember every beautiful thing about my Pretty Girl.

"Zhoe," I grab her hands placing soft kisses on her palms before I move her back onto the bed so I can hover over her. Kissing my way from her lips to her inner thighs, I place a wet kiss on her sex.

Zhoe lets out a soft mewl and I vow to remember that sound as well. Flattening my tongue, I lick a few laps over her lips and clit, tasting her, savoring her. Feeling how wet she is I move up her body. "I can't wait anymore, baby. I have to be inside of you."

"Please. Please, Jared." As soon as the words are out of her mouth I push into her softly.

I feel like my heart is being ripped to shreds. She's so perfect, it's like she was made for me and yet I plan to walk away from her. What the fuck is wrong with me?

"Jared, I need you to move." I didn't realize I wasn't. I'd been so lost in the way she felt, in the pain ripping through me I forgot what I was doing. I lost myself for just a moment.

Starting to move, I feel her wrap her legs around my waist bringing me deeper into her body. "You're so perfect, Zho. So damn perfect." I cup her cheeks in both of my palms, my body held up by my forearms and I just stare at her. I move my gaze all along her face, paying more attention to the emotions swimming in her eyes. I know she wants me to move faster, to help her forget, but that's not what this about.

It's not about forgetting, it's about remembering.

I need to remember every detail of this moment, of this sweet girl. I need something to remember her by, a piece of her to hold on to when she's no longer mine to have. Selfishly, I want to leave her with something to remember me by, too.

Sweat beads on our bodies, as our breathing picks up. I feel her nails dig into my back spearing me on. Her heels dig into my ass causing me to pump into her harder. Unable to hold back any longer, I slam into her over and over again reveling in the feel of her wrapped around me in every sense - legs, arms and pussy all wrapped tight around me.

Using all of my senses I take it all in. I watch her back arch of the bed, her eyes roll back. I feel her pussy clench around me, I hear her call out my name over and over again. "Jared. Yes, Jared." Reaching between us I rub her clit a few times until falls over the edge.

After a few more pumps I follow behind her, shouting out my own release, her name, a prayer of regret on my lips. "Zhoe, baby." I collapse on top of her feeling her tighten her hold around me with her arms and legs, like she's afraid to let me go.

Rolling onto my back I bring her with me. Our legs are entwined and I have one hand holding her hair keeping her head on my chest, the other running lines up and down her spine. Zhoe's arm is wrapped around my waist holding me close to her.

"Jared." I feel her breath hot on my chest. She lifts her head to look me in my eyes. "I love you, Jared. I love you so much." I never knew those words could hurt so damn much. My eyes close as the pain bounces around in my heart, shattering it. "I thought my father was going to kill you today," she continues. "I realized right then that I can't live without you. I need you, Jared. I can't survive without you."

Tears are streaming down her cheeks, crushing my already broken heart. I know she knows I'm going to leave her. She's always been able to see into my soul, see the real me – I should have known I wouldn't be able to hide this from her.

I reach up, wiping away some of her tears, my lips gently covering hers. We kiss passionately for several moments; moments that are gone too fast once again. As soon as she pulls away to catch her breath, I pull her head back to my chest, cradling her to me hoping I can hold onto this moment for just a little longer. Once her breathing evens out, I place a soft kiss on her forehead, closing my eyes, trying to push away the tears threatening to spill from my own eyes.

I want to tell her that I love her, but I can't do that to her. Zhoe has always been the strength in this relationship; tonight proves that. She knows I'm leaving but she was strong enough, brave enough to tell me those precious words anyways – afraid of me leaving without knowing. Why can't I do the same?

Would me telling her I love her and then walking away anyways hurt more or less if she knew how I felt? If she knew I did it *because* I love her?

I lay with her for hours, both of us squeezing so tightly it's borderline painful. Both of us trying to hold on to what remains of our broken relationship. Zhoe falls asleep quickly, but I'm too worked up to succumb – I can't turn my mind off, I can't breathe deep enough to find peace. My whole world is falling apart around me and there is not a goddamn thing I can do to fix it.

When the sun starts peeking through her window I realize my time is up – if I'm going to leave, I have to do it before she wakes up or I'll never be able to. Extricating myself from her grip I slip from her bed. Finding her notebook and pen that are always on her desk I leave her one last note before walking out of her room for the last time; before leaving behind the only girl I've ever loved. I knew this would hurt but I had no idea just how much.

I feel like I can't breathe, like I'm suffocating, like I'm dying. I take it all in, though because I deserve it.

Forty-Nine

Zhoe

It's been one week since I woke up to Jared's goodbye letter: *I'm so sorry Pretty Girl. I'll never forget you. – J.* As if saying sorry would make everything better, as if I could forgive him for walking away from me.

I never imagined we'd have our last kiss, yet we did. I'm still not sure what to do with myself. I'm not even sure who I am anymore without Jared. I don't know how to wake up in the mornings without my good morning note or text message. I don't sleep. My bed feels big, empty and cold without him in it.

I knew it that night that he was going to leave me. I could feel it in the air, in my heart. I could see it in his eyes and hear it in his voice. My emotions change with each day – anger and pain the most consuming of them all.

I hurt for him because I know he didn't really want to walk away from me. You don't walk away from someone you love and I know without a doubt Jared loved me. He may not have said the words, but I could feel his love in every touch, every caress. I could see his love in his eyes. I truly believe he walked away from me because he thought that's what was best for me – he believes he's not good enough for me.

I hurt for me because I gave Jared everything I am. I gave him my heart, my soul, my life but he walked away from it all.

I planned a future with him in my head. I could see us together forever, growing old and having babies. I could picture it so clearly and now it's all gone.

I think that's what hurts the worst. There will be no Mrs. Zhoe Roman, there will be no babies, no sitting together on the porch when we're old watching our grandbabies play together. Everything I ever let myself hope and dream the two of us could have is gone.

"Zhoe?" I hear Angelica's voice call for me through the bedroom door. "Are you up?" I've been staying with her for the last week since my dad stayed true to his word and kicked me out of my apartment and closed my bank account. The Registrar's Office has also informed me that my tuition is no longer paid for next semester. My father may be an asshole but he's no liar.

I've pretty much been sitting on Angelica's couch for the last week trying to decide what to do with my life. I've been looking for a job but haven't come across one just yet, although really I'm not in any hurry. I know Angelica and her parents will take care of me. I don't want them to, but I know they'll help me get through this.

I'm not really upset about the whole school thing since I didn't truly want to be there anyway. I've had dreams but my father has always pretended they didn't exist. Instead, he's shoved his dreams and his ideas for what my future should look like down my throat.

I should be able to find the positive in this situation. I finally have the opportunity to do what I really want, to live my own life. I just wish Jared were by my side to share the moment with me. To support me.

"So, I was thinking we could have a lazy weekend. Order in, watch chick flicks and stay in our PJ's until Monday morning." Angelica interrupts my thoughts. "What do you think?"

"Have I told you lately that I love you?" I try to smile and joke with her but it feels forced. Her plans for the weekend sound perfect, but I'm still unable to truly smile at her, the pain in my heart still too strong.

"You haven't, but you've been a little preoccupied." She grabs my hand, flashing me a small smile before turning back to the movies in her hand. "So I pretty much brought up every Nicholas Sparks movie ever made. What should we watch first? 'The Notebook?'"

I start shaking my head at her, that movie is forever ruined for me. Jared hated watching chick flicks with me. He did it because he knew I loved them, plus I watched all of the "Die Hard" movies for him.

"The Notebook" was the first one I made him watch. I spent more time watching him than the actual movie. He acted like it was pure torture, but at the end when they pass away together, I saw him sniffle and rub at his eyes. Of course he blamed it on allergies or something but I know it affected him.

Jared was like that – all hard on the outside but soft and sweet on the inside. He always said and did the sweetest things. His words would make me weak in the knees. Now I can only hear his sweet words in my dreams. In my memories of us.

"Not the 'Notebook,'" I finally say to Ang. "How about 'A Walk To Remember?'" That one never fails me, I always cry like a baby but thankfully I can't really relate it to my life so I shouldn't think about Jared too much.

"'A Walk To Remember' it is. Or, you could finally talk to me and tell me what happened?" She looks hopeful and I start to feel guilty. I really haven't given many details to my friend, simply telling her Daddy attacked Jared and then he left me claiming he wasn't good enough for me.

I guess I should really fill her in on everything else - his sordid past, his connection with Cole, all of it. Clearing my throat a few times I try to find the courage to get through this story. "I'm really sorry I haven't been open with you about all of this. I just needed time to process."

"I understand. You don't have to talk to me if you don't want to. I just want you to know that I'm here for you."

I smile at her, grabbing her hand I bring her back down so we're laying side-by-side facing each other on the bed. "I want to talk. Just promise to not freak out, it's a lot to take in."

She nods her head at me and I take one final deep breath before I tell her everything. I tell her about Jared's parents, his run-in with the law, his drug use and addiction. I tell her about the meetings he still attends so he doesn't fall back into that world. I tell her about Cole and how they were friends.

Tears are streaming down my face at this point. I can't seem to stop them. I hurt so bad for the boy Jared used to be. I hurt for the man he is now, still believing he's not good enough. "Shh. It's okay Zhoe. Shh."

I smile at my friend, thanking her silently for being there for me. "That's not it, Ang. This is the worst part." Deep breath. "He was with Cole the night he died." I pause letting that sink in for a minute.

"He what?" Her disbelief evident in the way her eyes go wide and her jaw drops open. "He was with him? How long have you known this?"

"Um, I found out that night at my parents' house. I didn't know before then."

"What the hell? Why didn't he tell you? I know you've talked about Cole with him." She looks angry and confused and I love her for it, but I don't blame Jared for not telling me.

"Ang, he was scared. He was scared he'd lose me."

Which of course he did, but he was the one to make that decision for me, for us. He believed I was going to walk away and instead he walked away from me. How dare he make that decision for me? How dare he ruin what we have because he believes something so untrue about himself?

He blames himself for Cole's death, but I don't blame him. I never really got to talk to him, though, so I don't exactly know what happened that night. I mean I can assume what they were doing but still, it would've been nice to have some answers.

"Holy shit." I laugh lightly at her reaction. Had Jared told me in a normal situation and I hadn't found out the way I did that probably would have been my reaction, too. "That's why he left, isn't it?"

"Yeah. He thinks he's not good enough for me. I asked him once to describe himself in one word; he chose damaged." I fight back another round of tears at the memory. Why didn't I press him for more information then? Why didn't I look into what made him damaged? I just let it go, hoping he would confide in me but he never truly did.

He told me things that contributed to him feeling that way, he told me things I know were hard for him, but he never told me the biggest reason; the one thing that connected us for all of these years.

"Zhoe, you have to go find him. I know you love him and I know he loves you. I saw it in his eyes. You have to fight for him to show him he's worth it. No one has probably ever done that for him before."

Oh my god. Why didn't I think of that? I let my own pain get in the way. I let my bruised ego and broken heart stand in the way of the one thing I want most in this world – Jared. I want him. I need him. And, he needs me.

"You're right. No one has ever shown him he's good and strong and worth it. I have to do it. I have to show him how much I love him."

FIFTY

Jared

    I knew leaving Zhoe would be the hardest thing I'd ever have to do, but fuck, nothing could have prepared me for this. Some days are better than others, but most days I feel like I can't breathe. I feel weak and tired. Sometimes when I picture her beautiful, perfect face I wonder if I'm going to collapse – a pain so strong, so deep cuts through my chest. I feel like there's a hole where my broken heart used to lie.
    It's been just over one month since I walked out on the only girl I loved, the only girl I'll ever love. Everyone, and by that I mean Rico, kept telling me it would get easier. She was just a girl. There were plenty more fish in the sea. At first, I was pissed he could say things like that about her. I mean he knew Zhoe; he knew she wasn't *just a girl,* she was special and unique and I fucking loved her.
    I've lived with regret and guilt all my life. But, I've regretted nothing as much as I regret turning my back on her; except maybe the fact that I never told her how I felt. I thought it would be easier for her to get over me if she didn't know I loved her.
    Deep down I know I was right in not telling her. But, the selfish part of me wishes I had because now those words will never pass my lips. Zhoe was it for me. I'll never love anyone else, and I'll never want to say those three little words to anyone else. It's always been Zhoe. It will always only be Zhoe.
    I haven't called her, and she hasn't called me once in the days since I left. I have however, gone past her place – sitting just down the block, hoping to catch a glimpse of her. I never did. What I did see was her asshole father with a locksmith changing the locks and movers taking away all of her furniture.

After that day, the hole in my heart got a little bigger, a little deeper. I have no idea where she is. I could always call her, or I could have Rico call Angelica, but I won't. I walked away for a reason – I'm not good enough for her. I wasn't good enough then and I'm not good enough now. It's best if I have no way of finding her, that way I won't be tempted to contact her.

I've thought about deleting her number from my phone a dozen times but each time, I freeze. Not having any way to reach her hurts too damn much to think about. So, instead of deleting her number like I know I should, I make a promise to myself not to call her as long as I can keep her number. It's illogical but it makes me feel better. Infinitesimally.

Deciding I need to get out of my own head for a bit I shoot Rico a text to see if he wants to go shoot pool and grab a few beers. We'll have to drive to the pool hall on the other side of town, since I can't go to the Slip and take the chance of running into Zhoe.

Me: Sup, man? You up for some pool and brews tonight?
Rico: Roman. I'm game. I've got some shit to take care of first but swoop by and pick me up in an hour.
Me: Cool.

I feel like a bad friend. Outside of work I've only seen Rico a handful of times since Zhoe and I broke up. I just haven't been in the mood to go out. Really I haven't been in the mood for anything, especially faking a smile even around my brother.

My days post-Zhoe have consisted of work, coming home doing a few circuit workouts –because I'm too much of a coward to go to the gym in case she's there – drinking beer and going to bed. Most of the time even those few mundane tasks feel like too much work, too much effort.

I vow to start getting back to living, beginning tonight. Beginning with Rico. I was only with Zhoe for two months and we've been separated half as long. How long is too long of a grieving period? How long of a grieving period am I entitled to when I'm the one that fucked everything up to begin with?

***

Pulling up in front of Rico's I honk the horn three times to let him know I'm here. It takes a few minutes before he finally makes his way to my truck. I know I've been stuck in my own head for a while but when did Rico lose so much weight? He looks like he's lost close to twenty pounds and a good portion of his muscle mass. He looks pale, too.

Hopping into my truck he flashes me his signature grin. "Sup, man? Nice to see you back in the land of the living."

Unable to hold it in, because beating around the bush is something we've never done I let my thoughts fall from my mouth. "Wish I could say the same about you, you look like shit."

"At least buy me a drink before you start hating on me. Asshole." He's still wearing a smile, but it's fallen a bit. Someone who doesn't know Rico as well as I do might not have noticed the change but I can always tell when something's on his mind.

I'm quiet for a minute, focusing my attention on the road ahead of me. "Look, Rico," I start unable to hold the apology in, "I'm sorry I've been so distant lately…"

Before I can even finish he cuts me off. "Don't go getting all pussified on me, Roman."

"Pussified? Is that even a word?" I can't help but laugh at him.

"It is now." I drop the subject. I vow to myself, however, to be a better friend, to keep an eye on him for a while. It's been a long time since Rico's had a relapse but that doesn't mean it's not a possibility.

As a former addict I know better than to come right out and ask him, especially if he's not using again. Doubting him could push him back in that direction and that's the last thing I want to happen. Biding my time, keeping my eyes open for the signs are the only ways I'm going to find out what's really going on.

We hop out of the truck and Rico turns to give me a huge grin as we make our way across the parking lot. "Let's go find us a couple distractions, huh?"

I can't help but laugh at him and his eagerness as we find a couple barstools near the end of the bar to claim as ours. Immediately, Rico waves the bartender over, and blatantly stares down her top as he orders a round of beers.

"So, what's been going on man?" Rico asks once she walks away.

"Not a lot. Trying not to wallow. What's up with you?"

"She's just a girl, Roman." He takes the beers from the bartender, flashing her a grin. "Thanks, beautiful."

She smiles at Rico, leaning over the counter so her ample cleavage is on display. "You boys let me know if you need anything tonight."

"What's your name, baby?"

"Tiffany," she smirks. "And yours?"

"Rico, and this is Roman. You just let us know if *you* need anything." With that she winks and walks away. "Damn, did you see her tits, dude?"

I ignore him, taking a giant swig from my beer needing something to numb the thoughts of Zhoe and her perfect body, her perfect tits. Fuck, I'm such a fucking idiot. Why did I let a girl like her go?

"Okay, that's it. I've had enough of this. What you need is to get wasted and get some pussy. A good lay is all you need to forget her."

"Fuck you, Rico. It's not that easy. I'm never going to forget about this girl."

Rico rolls his eyes at me waving down the sleazy bartender. He orders another round of beers and several shots of tequila. I down the first shot she pours, slamming the glass onto the counter. I wave my hand at the bartender to signal another round.

I'm not keen on Rico's idea, and I'm definitely not sleeping with some random tonight but a few drinks can't hurt.

I'm staring into my beer bottle lost in my thoughts when Rico slaps me on the back. I hadn't even noticed he was missing. I turn in my seat to find him standing behind me with a woman on each arm. I think they're pretty but I can't really tell at the moment, my vision's blurry.

"Roman. Meet Veronica and Stacey." He gestures first to the blonde and then the redhead. I'm surprised they aren't dressed to impress like most of the girls in the bar tonight – it is New Year's Eve after all. They are wearing jeans, high-heeled boots and tight shirts, and seductive smiles. Both look like they are on a mission.

"*Roman*. That's a sexy name," the redhead sidles up to me, placing her hand on my shoulder and her breasts on my arm. She takes a look at the bar top, taking in the empty shot glass and bottle of beer. "You know, I can help you take your mind off whatever's eating you, sweetie."

I twist in my seat a little; grabbing her by the waist I pull her onto my lap. "What are you offering, sugar?"

She leans into me, her lips brushing my ear. "Whatever you want."

I run my hand up her thigh, over her hip giving it a good squeeze. I look her over from head to toe. She's definitely got a nice body, pretty eyes and nice lips. I consider taking her up on her offer. For one minute.

For one minute I forget. I forget about the pain in my chest, I forget about the hole in my heart. I forget about Zhoe. But, then the girl places kisses on my jaw – just like Zhoe used to do – and I'm hit with a blinding pain.

She's not Zhoe.

"Get off me," I stand up quickly only caring in the back of my mind that she doesn't fall on her ass.

"Your loss, asshole," she shouts after me, but I barely register her voice. I don't give a shit what that girl has to say about me. She'll find some other guy to take her home in a matter of minutes and I'll be a distant memory.

"Jared, wait up. You can't drive, man." Rico catches up to me just as I reach for my driver side door. I hand him my keys, knowing he's probably right and walk to the other side of the truck.

I am so fucking ready for this night to be over. I want to go home and sleep this alcohol off. I want to feel every single ounce of pain, every crack in my heart because I deserve to feel pain. I broke Cole and Zhoe's family and I broke Zhoe.

I deserve this. All of it.

FIFTY-ONE

Zhoe

It's been thirty-six days since Jared walked out of my life, taking my heart with him. It's been twenty-eight days since I decided I was going to prove to him that he's worthy of my love. I hate saying it like that; it makes me sound so pretentious, so much like a Dawson.

In reality, he's the one who believes he's not worthy of me; thoughts like that have never even crossed my mind. Jared is a sexy, strong, wonderful, kind, loving person. What more could I want in a partner?

So, what's taking me so long to get back to him you ask? Me. I'm scared. I'm scared he doesn't want me anymore. I'm scared he's moved on. I'm scared he's fallen back into his old lifestyle. I'm just fucking scared.

More than fear though was the need to get my shit together. I've been focusing on finding a job, looking for a place to live that isn't with my best friend and trying to decide what my future looks like now that my father isn't telling me what to do.

So far I've checked off the job part. I'm working as the volunteer coordinator at the YWCA.

I love my job. I'm in charge of the volunteers and the community outreach events. I'm busy, which helps keep my mind off how shitty my life is currently. But, more than that, I'm doing something I've always enjoyed doing and getting paid for it. The problem? The pay is shit.

This is why I'm still staying with Angelica. She reassures me almost daily that she doesn't mind having me there. We've had a good time – every night is like girls night, complete with wine and chick flicks. But, I hate mooching off of her. I hate not having my own place to go. Mostly, I hate not having my own apartment to wallow and cry in without having to worry about being overheard.

Too many nights Angelica has had to come into my room to hold me and rock me as I loudly cry my eyes out. I thought it would get easier, that's what they say isn't? Time cures everything? But, it's not getting easier. It's hard and fucking hurts.

On those really rough days, the days I don't want to get out of my bed, the days where the tears seem endless – on those days, I wonder if trying to work things out is even worth it. He left me. He fucking left me. Why the fuck do I want him back?

Then I remember. I reread his sweet, dirty text messages; I dig out his love notes and reread those, too. I think about the knee-weakening way he used to kiss me. I think about the way we used to laugh. I think about all of the good times and it takes everything in me not to run out the door right that minute and go to him.

My heart hurts for everything we've lost, but it hurts more for Jared. I've lost my family now, too. I'm alone except for Ang, just like he only has Rico, but what he doesn't know is he still has me, too.

As much as I want to go to him today I know I have to wait until the time is right. I know my life, my heart, and my head need to be in the right place. Even though I know this, it's hard to stay away. I miss him. I need him. I can't help but wonder… does he need me, too?

The clicking of Angelica's heels coming down the hallway break me out of my thoughts, I turn to my friend and smile. She's dressed to impress tonight. Her long blonde hair is curled to perfection, her slim curves accentuated in the skin-tight black dress that barely covers the essentials. She's finished her look with sky-high red heels that match her lipstick. She does a twirl for me, grinning. "What do you think?"

"You are definitely drinking for free tonight my beautiful, slutty friend." It's New Year's Eve and she is heading out to paint the town, and pick up her newest conquest while I've decided to stay home in my yoga pants and wallow in my own self-pity.

"Zhoe, come with me," she says with a sad look on her face. She's been pleading with me all week to go out with her. She has told me on multiple occasions that I either need to go to Jared and get him back or move on. If only it were that easy. "You need to get out of this house. Come on, it'll be fun."

"I'm good. I have Channing to keep me company tonight," I wiggle the "Magic Mike" DVD case in front of her face. "Plus, copious amounts of wine and yoga pants. Sorry, but my night sounds way better than yours."

She turns an annoyed face at me and rolls her eyes. "Whatever. I'm leaving. Have fun tonight, loser."

"Love you. Call me if you need a ride."

"Love you, too."

***

My ringing phone wakes me from my slumber. I apparently passed out on the couch. I reach for my phone and before I even have time to say hello I hear my name being called through the other end. "Zhoe!"

The sound of Angelica's panicked voice knocks me into the hard face of reality. "Ang? What's the matter?"

"Rico," her voice breaks on a sob. "Rico. He's in the hospital. I'm at the hospital. Need you."

"Are you okay? Are you hurt?"

"Not hurt. Just please, Zho. I need you."

"I'm on my way." I hang up, jumping up as quickly as possible; willing my sleepy mind to wake the fuck up and move. My hands are shaking as I try to find my keys and purse. I have no idea what's going on. Angelica was a mess, which leads me to believe whatever happened, was bad. Really bad.

Ang is always calm, always the voice of reason. Even throughout everything that happened with Cole she never cracked or faltered. She was strong and collected. Hearing her cry and beg for me to be with her makes my heart race and tears surface in my eyes. This is not good.

Driving as quickly as I can to the hospital I'm lost in thoughts of *what if*. My car door is barely shut behind me before I take off running into the ER desperately looking for my friend. I find her in the corner curled into a ball in a waiting room chair. For a second I allow myself to breathe, seeing that she's okay – even though she told me she was it is still a relief to see her with my own eyes. I make my way over to her; squatting down in front of her I gently touch her leg, whispering her name. "Ang?"

She barely lifts her head off her knees to look at me but as soon as she realizes it's me, she flings herself at me, knocking me backwards onto the floor. "Oh, Zhoe!" She's hysterically crying. I try everything to get her to calm down. I whisper soothing noises; I run my hands up and down her back. I hold her as tightly as possible until after what seems like forever her tears slow enough for her to sit up.

I move us both into a sitting position, our backs against the chairs. I grip her hand in mine. "What happened, Ang?"

"Rico texted me that he wanted to meet up. I told him to come to the bar I was at but he never showed up. I went to his apartment to go off on him because this isn't the first time he's done this the last few weeks. He just doesn't show or call or answer any of my texts. But, when I got there the house was dark and I just knew… knew something was wrong. Oh god."

"Shh," I bring her down so her head is resting on my shoulder as another round of tears wracks through her body.

"I let myself in and found him passed out on his living room floor. He was barely breathing and wasn't responding to me. I don't think he was conscious. I called 911, and they said he overdosed on heroin. But, no one will tell me anything here since I'm not family." She sits up and slams her fist into the ground. "But he doesn't have any damn family."

"Does Jared know?" I ask. I'm terrified of her answer. I'm afraid for him to find out. This might break him to lose someone else.

"Yeah, I called him when I got here. I saw him when he first walked in, but I don't know where he went. Maybe they let him go to him." She looks at me and I've never seen my friend so broken, so scared. "I need to see him, Zhoe. I need to know he's okay."

"I know. We'll get you back there as soon as we can, okay?" She just nods at me her head falling back onto my shoulder. I feel completely helpless. I have no idea how to help my friend, so I do the only thing I know I can in the moment – I hold onto her for dear life.

I've always appreciated Angelica for being there for me during Cole's death and for being so strong but I never really realized how hard it truly is being the strong one. It's exhausting.

I hear a man clear his throat from above us, glancing up I feel like my heart is being ripped from my chest all over again. Jared stands there looking like a completely broken man. He has bags under his red-rimmed eyes, his posture is slouched and his mouth is turned down in a frown.

"Jare." My voice is barely audible. I need to say something, but I have no idea what to say so I just sit there silently staring up at the man that completely owns me. I watch as he slides onto the floor across from us. He doesn't say anything for so long I'm afraid of what the news is going to be.

Angelica asks for me, "Jared is Rico… is he…?" She never finishes her sentence but we all know what she's asking.

"He's alive. They gave him Narcan and are keeping him for observation for a few days while his body goes through detox. He's in room 313, he's asking for you."

"Oh, um. Okay." Angelica stands quickly, but pauses to look back at me. "Don't leave, okay?"

"I'm not going anywhere. I'll be right here when you get back. Love you."

She smiles at me softly. "Love you, too."

"How is she?" Jared gestures at Ang's retreating back.

I just shake my head. "Not good. She's pretty torn up about finding him that way." Jared nods, dropping his head into his hands. "Are you okay, Jared?"

"I'm fine." His cold, clipped voice sends chills down my spine. He's not fine. An awkward silence stretches between us. I have so much to say to him, yet nothing at all to say. Instead, we stare at each other, our pain reflected in each other's eyes. I want to go to him, to hold him and kiss him and tell him I love him. But, I'm terrified he'll push me away again. I don't think I can live through that again.

Finally, Jared breaks the silence. "Thanks for being here. For Ang, I mean."

"I'm here for you, too, Jared." His silence is deafening. If I've learned anything it's that life is short. We never know when our last day is going to be and I'll be damned if my last day with Jared is spent like this. I love him too much. Despite him walking away from me, from us, I want him. I need him.

I move from my spot on the waiting room floor, sliding up next to him. I grab his hand in mine and squeeze. Instantly, Jared breaks. I've never seen a grown man cry. My father didn't even cry when Cole died, which considering his cold heart really shouldn't surprise me all that much. Watching Jared cry is the hardest, most painful thing I've ever experienced. I reach up and position him much like I did Angelica. I push his head down until it's resting on my shoulder. Jared surprises me by wrapping his arm around my waist pulling us close.

"I was so scared, Zho. I thought I was going to lose him. I have no one left. I can't lose him, too."

"Shh. You have me, Jare. You'll always have me."

"Always?"

"Always." I brush a soft kiss on head, taking a deep breath, inhaling the scent that is all Jared. I never thought I'd have this again with him. I never thought I'd be able to hold him and smell him and kiss him. I don't know what this means, but for now I'm going to soak it all in. I'm not letting him go for a long, long time.

"Don't leave me, please," Jared whispers against my neck.

"I'm not going anywhere, baby."

After what feels like a small eternity, but still isn't long enough, Jared moves from his position and looks at me. His eyes hold so much emotion, they always have been his tell. I can see his worry and his pain; I see regret and maybe something that looks like love. I don't let myself focus on that though. Today isn't about me; it's not even about us. I'm here for my friends – including Jared. Though, it's painful to categorize him that way.

Jared moves to stand. Reaching down he grabs me under my arms and lifts me until I'm also standing. "Come on, you don't need to be sitting on this floor." He walks us over to one of three couches in the waiting room, which surprises me and excites me at the same time. He sits down, pulling me onto his lap and holds me tight once again.

"Tell me if this isn't okay," he mumbles into my hair. "I just really need to hold you right now."

I wrap my arms around his neck and squeeze. "I don't ever want you to let go."

Fifty-Two

<u>Jared</u>

Several hours later Angelica met us in the waiting room again, telling us she planned on staying the night with Rico. Reluctantly, Zhoe and I left. There really was no point in us sleeping in the waiting room. Angelica promised to call us in the morning or if anything happened during the night.

The doctors and nurses felt he was going to be okay, though. If Angelica hadn't gotten there when she did, I don't know what we would be facing today but I don't want to think about it.

I stood with a sleepy Zhoe still wrapped around me and carried her to my truck. Once she was tucked safely inside, I looked over at her taking in her beautiful face. God, I missed her. Why the hell had I ever let her go?

"Zhoe, baby. I know I have no right to want anything anymore when it comes to you," I say softly, my voice still too loud in the cab of my truck. "But, I really need you tonight. Will you come back home with me?"

Zhoe being Zhoe smiles a soft, sweet smile at me. "There's nowhere else I'd rather be."

I don't hesitate. I don't give her a moment to regret her decision. I just drive. I drive us straight to my place. The cab of the truck is completely silent as she fights sleep, and I fight the urge to pull her into my arms. Losing the battle, I carry her out of the truck and inside, because I need to keep touching her, I need the reminder that she's here. With me.

Waking up this morning I feel like death. My mouth is dry, my head is pounding and my stomach is growling, but really I'm just fucking exhausted. Getting a phone call that your best friend, your brother, is in the hospital because of an overdose is terrifying and sucks the life right out of you.

Driving to the hospital last night I felt completely weighed down with guilt. I've already failed one friend – I couldn't get to Cole in time to save him. I couldn't bear the thought of letting another friend down, especially since I should have been with him.

I've been so distant from Rico, from everyone really. Lost in my own world of self-pity, and heartache that I failed to really notice the signs. I knew something was going on with him but I continued to ignore the signs.

Relieved that he's alive doesn't even begin to cover the way I feel. I need to be a better friend. I need to be there for Rico, more than anything right now.

All I want to do is lay here and sleep for days, needing the energy to deal with what today is going to bring, but apparently, my body has other plans. Opening my eyes just a crack I realize my head isn't on my pillow but instead on a warm, soft chest. Opening my eyes farther I feel the breath get ripped out of my lungs.

Zhoe's perfect face is right next to mine. Her eyes are closed, her breathing slow and steady like she's sleeping. Her arms are wrapped so tightly around my upper body I don't know how I could breathe at all. I continue staring at her, taking her in. Savoring her. I almost forgot how good she smells, taking a deep breath I inhale her sweet vanilla scent.

I must be dreaming. There is no other explanation for it. Why the hell else would this gorgeous girl be in my bed? Especially after I walked out on her and have avoided her for months? She wouldn't be, she couldn't be. It's a sick, cruel dream my mind is playing on me. Haven't I suffered enough? I'm being taunted with the one thing I want more than anything but can't have. Fucking cruel.

I would give anything to be a different man, to be good enough for this girl. I didn't realize how much I missed her and needed her, until I had her back for a moment, even if it's not real. My heart hurts with how much I've missed her.

I love her. I've never loved anyone in the world, but I love her.

She opens her eyes, piercing me with her bright blue gaze. She reaches over to brush a tear I didn't realize had fallen off my cheekbone. As soon as her hand touches my face I grasp the fact that I'm not dreaming, she's really here.

"You're real?" I question through the lump in my throat. She looks at me like I'm crazy but doesn't say a word, just continues to wipe away my tears as they fall harder. "I thought I was dreaming. I... what are you doing here, Pretty Girl?"

"You needed me." She says it like it's so simple, like it was a stupid thing for me to ask. Of course I needed her. I need her every fucking day of my life. But, that doesn't explain why she's here after everything I did to her.

"But, I left you. I hurt you. I walked away. But, you're here..." I trail off. I'm not making any sense and I know it. I just can't understand why she's here. This just proves that I'm not good enough for her. She'll always be a better person than me.

Hugging me closer, she tucks my head into the crook of her neck, her fingers massaging the back of my scalp. "I never left you. We both needed time and space to figure things out but I never planned on letting you go."

"Zhoe."

Her voice is nothing more than a whisper. "Shh. I'm here Jared. I'm not going anywhere, okay? I love you."

She loves me? Still? Pulling back I look down into her beautiful eyes and tell her the one thing I should have told her months ago, the only thing that really matters. "I love you, Zhoe. I'm sorry it took so long for me to tell you, but I'm crazy about you. I love you so much it fucking hurts."

Tears start running down her face, leaving tracks and smearing her mascara but she doesn't seem to care or even notice. Instead she reaches up to cup my face in her hand and says something so Zhoe like it makes me smile. "I know."

I bark out a strangled laugh. It sounds odd because it's been so long since I've laughed and it's mixed with my tears and my pain, but I still laugh. "Only you, Pretty Girl. Only you could make me smile on a day like today. Thank you for being here."

"I wouldn't be anywhere else." Moving one arm to the other side of her body, I cage her in, holding my weight up on my arms. Leaning down, I place my lips gently over hers. I know she just said she still loves me, I know she said she's not going anywhere but that doesn't mean she's mine anymore. That doesn't mean I get to kiss her whenever I want, not yet anyways.

But when she leans forward, her hands pulling my mouth closer to hers, I realize she is still mine. I never thought I'd have this again, but I'm not going to let her go this time. I revel in the feel of her soft lips as they move perfectly against mine. I take in her taste and her smell and the way she feels lying underneath me.

"I missed you so much," I whisper against her lips. "I'm so sorry. So sorry."

She tilts her head away from me so my mouth can no longer reach hers. "Stop. We'll talk about all of that later. Right now I want to feed you and hold you and comfort you. Okay?"

"Okay." I nod at her and give her a little smile. I'm so glad she came back to me, so glad she's strong enough for the both of us.

After a few more stolen kisses we head down the hall towards the kitchen. Zhoe orders me to sit on the couch while she makes us scrambled eggs and toast. I can see her in my kitchen from my spot in the living room and even as shitty as today has been, I can't help the smile on my face.

I could definitely get used to her being in my kitchen, barefoot, cooking for me every day. Zhoe's not a great cook but she's learning. She cooked for me when we were dating a few times, and each time she got a little better. Of course I ate everything she gave me and praised her for it, and truly I don't mind her terrible cooking. I just like her cooking for me.

"What are you smiling about?" she asks, walking into the living room with a plate and a coffee mug in her hands.

"I like having you cook for me in my house." With a quick kiss to her cheek, I grab the dishes out of her hands. It takes everything in me to not chuckle at the eye roll and slight blush I get from her at my answer. Confident and shy, only my Zhoe can be both simultaneously.

"Don't get used to it," she calls over her shoulder, going back to pick up her food from the kitchen. Our easy banter makes me grin. This is how it's always been with us. Easy. How could I ever think I could live without her?

We spend the next several minutes sitting close to each other on the couch, eating our breakfast in relative silence. I can't help but steal glances at her every once and while. I kind of want to pinch myself to make sure this is real.

For so long I've dreamt of her, willing her to stay in my dreams and my memories. I knew I didn't even deserve those precious moments she gifted me with but I was taking them. I never wanted to forget a single moment with this girl.

But, having her back is surreal. It's almost too good to be true. It's also pure fucking torture sitting next to her and not touching her. I want to pull her into my arms, kiss her until we can't breathe and then make love to her until we're both too tired to walk. All the while telling her over and over how much I love her. Praying she believes me and it's enough, because as greedy as it is of me – I've lived without Zhoe and I never want to again.

Fifty-Three

Jared

Not really wanting to bring it up but knowing it needs to be discussed soon, I decide to dive in headfirst. "How have you been, Zho?"

She leans back into the corner of the couch, pulling her knees up she wraps her arms around them almost like she's protecting herself. She doesn't answer right away. Instead she gazes at me intently like she's trying to decide how honest she wants to be. "I'm surviving."

Well, that's about as honest as you can get. I know she means it because I feel the same fucking way. Every day without her was just another day to get through, another day I could mark off the calendar. I had nothing to look forward to, no one to go home to or wake up to in the mornings. It was just another day.

"I'm sorry," I offer. I know it's not much but I have to at least try to apologize.

"For what exactly?" She's been so calm and quiet and supportive today her sudden anger surprises me. I know I deserve it, I know it's warranted, but I wasn't prepared for it.

"What do you mean 'for what??' I'm sorry I left you. I'm sorry for everything that happened that day. I'm sorry for not saving Cole." I have so much to be sorry for I don't know where to start or when to stop. "I'll never stop being sorry, Zhoe. I have so much to make up to you."

"Are you sorry for thinking you're not good enough?"

What? Of all the things I need to apologize for that was not one of them. I'm not good enough for her, so there's no way I'm going to apologize for that.

"No. I'm not. I'm not good enough for you, Pretty Girl. How can you even want someone like me? I'm messed up. I'm damaged, broken. But you? You're so fucking perfect it hurts. You deserve someone just as perfect as you, not a fuck up like me."

She crawls over to me, straddling my lap, her hands on my shoulders. Her eyes are serious as she tells me quietly, "I don't want a perfect person. I want *my* perfect person. I want someone that makes me laugh, makes me feel sexy and special. I want someone that looks at me with love in his eyes. To me, that's perfection. To me *you're* perfection."

"I love your laugh, I'll do anything you want if it makes you laugh all day, every day. You are so fucking sexy I can hardly keep my hands to myself when I'm around you. I look at you with love in my eyes because I love you with more than my heart has room for. I want to be that guy for you, Zho, you have no idea how much I want to be that guy for you."

Even though I told her I didn't want to see her cry anymore, tears are falling endlessly from her eyes, but they are bright and her face is adorned with a beautiful smile. "You're the only one stopping you."

Smiling back at her I grip her face in my hands pulling her close to me, close enough she can hear my whispered promise. "I'm not good enough for you. I never will be, but I'm selfish enough to keep you anyways. I'm not letting you go again, Zhoe."

"Good, because I'm not going anywhere. I love you, Jared." The look in her eyes is so sincere and real. I've never really known love – my parents left me, my friends ditched me. But, this is real, I know it. I can feel it and I vow to myself right then and there to never, ever let this go.

"I love you, too."

I pull her down until her lips are on mine; starting off gently I rub our lips together until she opens up to me. Plunging my tongue into her warm cavern, I take it all in; the way she smells and feels and tastes and sounds.

Standing up from our spot on the couch I let her slide down my body until her feet touch the floor. I need to show her with more than words how much I love her, how much I need her. Leading the way to the bedroom I stop near the side of the bed.

Taking my time I tease her lips with feather light kisses the same way I tease her stomach under her shirt. I bring her shirt with me as I skim my fingers up her sides, loving the smoothness of her skin.

Her head falls back as I skim the pads of my fingers over her puckered nipples. Taking one breast in my mouth I savor the light moans escaping her parted lips. Releasing it with a quiet pop, I move my mouth South. I fall to my knees in front of her as I kiss my way down to the waistband of her pants.

"Step out, baby," I ask as I drag them down each leg slowly, carefully.

Starting at her ankles, I kiss my way up her left leg. I place a closed-mouth kiss on her mound, before trailing kisses back down her right leg.

"Lay down, Pretty Girl." I stand, ridding myself of my clothes as she complies. Once we're both completely naked I follow her down onto the bed, hovering above her.

I start kissing her arms caressing my way up and down, paying attention to her palms and the soft skin on the underside of her wrist. "Jared."

"Shh. I've got you." Looking down at her, I take a minute to appreciate her beauty. "You're so beautiful. I need to be inside of you, right now. I'll make it up to you later," I tell her between kisses on her chest and belly.

"Okay," she says around a sexy grin. With one last kiss on her luscious lips I slide into her inch by inch until I'm seated fully inside her body. "Jared. Move, please."

I slide out of her almost all the way before slamming back into her, hard. Her entire body moves back several inches with the force of my thrusts. I know I'm probably hurting her, but I can't seem to slow down or stop. "You feel so good, baby." Leaning down I take one nipple into my mouth, sucking and biting, until she calls out my name. "That's it, baby. Louder. I want everyone in this building to know my name, to know you're mine. Let me hear it."

Being inside of her is pure perfection. We fit together so flawlessly. She's so wet and tight and hot. Her legs are wrapped tightly around my waist, squeezing with every clench of her inner muscles. Her hands are gripping my back, her nails digging into my skin.

Reaching between us, I circle her clit, with a few final thrusts of my hips and a last painful bite to her nipple she shatters around me, screaming loud enough for everyone to hear just like I asked her to. "Jared!"

My name sounds like a mantra coming from her lips. It's by far the sexiest, rawest experience of my life. I come hard seconds later, shooting everything I have into her. As soon as I finish, I collapse on top of her, my weight probably crushing her but she doesn't seem to care. Her legs and arms wrap around me holding me to her.

We're both sticky with sweat, our hearts pounding against each other through our chests, our breathing rapid and shaky. Still, I feel whole again, complete. Loved. "I missed you so much. Every day I missed you." I need her to understand how much I care about her. I didn't leave because I didn't care – she has to understand that.

"Don't let me go again, Jared." Her voice is shaky, and I know she's fighting off tears. I roll to my side keeping her tucked against me; I hold her tight trying desperately to keep us from falling apart again.

"I won't. I can't. Love you, Pretty Girl."

She replies sleepily, "love you, too," before drifting to sleep. My own slumber not far behind.

Fifty-Four
<u>Zhoe</u>

Opening my eyes I feel a little disoriented. It takes me a few minutes to realize I'm naked in Jared's bed, wrapped in Jared's arms. It takes me longer to realize it's three in the afternoon; I knew we were both exhausted from the events of yesterday but holy shit we slept the day away.

I try rolling to my side but find I'm completely trapped beneath the giant that is Jared Roman. Jared is lying on his stomach his gorgeous face inches from mine. Most of his body is on top of mine, with very little touching the bed. I have no idea how I didn't suffocate to death.

I realize belatedly I'm sweating to death. Moving my right arm, since my left arm is still trapped, I try to push Jared off of me. I'm not gentle about it because I feel trapped, claustrophobic. "Jare. Get up. You're crushing me."

Jared just grumbles something unintelligible before pulling me unbearably tighter underneath him. "Fuck, Jared! Get up!" This time he opens his eyes and for a moment I forget my panic, not sure if the lack of air intake is from his weight as it threatens to crush me, or his gorgeousness. He really is a ruggedly beautiful man.

"Morning, baby." He smiles at me lazily.

"Jared," I'm trying to remain calm but the words are being gritted from between clenched teeth. "If you don't get up, I seriously might die, then come back to haunt you forever for fucking killing me with your dead weight."

It takes him a minute to process everything I've just said, but slowly he looks down at our joined bodies comprehending the fact that he's fucking crushing me. The second it registers he jumps up and off of me. "Shit! Zho, are you okay? Holy fuck. I seriously could have killed you. Are you okay?"

I can't help but laugh at him. His face is full of fear, his eyes are still partially closed with sleep and he's naked and rock-hard. As soon as I see his morning, or well afternoon, wood I forget about everything else. Crawling on my hands and knees I make my way to where he's standing on the side of the bed.

Without any preamble, I close one hand around his impressive erection, my other hand fondling his balls for a few short seconds before I take him into my mouth. "Fuck. Zhoe, baby. As good as this feels..." He grabs my hair in his palms pulling it in a makeshift ponytail so it's out of my face, "I need to make sure you're okay."

It's a heady thing knowing I can affect him so completely that he can't even think straight, can't form complete thoughts and sentences. But, even still he's thinking of me – caring about me. Jared fucking Roman – hard and scary on the outside but I swear that boy has a heart of gold and I love him for it.

Taking him as deep as I can I work him over with my mouth. Sex with Jared is always hard, and giving him head is no different. I hallow my cheeks sucking with as much force as I can, before gently teasing him with just my tongue licking hot paths up and down his shaft. Most guys hate the feel of teeth during oral, but I've learned that Jared loves it. I don't bite him hard, applying just enough pressure to scrape my teeth once or twice as I pull him out of my mouth usually does the trick.

"Fuck. God, you're so fucking good at that, Zho. Don't stop. Take me deep." Jared's low, rough voice is sexy all the time but Jared's voice when he's turned on? It's so damn sexy I think about recording it to pull out when I'm lonely, just his voice could get me off.

I look up his body only to find the sexiest sight I've ever seen. His eyes are closed, his hair still messy from sleep. His perfect chest and abs are on display, covered only by his tattoos that are moving with each contraction of his muscles as he desperately tries to keep himself from thrusting into my mouth.

I massage his balls as I take him once, twice more down the back of my throat; that's all it takes to send him over the edge. He fills my mouth, my throat, with his salty come. I've never cared for swallowing, but even his come is delicious. Is there anything about Jared Roman that isn't pure sexiness?

As soon as he's finished he grabs my shoulders pushing me back onto my back on the bed before coming down over me. "Hi, Pretty Girl."

I smile coyly at him. "Hey yourself, handsome."

"So, after that I'm really glad I didn't smash you to death," he says with a light chuckle. After everything we've been through, after everything he dealt with yesterday, I'm glad to see things are back to normal between us. I'm so fucking happy we fell back into our easy banter, laughing and joking with each other. "We need to get up to the hospital."

I stand up. "Okay. I can't believe we slept all day." He places a kiss on my forehead and heads to the bathroom. After showering I put the clothes back on I was wearing last night, thankful I was wearing yoga pants.

It's not until we're climbing into his truck that Jared notices my lack of clean clothes. "Do you need to run by your place to get clothes?"

"Um, well I'm staying with Ang right now. So..."

Jared turns to me now. "Okay, confession. I saw your dad and a bunch of movers at your place one day, because apparently I turned into a stalker for a little while there. I didn't realize you were moving in with Ang. Why did you?"

"My father changed the locks on me, he pretty much took everything away from me except the cash I took out of my account and my car because it's in my name, thankfully."

Jared looks like he's fighting an internal battle. "He did what?" He's not quite yelling but he's not quiet either. "He locked you out of your place without letting you know first?"

"I mean, I knew he was going to do it," I answer him without making eye contact. "Ang and I got everything out that I wanted before he could do it. So, it's not really a big deal. It's not like I didn't have anywhere to go."

"It is a big deal, Zho. What kind of father does that to their kid? And what do you mean you knew he was going to?" He looks at me incredulously.

Fuck. This was the part I didn't want to tell him. Jared blames himself for too much already, the last thing he needs is more guilt. I know it's not his fault, he didn't force me to choose him over my family, in fact he's probably going to be pissed that I did, but he'll find some way to blame himself.

"Tell me, Zhoe. Right now." His voice comes out through gritted teeth.

"Remember when he came up to me and tried to stop me from getting into the car after your fight?" He just nods at me. "He pretty much told me it was you or him, which really meant you or his money."

Fifty-Five
<u>Jared</u>

God fucking damn it. I don't respond to Zhoe, I can't. I'm fucking livid. I'm not sure who to direct my anger towards though so I chose to just drive, to take her to her friend's house to get her clothes.

I'm really fucking pissed at myself. If I were a better person she wouldn't have had to choose. With the way her parents are it's doubtful we'd ever be a big happy family, but they would have at least accepted me as a part of her life. I'm pissed that I left her after she made that sacrifice for me.

I'm pissed at Zhoe for choosing me over her family. I'm fucking pissed that she would do something so stupid and careless. She may not have had the best family in the world, but at least she had someone to fall back on. Someone other than me.

I'm pissed at her father. Who does that to their kid? Who makes their daughter chose between the man she loves and her asshole family? As if that wasn't enough he took everything away from her – her home, her money, her school. Fuck her school!

"What about your schooling, Zho?" I didn't mean for the words to sound so harsh but, of course, they do. My anger is suffocating me, making it impossible for any other tone to leave my mouth.

"Yeah, that too." Her voice is a whisper, she sounds sad and distant. I knew we were going to have a lot to talk about today and I knew most of it was going to be hard to hear but this fucking sucks. This girl gave up everything for me. She chose me over everything else in her life, her fucking future even.

"Baby, look at me." We're stopped at a red light, so I have a second or two to try to get control of this situation again. As soon as she looks at me, her face void of emotion I tell her, "I'm sorry. I will find a way to get you back into school. I'll pay for it myself, even if I have to work three jobs. You're not throwing away your future for me. Do you hear me?"

For a second she just stares at me but then her mouth twitches and I can see she's trying not to smile. "Quit. I'm fine. I chose you and I'd choose you again." I swear this girl drives me insane. Any other girl would expect me to do what I just promised her I would. Shit, any other girl would have been banging on my front door telling me what they gave up for me, begging me to take her back.

But, of course Zhoe doesn't do that.

She's too fucking strong for that shit. If I didn't want her she wasn't going to beg me to take her back. She made those decisions; I didn't make them for her; so she wasn't going to hold them over my head.

I promise myself to make it up to her anyways. The only way I can, the only way that will be good enough for her – I'm going to love her. That's all she's ever really wanted anyway, so I'm going to give it to her. I swear I'm going to love that girl with every single fucking ounce of my shattered heart and my damaged soul until the day I take my last breath.

I will make up for every mistake in every touch, every kiss, and every word spoken. It's the only way I can right my wrongs. More importantly, it's what my girl deserves.

"Is Angelica home?" I ask nervously. I'm afraid of that girl a little bit. She's feisty and she loves her best friend, so I'm sure she's furious at me, she has every right to be but that doesn't make me any less jumpy. She was too distracted last night with Rico to acknowledge me, but I'm sure I'll have her undivided attention the next time I see her.

"Yep," Zhoe answers animatedly, making a popping sound on the P at the end of the word. Glancing at her I notice she's got a huge grin on her face.

Fuck, I'm screwed.

As soon as we walk in the door Ang is on me, pulling Zhoe out of her way she gets right in my face, giving my chest a decent shove. "You fucking dickhead. What the fuck is wrong with you? Do you know how much she loves you? Do you know how long it took me to get her to stop balling her eyes out every fucking night? Do you? Of course you don't know because you were too busy sticking your head up your ass. Asshole."

Holy shit. Does the girl ever breathe? I look over her head at Zhoe who is leaning against the wall with her arms and legs crossed, her posture exudes calmness, but the look on her face tells me she's anything but. It looks like she's trying her damndest not to cry. I try to get to her, attempting to sidestep Angelica but of course the girl is having none of it.

"Oh no you don't. I'm not done with you, fucktard." Where does she come up these words?

Not taking my eyes off Zhoe, willing her to look at me I answer Angelica's eloquently posed questions. "You're right I am a fucktard, a dickhead, an asshole. I did have my head up my ass." Zhoe is smiling slightly now, it's not a real smile but it's a start. "I promise you I learned my lesson. I've learned what life without Zhoe is like and it fucking sucks. It felt like I couldn't breathe. I never, ever want to feel that way again. So I'm sorry, to both of you, but I mean it when I say I'll never make that mistake again."

At some point during my speech Angelica moved to the side enough for me to get to Zhoe. Zhoe may not be crying but the pain from the weeks apart is evident on her face. I drop to my knees in front of her, desperately gripping her hands in mine. "I love you so fucking much, Zho. I'll spend the rest of my life making it up to you. I promise."

"Get up here and kiss me, handsome." I can't help but laugh at that. There's my girl – my strong, confident, stubborn girl. Doing what she asked I stand up quickly, pinning her against the wall with my body before kissing her deeply, fully, completely.

I hear Ang clear her throat several times but I do my best to ignore her, instead focusing on the sweet, soft lips I'm currently devouring.

"Okay, seriously. Will you two get a room?"

Reluctantly I pull away from Zhoe with one final chaste kiss I shoo her away. "Go get dressed, baby." She smiles at me and walks down the hall. As soon as she's out of earshot I turn to Ang. "Thanks for having her back. She just told me about her family, so I'm glad she has you."

"She'll always have me. Don't fuck this up again, okay? I want to like you and I want Zhoe to be happy, she deserves that." For a little thing this girl sure is feisty, I love it.

"Believe me, no one knows what she deserves more than me. Those weren't just words, Ang. I'm going to spend forever making this up to her, every single fucking day of my life I'll make it up to her."

For the first time since I got here she finally smiles. "Good."

Zhoe chooses that moment to walk back into the room, knowing her she was probably around the corner listening to our conversation the entire time. She's changed into a pair of jeans, a long sleeve shirt and a scarf. She looks stunning.

Forcing my attention away from my beautiful girl I look back to her friend, "How is he Ang?"

"He's okay. Pissed and cranky, but he's alive." She offers me a small smile and I can't help but feel grateful for another reason.

I take the few steps across the room to her; wrapping her in my arms I hug her tight. "Thanks for staying with him, Ang. Thanks for being stronger than I was."

She whispers back, "You had other problems to fix. Thanks for loving my friend." She steps back and gives me a teary eyed smile. "No, I will not have a three-way with you, perv." I recognize the defense mechanism; I use it all the time. I wink at her and laugh.

"We were just getting ready to head up to the hospital, do you want to come with us?"

"I'll follow. He's still in ICU, so I'll probably just stay there again tonight."

Grabbing our winter coats the three of us bundle up ready to head out to see our friend. My brother. Now that I have a clear head, now that I know he's going to be okay I kind of want to beat his ass. He's not going to be happy after seeing me.

FIFTY-SIX

Zhoe

We walk into the hospital together, hopping on the elevator and taking it to the third floor. When we step off, Angelica leads us down the hallway toward Rico's room. There's a small waiting room at the other end of the hall, so I tell Jared I'll wait for him there.

"Baby, you can come in with me."

"No, you need time alone with him. I'll be just down the hall waiting for you. Take your time though, okay?"

He places a sweet kiss on my forehead. "Love you, Pretty Girl."

I lean up giving him a soft kiss on his lips. "Love you too, stud."

Ang and I walk hand in hand down the hallway sitting next to each other on the couch. I keep a firm hold on her hand. "How is he really, Ang?"

"He's here, but I'm worried about him, Zho. I think he needs to go to rehab but he keeps insisting it was an accident and he doesn't have a problem."

"Hopefully Jared can talk some sense into him. I think he's really worried about him, too." She just nods as tears fill her eyes. "Okay, you need to tell me what's going on with you two. This seems more serious than just friends with benefits."

She takes several long deep breaths; tears falling freely down her face. "I want to love him, Zho. I think he wants to love me, too. But, we can't be together for the long haul. We just can't."

"But, why? I don't understand."

"We're too broken together. I'm too broken to try and fix someone else. I need a man that has it together, that knows what he wants and where he's going. I need a man that can pull me back together. But, Rico, he is the opposite of that and needs more than I give him. I don't have time to fix him right now."

I look at my friend for a long time trying to figure out what the hell she's talking about. We've been friends our whole lives, we've never had secrets between us but it feels like a huge secret is looming over our heads. She's not telling me something, something big. But why? And what the hell does she mean she's broken? I've never known someone that has it together as much as she does. She's never questioned what she was supposed to do in life, never questioned who she is. So, why now is she thinking these thoughts?

"Ang, you are the farthest thing from broken. What are you not telling me?"

"I can't tell you, not yet anyways. Someday I promise I'll tell you the whole story. But, not now."

I pull her close, wrapping her in my arms. "I just want you to be happy. You know I'm always here for you and you can tell me anything, Ang."

"I know. Thanks." She sniffs, sits up and wipes her tears away. "So the L-Word was dropped, huh?"

"Yeah." I can't help the smile that crosses my face. "We haven't talked it all out yet, but I think we'll be okay. I can't be without him, Ang. He's it for me, you know?"

"Is he your forever?"

"Yeah, he's my forever, my always, my everything." She flashes me a small, awkward smile before turning away from me. I let her have that moment to gather her thoughts, afraid of pushing for too much.

If there's one thing I've never understood about my friend it's her resistance to love. Her parents have a great marriage and they've always showered her in love. Still, the only time I've ever seen her close to a guy, in more than a sexual way, was with Cole the summer before he died.

The three of us spent most of the summer up at the lake house. There were many times when I caught the two of them sneaking off to a bedroom, or getting cozy on a couch or the beach. At the time I blew it off as a summer fling, a means to an end for both of them. Now, I'm wondering if maybe it was more.

I should ask her, I should have asked a long time ago, but I've always been leery of the answer for some unknown reason. If she didn't tell me about them she had her reasons. I just need to trust that one day my friend will come clean with me.

Pulling my phone from my purse I realize we've been here for nearly two hours, it's pushing one in the afternoon. Turning to Ang I ask if she wants to grab lunch in the cafeteria.

She's still quiet as we make the trek to the cafeteria. We pick up our food, and I grab an extra sandwich for Jared. Angelica chooses a small table near the back of the room, away from the chaos of the main dining area.

"Are you okay, Ang?"

She takes a bite from her turkey wrap, as if contemplating her answer before making eye contact. "Yeah, just worried. I think he really needs rehab, but I'm afraid he doesn't want to admit he has a problem."

I nod at her unsure of what to say. I've never had to deal with problems like this before. I know Jared has had his issues, but it's not something we've talked about a whole lot. "Jared won't let him get away without going. He was pretty upset last night. Rico's all he has left, you know? I'm sure he'll get him there."
"Thanks for being here today. I don't think I could do it on my own."

"I'm always here for you Ang."

The rest of lunch is spent in silence. Angelica eats much quicker than normal anxious to get back upstairs to Rico. As soon as she finishes her last bite she stands from the table asking if I'm ready to go back.

We've only been back in the waiting room for a short time when Angelica and I both look at the same time, sensing Jared creeping in on our moment. With a quick kiss on my cheek he takes the chair next to me. "Sorry, I was gone so long."

"You're fine. How's he doing?"

I may have asked the question but the answer is all for Ang. "I think I've convinced him to go to rehab."

"Really?" Ang looks equal parts excited and skeptical.

"Yeah, there's actually one in town I think would be a great fit for him. He'll be allowed visitors after a certain period of time, assuming he's doing well enough to have them."

"When will he leave?"

"In a few days. They want to keep him here to make sure his body adjusts to the detox before they send him out."

Angelica closes her eyes and takes a deep breath. She looks over at Jared giving him a tentative smile. "Thanks, Jared. Really." Jared doesn't respond but then he doesn't have to. It's his best friend; he would have done anything to get him the help he needs. "Take care of my girl, okay?"

"Always. Call us if you need anything."

Angelica stands and starts to make her way out of the room. "I will. Love you, Zho."

"Love you, too, Ang." Once she's gone Jared and I turn to look at each other. "Hi," I whisper.

"Hi. What do you want to do today?"

The million-dollar question. Part of me wants to go home and curl up in bed with him again, blocking out the world and its problems, our problems. The other part of me wants to get our problems out there so we can move on, move forward. "Are you up for talking about everything?"

Jared sighs, running his hand through his hair before turning back to me. "Yeah. I think we need to. Get it all out there, you know?"

I just nod at him. "Not here though, okay?"

"No, not here." He stands with my hand in his, he pulls me to my feet. "Come on, there's something I want to show you."

Fifty-Seven

Zhoe

"Here you go," I hand him the sandwich I picked up for him once we're in the truck, "I grabbed this for you when Ang and I went to the cafeteria."

"Thanks," he takes it, before turning back to the road. He starts driving to some unknown destination. I'm not really paying attention, too lost in my own thoughts to really care where he's taking me.

What he said back at Angelica's keeps playing on repeat in my mind. It's not that what he said wasn't sweet and perfect, because it was. It's just I'm having a hard time coming to terms with everything that's happened, is happening, between us.

Two days ago I didn't have Jared in my life and wasn't sure I ever would again. Today he's professing his love for me and promising me a lifetime with him? It's too much.

Don't get me wrong, when I picture my future I see Jared but I'm afraid he doesn't really want that. I'm afraid he's just promising me those things because he thinks that's what I want to hear.

"Where ya at, Pretty Girl?"

Jared's voice breaks me out of my thoughts. "Hmm?" I have no idea how long I was zoned out, but I was far enough away to not realize we were stopped and parked along the side of a country road; there is nothing but snow-covered fields and a few barren trees alongside the road. Where the hell did he take me?

"Where'd you go? You looked deep in thought there."

I risk a glance at him, not sure if I should tell him where my thoughts were or not. Considering today is about putting it all out there I might as well go for it. "I was just thinking about something you said earlier. About spending the rest of your life making it up to me."

"What about it?" Jared asks, sounding as confused as I feel.

I take a deep breath before diving in, looking straight ahead rather than at the beautiful man that has me all tied in knots. "It was a nice thought, but I don't expect you to give me forever. I know it's not something you've ever really wanted before and that's okay. I'll take you for as long as you'll have me." I pause, my shaky voice giving away my true feelings. The thought of Jared getting rid of me, be it tomorrow or twenty years from now is enough to knock the air out of my lungs. "But, just don't make me promises you can't keep, okay?"

Jared doesn't answer. Instead, he opens his driver side door and hops out of his truck. I don't move. I'm afraid he needs minute to think, to clear his thoughts. Before I can dwell on it any longer my door is being ripped open scaring the shit out of me.

Jared grabs me around the waist hoisting me out of the truck. He flips me over his shoulder carrying me fireman style to the back of the truck. "Put me down, Jared. What the hell are you doing?"

Still he ignores me, lowering the tailgate he plops me unceremoniously on to it. Spreading my legs with his knee he fills the space he just created, crowding me. He grabs my ponytail, tilting my head back so I can look up at him. "Listen good, Pretty Girl. I'm only going to say this once."

Where did this Jared come from? I've seen him be controlling and demanding in bed but never like this; outside of the bedroom he's usually insanely sweet. Too stunned to talk, I just cock an eyebrow at him, silently willing him to continue with his little tirade.

"You. Are. It. For. Me." He speaks slowly, deliberately. "Before you, forever was an abstract thought, it was something I never thought I wanted but more than that it was something I never thought I could have. But, with you that's exactly what I want. I'll never make a promise to you I don't intend to keep. So listen up…" I tip my head even farther back, making sure I'm looking directly into his eyes as he speaks his next words. "I'm not proposing…yet. But I fucking promise you I'm going to marry you one day. You are mine. Forever. Got it?"

Again, I'm too stunned to talk. How did we get to this point? How did this scary man I met at a bar, who walked away and broke my heart become the guy promising me forever? How did he become the only guy I could ever picture forever with?

Finally finding my voice, I whisper the only thing I can in this moment. "Got it."

Jared growls before lowering his head to mine. The second his lips touch mine everything else is forgotten. I forget that I have no idea where we are, what we came out here to do, I even forget the reason he's kissing me so passionately. All I can focus on is the way he makes me feel. Complete. Loved. Happy.

Pulling back enough to rest his forehead on mine, Jared sighs softly. "I love you, Zhoe."

"Love you, too, Stud."

***

It's barely evening but the winter sun has dipped just slightly causing the air to cool a few degrees. Huddling into my winter jacket I lean closer to Jared's side. He's extricated himself form between my legs to join me on the back of the truck. For a while we just sit here letting the quiet blanket us, giving us room to think.

"So..." Jared starts. We both chuckle lightly at the awkwardness of the situation. "This used to be my favorite place in the world."

"Where are we exactly?"

"In the middle of nowhere. Down that way," Jared points into the thick tree line to his right, "there's a pond. I have no idea who owns it but it's always clean and well maintained. It's completely surrounded on all sides by trees. It's definitely man-made because one side is much shallower than the other side."

"How'd you find this place?"

"One night in high school I left my house desperate to get away from all the bullshit. I borrowed a friend's car and drove around for a while, not really going anywhere. I found this place. It was the one place I could breathe, no one knew where I was."

I glance over at him to see Jared staring down the empty dirt road, not really seeing anything – probably lost in memories of his childhood. I'm glad he had a place like this, somewhere he felt safe and free. "Who did you come here with?"

He looks at me out of the corner of his eye. "No one. That was the beauty of it. It was all mine. I've never actually brought anyone here before, not even Rico."

"When was the last time you were here?" I don't know why that matters but for some reason it does.

He shakes his head, covering it with his hands. "Last night. I went out with Rico for a little bit but it was a fucking disaster. He drove me home and then left to meet up with Ang. I stupidly drove out here desperately needing to get out of my own head for a while. I should have been with him last night, Zho."

Reaching over I grab one of his hands, pulling it off his face and into my lap; entwining our fingers together I squeeze tightly. "It's not your fault what happened."

"I know that, but if I was stronger I would have been over my own shit enough to see that he was in trouble."

"Jare, look at me." I wait several seconds before he finally turns his head enough to make eye contact. "You're right. He might not have done it that night, but he may have the next day or the next week. He was in a bad place. It's not your fault or your responsibility to take care of everyone. You have to worry about you sometimes, too."

"And what about Cole?" he asks not taking his eyes off of me. "Was that not my fault either?" His voice is laced with anger, bitterness. Guilt.

I have to look away for a minute. Talking about Cole was the main reason we're here, but it's hard. I miss my big brother. I miss him even more now, knowing he and Jared were friends and would have been happy I've found someone to love so completely, someone that loves me back. It hurts every day and I wish he were still here but that doesn't mean it was Jared's fault. "No, that was not your fault either."

Jared jumps up from the truck then. He doesn't say anything for a long time, instead choosing to fight this internal battle with himself. He paces back and forth, occasionally gripping and pulling at his hair; but still no words leave his mouth. I pull my legs up, wrapping my arms around them trying to stay warm. My teeth are chattering with the cold now that my personal space heater has moved, but I won't bring myself to complain. He needs this time to work things out. I watch silently as Jared fights his inner demons, struggles with the guilt that has plagued him for too long.

For too long Jared has been told things are his fault. If he weren't born his mother wouldn't have been so poor. If he didn't need to eat they would have had more money for drugs. If he didn't take Cole down there that night he would still be alive. But what he needs to understand is that none of those things are his fault.

I hate that he's had the life he has. It's not fair to anyone to grow up the way he did, hearing and seeing the things he did. But, selfishly? I'm grateful for those things because they made him the man he is today. Selfless, strong, determined, loving. How can I fault him for being any one of those things, let alone all of them?

Finally, Jared stops pacing and drops to his knees in front of me. "I am so sorry, Zhoe. It should have been me that night. Cole had a good life, a good future. It's not fair that he died when he did. It's not fair…"

"No, it's not fair, but life never is. You have a good life and a good future, too. You deserve to live. You have a great job, you're healthy, and you have me. Those are all things worth living for. I'll never stop missing my brother. I'll never stop wishing he were here. But, I'll also never stop being grateful that you *are* here. I love you, Jared. No matter what you did in the past, no matter the choices you made back then, you're here now. And I fucking love the man you are. So thank you for not giving up. For living."

Fifty-eight

Jared

Staring up at my beautiful girl from my spot on the ground I'm awestruck. How the hell did I get so lucky? I don't even know if she understands the impact her words have on me. My whole life I've been told I'm nothing, a no one. I'd never amount to anything. I wasn't good enough. To hear this perfect, gorgeous girl tell me the opposite is life changing.

"You mean all of that, don't you?"

She looks down at me, her eyes full of love, her face twisted in confusion. "Of course I mean all of that."

She acts like it's so simple; like this is exactly where I'm meant to be. The longer I look up at her, the more I start to believe her. Is it possible that I was spared that day just so I could love this girl? So I could make her happy?

"You are so beautiful, do you know that? Inside and out. What did I do to deserve you?"

Zhoe doesn't say anything. She just smiles at me, a soft, sweet smile, a smile that breaks through the wall I've carefully constructed around my heart. Little by little this tiny girl knocked down those walls; walls no one has ever been able to get through, but she did. And right here, right now she knocked down what was left.

My heart is crippled and decayed from being alone in the dark for so long, but if she wants it, it's hers. Completely. I know I just told her I wasn't yet proposing but fuck if I don't want to. I want this girl to be mine, forever. "Move in with me." It's not a question because I'm not taking no for an answer. She's not ready for marriage yet; our relationship isn't quite ready for marriage yet, so this is the next best thing.

"What? Are you serious?"

"I know what it's like to live without you Zhoe and I don't want to do it again. I meant everything I've said today. One day you're going to be my wife, not yet, but one day. So, why not start our lives together now? I want to fall asleep with you sated and sleepy in my arms every single night." She giggles when I say sated, though I'm not joking. My favorite place in the world is buried in Zhoe.

"I want to wake up to your grumpy, adorable self in the mornings. I want to be the one to bring you coffee and breakfast. I want to be the one you cry to and laugh with and I don't want that only sometimes, I want it every fucking day. So, what do you say?" I finally stop, taking a deep breath. What is it about this girl that makes me give long speeches and declarations of my feelings? She's turning me into a pussy-whipped bad ass and I love every second of it.

"I say hell yes!" She laughs loudly before throwing herself at me. Wrapping her arms around my neck she hugs me close to her. "I love you, you know," she mummers against my cheek.

"I was kind of counting on that, Pretty Girl," I move our faces so our lips are lined up. "I love you more than you'll ever know." I press light kisses on her lips, her nose and her chin, unable to stop tasting her soft skin.

"So what now?" she asks, pulling back enough to look at me. I can't help but laugh at the situation we're in. My tailgate is down yet I'm sitting on the frozen ground, practically in the middle of the street with Zhoe wrapped completely around me, her lips nearly blue from the cold.

"Now, we get into this truck before you freeze to death. Then we go back to Ang's and pack up all your stuff." Zhoe squeals before jumping off of me and running toward the passenger side of the truck. "Did you just squeal?" I ask once we're both inside the truck.

"No, nope. I don't squeal," she tells me sternly. But we both know she did and we both bust out into a fit of laughter. I've never in my life been happy that I'm still alive but in this moment I've never been more grateful of anything.

Life is good. Life is worth living and it's all because of the girl sitting next to me.

FIFTY-NINE

Zhoe

Waking up in Jared's arms this morning was amazing. No, it's not the first time but this time felt different. Knowing I'm going to be living here and I get to wake up like that every day from here on out is a heady feeling.

After our big talk last night we went back to Ang's to pack a few necessities. Since I only took personal belongings from my old place it won't take long to move the rest of my stuff over this weekend. We were both anxious to take this next step, so I officially moved in last night.

People always talk about how great it is to be in love. They also talk about how hard it is to be in love. But what they don't talk about is the overwhelming sense of peace and security that comes with knowing someone else loves you the same way you love them. I've never felt happier, more content, more relaxed than I do right now.

I couldn't concentrate for shit today at work. I just wanted to go home to my man. Well, really he'll be coming home to me since I get off before he does. All day I've been planning a special meal for him, something to say thank you for loving me, for wanting to live with me and share your life with me.

The problem is, I'm a shit cook. So, I decided to take a trip down memory lane. I called the Ale Shack and ordered the same meals we did on our first date. I also picked up a six-pack of their homemade brew before heading back home.

Home.

Who knew Jared and I would ever get to the point in our relationship where we'd share a home? Jared's place is so different from my old place and especially from Angelica's, yet it feels homier, more comfortable than either ever felt to me before.

Walking in the door I place the beer in the fridge and the burgers in the microwave hoping to keep them warm. Checking the clock I realize Jared should be home any minute. I start to feel giddy, not sure what to do with myself I stand awkwardly in the middle of the kitchen for a few minutes before busying myself with the dishes we left in the sink this morning.

Just as I'm finishing up, I hear keys jingling in the door and any semblance of calm I found cleaning has disappeared. I know Jared wants to move our relationship forward as much as I do but I think part of me is afraid he'll freak out realizing he doesn't actually want me here invading his space. Fuck. That would be devastating.

"Honey, I'm home!" Jared yells with a smile in his voice through the apartment. I mentally shake my head at myself. I'm so stupid for ever doubting his feelings for me. "Zho?"

"In the kitchen," I yell back. I start to tell him I picked up dinner but when he walks around the corner all thoughts leave my brain, except one – I want him. Now.

Jared looks so fucking hot right now. All I want to do is jump his bones right there in the middle of his kitchen. I've never seen him dirty and tired from work, he always insisted on picking me up after he showered.

But, holy shit have I been missing out. I lick my lips like a starved woman as I take him in. He's wearing tight jeans that cling to his impressive body perfectly, especially where they are torn giving a slight glimpse at his muscular thigh. His bright green T-shirt is covered in dirt but accentuates his tan; even the dirt smeared on his forehead and cheeks is sexy.

He looks like a man, I think to myself. This is what a man should look like when he comes home from work. Fuck a shirt and tie; he should come home dirty and exhausted – needing a woman to take care of him. And lucky me, I get to be that woman.

I have no idea how much time has passed but Jared quickly picks up on my mood as he leans back against the counter, crossing his legs and arms and quirking one eyebrow up at me. "Like what you see, beautiful?"

Again I just nod my head and lick my lips. Finding my courage, I take several determined steps across the room until I'm standing directly in front of him. Without words, I lower the zipper on his jeans before reaching my hand inside to pull him out. I'm too starved, too impatient to take his jeans off.

Feeling the weight of his cock in my hand I tell him the only thought I've had since he walked in the door. "You look so fucking sexy all dirty and tired from work." I stroke him several times before leaning in and taking his lips between mine.

He lets me have my fun for a moment before pulling away with a hard slap on my ass and a sweet kiss on my forehead. He places me on the counter before sliding between my legs, and placing his hands on the counter on either side of me.

"I need to shower, then you can play with my cock all you want."

I can't help the cocky smirk on my face as I watch him reach down, tucking himself back in his jeans. "Sounds like a plan to me."

"How was your day, Pretty Girl?"

This is one of those things I love about Jared; he's always thinking about me. Always genuinely interested in how I am. "It was good. We signed up a new school today, which means I have twenty new volunteers to call on, which is always a good thing. How was your day?"

"Long. We were short a few guys so there was a lot of extra work. I'm starving, what do you want to do for dinner?"

"Oh, I almost forgot!" I give him a little shove to his chest so I can jump off my perch on the counter, "I picked up some Ale House. Go hop in the shower and I'll warm it up for us."

He saunters over to me, placing a gentle kiss on my forehead. "Thanks, baby. I'll be out in ten."

Sixty

Zhoe

I wake up the next day with a huge grin on my face. I can't help it. I'm fucking happy, okay? Can't a girl be happy?

Rolling over I notice a certain sexy man is missing. Prolonging my moment of bliss a little longer, I take a second to stretch my overworked muscles before climbing out of bed. I pad my way down the hall following the scent of fresh brewed coffee. This man really knows the way to my…

"Holy. Shit." If I thought Jared coming home in his dirty work clothes was the sexiest thing I've seen, I was sadly mistaken. Slowly my eyes devour Jared starting from the floor up. He's standing in front of the stove wearing nothing but a skin-tight pair of black boxer briefs. "Are you trying to kill me?"

Jared turns only his head to flash me a cocky smirk before focusing his attention on the eggs in the frying pan. I swear this man is too sexy for his own good. His muscles and tattoos are on full display, and his boxers leave very little to the imagination. Instead they highlight his very firm, very defined, very fine ass.

For several long moments I stand there drooling over said ass. Since I'm so focused on his body, I notice the exact second he turns in my direction, catching me staring. I notice because it's the same time another part of his delicious body catches my attention.

Snapping my attention up to his face I notice his eyes have darkened with his desire, as I'm sure mine have. He's stalking in my direction slowly. "Are *you* trying to kill *me*, Pretty Girl? Do you have idea how fucking sexy you look wearing nothing but my T-shirt?"

As soon as he reaches me he grabs me around the waist, hoisting me onto the counter. "Good morning, beautiful."

"Morning, Stud." I smirk back at him. All of this feels so normal, so natural. So right. I can't help but smile, constantly. Leaning in, I take his lips prisoner, kissing him like I've been deprived of it.

Jared wastes no time catching up to me. His hands trace a fiery path from my knees up to the juncture of my thighs, pushing my shirt up in the process. As soon as he feels my wetness he growls into my mouth before plunging two fingers into me, I can't help but call out his name at the feeling.

"I need you, baby. Right now," Jared tells me huskily against my neck where he's currently tasting me.

"Then take me." I don't understand this insatiable need for him. I've never been this way about another man, or about sex, but with Jared I can't get enough. When he's not filling me, I need him to and when he is, I need him deeper, harder. More.

As if he's privy to my thoughts, Jared voices them out loud as soon as he's seated inside me. "You feel so good, baby. I'll never get enough of this, of you."

Sitting on the counter my eyes are level with Jared's. I can't help but get lost in the brown depths of them. His eyes hold so much emotion. They tell me things words never could. Jared has never had a problem telling me how he feels, but if ever I question what he's saying all I have to do is look into his eyes.

Right now his eyes are reflecting everything I'm feeling. Love so strong, so deep it's breathtaking, earthshattering, soul crushing. I never knew a love like ours existed. I can count on one hand the number of times Jared has made soft, passionate love to me and every time is beautiful. This one included.

Jared continues to pump his hips into mine slowly, never taking his eyes off mine. "I love you so much." I can't help but whisper the declaration to him. The emotion this man makes me feel is overwhelming. I feel like I tell him how much I love him constantly, but I can't seem to help myself.

"Love you too, baby."

He reaches between us to massage my clit, which was apparently what I needed in that moment. The second he touches me I break apart, quietly calling out his name. Jared follows soon after but neither one of us are in a hurry to separate.

We're both silent as we try to catch our breaths, our eyes never breaking contact. I lean my forehead against his, "I didn't know I could be this happy."

"You make me happy, too, Pretty Girl. So fucking happy the guys at work keep ribbing me about the lovesick grin I'm always wearing."

At that, I laugh my ass off. "Poor baby. I didn't know you were getting teased. Whatever should we do about that?"

"Hmm, you could come to work with me one day. Once they see how damn sexy you are they'll understand what I'm so happy about."

"I can do that. Want me to bring you lunch today?"

"Really?"

He looks so damn cute, so hopeful, and so young I can't help but give him what he wants. "Yeah, I have a few meetings this morning but I'm free this afternoon. What time should I come?"

"About five minutes ago." He deadpans.

"That was your one for the day. Awful, so bad," I shake my head at his corny joke, unable to stop myself from laughing.

He just laughs at me and shakes my insult off. "How about one o'clock?"

"Perfect," I tell him, pushing off the counter to get showered. "See you later, lover boy."

Sixty-One

Jared

I've been distracted all damn day. All I can think about is Zhoe walking her sexy ass onto this job site, flaunting herself for all the guys to see. I can't wait to see her and show her off, but the caveman in me wants to keep her locked up in my house for the rest of our lives, keeping her only for me.

"Roman!" I turn at the sound of my name being called. "Where the hell is your head today?" Dave Holster shouts at me. Dave's been around for a while, he started not long after Rico and I did and we've worked on several jobs together.

"Sorry, man. I had a long night." I can't help the smirk that comes to my face. Yeah, I definitely didn't get much sleep last night. Zhoe was ravenous. After her welcome home surprise we ate dinner and then went straight to bed; only we didn't get much sleep. My girl loves sex as much as I do.

"Jesus, that fucking smirk again? Seriously, dude. You better man up before the guys around here start thinking you're some pussy-whipped douche bag."

Fuck. He's right. I love my girl and she makes me happy as fuck, but I need to man up on the job site, especially if I'm going to take over soon. I need these guys to respect me.

Right that moment I hear a delicate throat clearing, both Dave and I turn around to find Zhoe standing there looking sexy as ever. She's wearing a skin-tight pencil skirt, a white frilly blouse and sky-high red high heels.

The way she's dressed and the way she's standing, scream confidence, but the way she looks at me from under her lashes and the shy little smirk she's wearing, exudes her shy side. I almost laugh because I know she heard everything Dave just said and all of this is a show, but fuck if it isn't working. My work jeans are suddenly way too tight.

"Hi, baby," she says in her low, raspy bedroom voice. Fuck. Me. She walks straight up to me and plants an indecent kiss on my lips before turning in Dave's direction. Her hands are still planted firmly on my chest, letting everyone know that she's mine. Have I told you how much I love this girl? "Oh, sorry. I'm so rude. I'm Zhoe." Then she smiles. Her full on Zhoe-I-Light-Up-The-World smile.

"Holy shit," is all Dave can mutter as he slowly rakes his eyes all over Zhoe's body. Normally I'd be pissed some other guy is looking at what's mine; but the way she's wrapped around me lets everyone know she's mine, so I know I have nothing to worry about.

When it becomes obvious Dave isn't going to add to the conversation she turns back to me with knowing smirk on her pretty face. "Hungry? I picked up some subs from the shop down the street."

"Starved. Come on, I'll show you off... I mean around." I know my one-liners are awful but they always make Zhoe laugh and that's what I'm shooting for.

"You better show me off, you think I suffered in these shoes all day for nothing?"

"Oh, about those sexy fuck-me shoes," I lean down to whisper in her ear, "you better be wearing those and nothing else when I get home tonight, got it?" I give her a little bite on her earlobe to drive the point home.

"Yes, sir." She grins up at me. I should have known Zhoe wouldn't let me be the only one having fun today, though. "Good luck getting any work done this afternoon while you picture me at home, in our bed, naked except for the shoes. What time do you get off again?" She finishes her thoughts with a come-hither smile.

"You are a cruel, cruel woman."

***

Driving home is fucking torture; my dick has been hard since I got into my truck and left the jobsite. Just like Zhoe promised the rest of my day dragged on. All I could think about was the picture she painted for me.

I practically sprint up the walk to our apartment once I'm out of my truck. Bursting through the door I kick my boots off, dropping the rest of my clothes as I make my way down the hall to our bedroom. "Zho?"

"In here," she calls, practically fucking purring the words.

Damn. I stop dead in my tracks in the doorway, mentally willing myself to slow down and savor this moment. I've never seen a sexier sight in my life. Zhoe is lying in the middle of our bed just like she promised she would be – completely fucking naked save the red heels. She is lying on her side, her head propped up with one hand. Her other hand, however, is the star of the show.

Her left hand is running a lazy path down her body. Starting at her perfect breasts she rubs one, then the other paying special attention to both nipples. Then it moves lower, over her ribs and waist, down her thigh and then back up to the one spot I'm dying to see. Of course I can't see what she's doing to herself because of the way she's laying, but fuck if I don't want to. Especially when her eyes close and a soft mewl leaves her lips.

"Are you going to stand there all night, Stud, or are you going to help a girl out?"

"You look like you're doing a good job all on your own. Are you sure you need me?"

Opening her eyes she pins me with the sexiest look, telling me everything I need to know. She bites on her lower lip for a second before purring the words I wanted to hear. "I'll always need you. Get over here and take care of your woman."

You don't have to tell me twice. Moving swiftly, I pounce. Grabbing her ankles I pull until she's flat on her back. My hands make the same path Zhoe's did, but in the opposite direction. Slowly I move my way up her body. Gripping her wrists in one of my hands, I pull her arms above her head and pin them there, while my other hand pulls and pinches at her nipples.

"Jared."

"What's the matter, Zho? You think you're the only one that can tease around here?"

She starts wiggling underneath me, trying desperately to get away or at the very least get some friction. "Fine, you win. Now fuck me already would you?"

"Oh, I fully intend to. Just not yet." Leaning down I retrace my path, this time with my tongue. I nip and lick and bite my way down her delicious body until I reach her center. I place several closed mouth kisses on her mound and her lips before spearing my tongue inside her warmth.

"Yes, finally." Zhoe stammers out in between her ragged breaths. She's always so ready for me – always so wet and warm. I don't stop tasting her, devouring her with my mouth until she's screaming out my name.

As soon as she comes back down, opening her eyes to look at me I reluctantly pull my mouth away. "Slide up the bed, baby. Grab onto the headboard and don't let go. You let go, I stop."

Without a word she does as told. I love my stubborn, strong woman, but when Zhoe submits to me in the bedroom there is no greater turn on. Standing, I look down at her from my spot at the foot of the bed. Just looking at her gets my dick hard enough it hurts.

Quickly I rid myself of my own clothes, dying to get near her. Dying to feel her soft skin rub against mine. Taking my rock hard erection in my hand I start to stroke it, relishing in the way her eyes never leave my dick. Loving the way she licks her lips like she wants a taste.

"Tell me, Zho. Were you thinking about this all day, just like me?" She nods her head at me. I didn't have to ask, she's just as sexual as I am. She was soaking wet before I even walked in the door. "Tell me what you were thinking about."

"You, Jare. Always you."

"What do you want me to do to you?"

My confident girl makes an appearance. "I want you to fuck me. Hard." I had planned on playing with her some more, making her squirm until she couldn't take it anymore. But, hearing those words come out of her mouth and all my plans disappear. All I can think about is giving her what she wants – hard, dirty sex.

Crawling back up her body I brace my arms on either side of her head, leaning down I take her lips between mine before slamming into her in one hard thrust. I see her readjust her grip on the bed, "don't let go, baby." She looks so damn sexy like this; eyes closed in ecstasy, hands holding on to the bed, open for me, trusting me. So damn sexy.

Moving so I'm resting on my shins, I grab her plush thighs in my hands and push them back until they are nearly touching her chest, her calves resting over my shoulders. Using her legs for leverage I pump ruthlessly into her, taking everything she's so willing to give me.

"Holy shit. Yes, Jared. God, you're so deep like that. Please don't stop." Her words only encourage me. I slam into her over and over and over again. I could live here, just like this with her wrapped around my body.

"As much as I loved your little games today, that body is only for me to see. Do you understand me?"

"Yes. Yours," she pants her acquiescence.

As if to drive my point home I rear my hips back and slam into her with enough force she moves back a few inches on the bed, her hands on the headboard the only thing stopping her head from hitting it. The loud moan she lets out feeds the insatiable beast within me, like a man possessed I take her hard and fast. Burying myself to the hilt in her hot, silky channel until she's calling out and tightening around me.

I'm quick to follow with my own release, quietly panting out her name. "Zhoe. Yes, baby. Fuck."

I make quick work of untangling our bodies, freeing Zhoe's hands from the headboard. As soon as she's free she spears her hands into my hair, and gazes deeply into my eyes for several moments before speaking. "I love you, Jare. I know I tell you that a lot, but I need you to really understand how much you mean to me. You make me crazy happy. I need you in my life. You make me stronger, better."

Leaning down I place several closed mouth kisses on her sweet lips. "No, baby. You make me better. You're the best person I know and I'll never stop being grateful that you're mine. Mine, Zhoe."

"Yours, always," she whispers back.

I roll to my back and Zhoe instantly takes her place curled up next to me her head on my chest. I let out a contented sigh. Fucking perfection, my life with Zhoe is perfection. I'll never let this go. Not without the fight of my life.

Sixty-Two

Zhoe: 6 Months Later

When I think back on the last year of my life I'm bombarded with a surplus of emotions – happiness, love, sadness, anger. Jared and I have gone through so much but still we managed to make it.

Really, we've done more than make it – we've made a great life together full of laughter and happiness and love, so much love. It amazes me every day how much love Jared has to give. He's always thinking of me first, he's always making me feel special and cared for. Don't get me wrong, he's still overpowering and controlling in bed and it's sexier than ever, but he is seriously the sweetest man.

Both of us landed our dream jobs. I was promoted last month to Director of Outreach for the YWCA. My old boss retired, so I took her position. My job duties are essentially the same but now I have several people working underneath me. It's still not much money, but we make it work and it's plenty for the two of us to be happy and live off comfortably.

I'm still going to school part-time though. Even though I already have the job I wanted upon graduation. I feel funny, incomplete almost, not having my bachelor's degree. It was important to me, but also to Jared that I finish school. He's been so supportive of all of my choices, always pushing me to do more, be better, but more importantly pushing me to be happier.

Yesterday, Jared finalized the contract in which he took over half of Porter and Son Construction Company. He's officially a business owner!

Okay, sorry I know that was a little dramatic, but I'm so damn proud of him. He's had to struggle with so much, had to fight so many battles and demons along the way but he made it. He got out of that life he thought he was destined for and made something of himself.

"Zhoe, baby? Are you ready? We have to go." Jared calls for me down the hall of our new apartment.

We are meeting up with Angelica and Rico for dinner. Rico was released from rehab today, so it's a celebration dinner. I am so proud of him for realizing he has a problem and fixing it. I didn't visit him, feeling like it wasn't my place; but Angelica and Jared both went regularly and kept me up to date. From what I've heard he did really well.

"I'm coming!" I call back. I reach behind me to zip up my red and white flower sundress. I opted to wear my hair up in a French twist since it's the middle of July and hotter than hell out. The only makeup I have on is mascara and a clear gloss, figuring it'd just melt off if I put anything else on.

"Zhoe!" Jared growls for me.

"I'm coming! Geez, a lot of work goes into my looking this good." I finally walk downstairs to find him leaning impatiently against the kitchen counter.

He smirks, sauntering up to me and wrapping me up in his arms. "You could wear a plastic bag and still be the most beautiful woman there, baby."

I roll my eyes at him before leaning up to place a quick peck on his lips. "Whatever. Let's go, Stud." We hop in his old Chevy truck, and take off for the restaurant.

Not long after moving in with Jared we realized his place was too small for the both of us. We found a cute condo within walking distance of both campus and the YWCA. The condo is large compared to his old place, but still cozy. It has a large living room, a huge beautiful kitchen with a breakfast bar and a dining room. The upstairs has two bedrooms, a laundry room, and two full bathrooms. We even have a basement for storage. I freaking love it here.

We pitched or donated pretty much everything we had before, opting instead to furnish the new place together. It's been fun and stressful merging our personalities and tastes but I think we've found a happy medium. All of our mismatched pieces make me smile, it feels like home.

Our home.

Jared reaches over entwining our fingers. "What's the smile for, Pretty Girl?"

I look over at him, my smile growing as I take him in. He's seriously so freaking sexy. He's wearing dark jeans and a cobalt blue button up that highlights his tanned skin. So sexy. "I was just thinking about apartment hunting and furniture shopping."

"You want to move?" he asks, with a crinkle between his eyes.

I can't help but laugh. "No, not at all. I love our place. I was just thinking about how we have a home together, and how crazy it was trying to merge our styles."

It's his turn to laugh. "Yeah well, if you didn't have the taste of an eighty-year old woman it would have been a lot easier."

"What?" I pretend to be offended. "It's called shabby-chic," I say in an annoyed tone.

Jared just laughs at me, and squeezes my hand tighter. "As long it makes you happy, baby."

We spend the rest of the ride in comfortable silence. I can't believe I've known him for almost a year already. It feels like just yesterday we were eye-fucking each other from across the room, which we still do regularly. Thankfully. Everyday has been interesting and fun and full of love.

We fight just like every other couple but it always ends up with us making up in bed, usually more than once. I can only hope that it's always like this. That I'll always love him this much, that he'll always make me smile and laugh; and that we always want each other.

Jared helps me out of the car, his hand on the small of my back as he guides me toward the restaurant. We're just about to the door when we hear Rico call for us, "Roman!" We turn and spot him and Angelica walking toward us.

I take a minute to really look at him. My heart feels full watching his smile spread across his face. He looks healthy and happy, which is a far cry from the last time I'd seen him. When we said goodbye to him at the hospital before he left for rehab, he looked awful, sickly.

Even after three days at the hospital, being forced to eat and drink liquids, he still looked rough. His skin was pale and had an almost grey tint to it. He was thin, too thin. You could see his cheekbones in his face. His eyes were sad and tired.

But, looking at him now as he and Jared share a man-hug, he looks good. Really good. He's gained weight and if I'm not mistaken he's put on some muscle mass, too. His skin is tan and healthy, but more importantly his eyes are bright.

"He looks good, right?" Angelica whispers in my ear.

I clear my throat. "Has he been working out?"

"Mmm, hmm." She gives me a salacious grin and I can't help but laugh at her. "He almost has one of those V-muscles now. I've never seen one in real life before."

I smile inwardly, I know exactly what she's talking about. It's one of my favorite parts of Jared's body. I could stare at it and lick it all damn day.

"Wait, didn't he just get released a few hours ago? How have you already seen his naked body?" I turn to Ang with an eyebrow raised. She just shrugs and laughs. Dirty, dirty girl.

Epilogue

Zhoe

"I can't believe how good he looked," I say to Jared once we're in the truck. Dinner was great. We laughed and talked and filled each other in on all the things we've missed in each other's live.

Turns out Rico is going to move in with Angelica. He said he needs someone to keep him on track and of course she's just crazy enough to do it. I asked about their relationship and both assured me that while they care about one another, they realized their friendship is more important.

That being said, I'm sure their friends with benefits arrangement is far from over.

"Yeah, I'm glad he's doing well," Jared says. "Are you up for a pit stop?"

"Sure." We drive for a long while and it takes me a minute to realize we're heading out of town. "Where are we going?" I ask him, curious as to what he's planned – especially when I see him grin over at me like the devil himself.

"It's a surprise. Now, hush. No more questions."

After driving a little longer it starts to dawn on me where we're headed – Jared's pond. As soon as the realization hits me I whip my head in his direction. "The pond? Why?"

Jared doesn't answer me, he just reaches over grabbing my hand in his, flashing me a reassuring smile.

I sit in the passenger seat trying to still my nerves. I have no idea why I'm nervous. I only know that I should be. Jared used to come out here to escape, what could he possibly be bringing me out here for now? The last time we were here he made me promise to move in with him, to love him and stay with him – did that one happy memory erase all of his darker ones from this place?

After what felt like a small eternity, we finally come to a stop at the same the spot we parked so many months ago. Still wordless, Jared climbs from the truck walking slowly around it to open my door. Gently he lifts me by the waist placing me on my feet in front of him.

He grabs my hand and pulls me towards the woods. "Are you going to kill me?" I ask, trying to break the lingering silence stretching between us. I was only joking, but as I take in our surroundings I don't know that I'm too far off the mark.

We're walking carefully through a heavily wooded area. The sun is just starting to set so it's still light out but there is nothing but quiet wildlife surrounding us for as far as I can see.

Jared barks out a laugh, one so loud birds take off from some of the trees nearest us – hiding from the danger. "I'd never kill you, Pretty Girl." He stops in front of me, his eyes raking up and down my body. "I'd miss this sexy body of yours too damn much."

Rolling my eyes at him I mutter under my breath, "gee, thanks." But, the smile he's wearing is infections and I can't help but smile back at him.

"Patience, Zho. It'll be worth it... I promise."

He turns his back on me, dragging me behind him again to some unknown destination.

Finally, we break through the shroud of trees and I take in a sharp breath at the sight in front of me. A large pond sits in the middle of a huge wide-open field. The sun is hanging low in the sky casting a gorgeous orange-pink light over the scene.

Jared keeps walking us toward the pond, stopping once we reach the water's edge. The pond is clear – clearer than most pools. I can see the bottom and the hundreds of fish swimming blissfully in circles. The edges of the pond are lined with large sandstone rocks and a small garden has even been planted on the side nearest us with a weathered wooden bench placed in the midst of it. Whoever owns this definitely takes pride in their work – it's gorgeous here.

"Jare," it's all I can get out. I'm suddenly overcome with emotion. I understand now why he came here, of all places, as a child desperately seeking peace. Closing my eyes I take a deep breath feeling that same feeling of peace wash over me.

***
Jared

I take second more to find the sense of peace I've always found when I come here before turning to the beautiful girl that brings me more peace than any place in this world ever could.

I step up to her, taking both of her hands in mine for long seconds as I just stare into her perfect blue eyes that are full of so many questions, willing my heart to slow down. This is exactly where I'm supposed to be, exactly what I'm supposed to be doing – there's no need for nerves.

"Zhoe, baby. I love you – I hope by now you know how much. You make me so damn happy. You make me a better man. Before you I was lost, completely fucking lost just trying to get through each day without giving into the temptations, the loneliness."

I stop, reaching my thumb up to wipe the tears that have started falling from her eyes.

"When I was younger I used to come here to escape, to find some semblance of peace. A meaning to my shitty life. I know I told you I've never dreamed of a future – one with a wife and kids, but that was a lie. I used to come out here and dream of finding you."

"Jared."

"I used to dream of a gorgeous girl that would love me. I used to dream about what it would be like to marry that girl, to make beautiful babies with her."

I drop to one knee in front of her, careful not to let her hand go – desperately needing her touch to soothe my nerves. Reaching into the front pocket of my jeans I pull out a small diamond ring. It's a one-carat solitaire princess cut engagement ring – simple and stunning just like my girl.

As soon as she sees the ring Zhoe gasps, her free hand fluttering up to her mouth. Her tears are falling freely now and as much as I hate to see her cry, the love shining through her wet eyes and the smile she can't seem to erase, makes the tears almost worth it. "Jared," she lets out on a soft whisper.

"You saved me, Zhoe. You helped me conquer my past, my fears and insecurities. You are my strength, my breath, my heart. You are my whole world. I was broken but you helped pick up the pieces and put me back together. The only thing I need to be complete is for you to become my wife. Marry me, baby and I'll spend the rest of forever making you deliriously happy."

Zhoe wastes no time with her answer, thankfully because the slightest pause would have done me in. "Yes!" she shouts for the world to hear, making me feel like the strongest, luckiest bastard in the world.

As soon as I slip the ring on her finger she pounces, her arms sling around my neck as she presses her lips against mine. I'm so unprepared for her attack I end up falling on my back bringing her down on top of me. "I love you so much, Jare."

"I love you, too, Pretty Girl. So fucking much."

At one point in my life I questioned my faith on a daily basis, but when Zhoe crashed into my world I once again became a believer. I'll never stop thanking God for bringing this sweet, confident, shy, beautiful girl into my life.

I'll never stop thanking Zhoe for loving me, for saving me and wrecking me in the most amazing of ways. I'll never stop loving her; I couldn't even if I tried. She's a part of me. Take away my love for her and I'd die, perish, cease to exist.

"I'm going to love you until the day I die, Zhoe. I love you with everything I am, even the broken, damaged, unworthy pieces of my heart love you. You're it for me; you're a part of me. I'm never letting you go."

"Promise?"

THE END.

Acknowledgements

Firstly, thank you – the reader – for taking the time to read my book. Thank you from the bottom of my heart for giving Jared and Zhoe a chance. There are so many amazing books to choose from I'll always be grateful you chose mine.

Thank you to my husband, who stood by my side supporting me all the way. Thank you for dealing with the nerves and the frustrations. Thank you for allowing me to live out my dream.

I have to thank my best friend, my blogging partner, and my beta reader for being so amazing. Seriously, Betsy, I couldn't have done this without your help. I can't count the number of times I called or texted you asking opinions, or running scene ideas by you and while sometimes you laughed you always had an answer, or words of encouragement.

Thank you to my friends, in particular Kim and LaKeysha, for keeping me on track, and keeping me motivated. Thank you to my friends and family that read Vanquish early and provided priceless feedback.

To Tee Tate, my editor - thank you. Thank you for letting me bounce ideas off of you, for being so thorough and for being a great editor.

Finally, a huge thank you to my fellow bloggers that not only read Vanquish but also took the time to review it and share it with your readers. Wherever, Jared and Zhoe's story ends up know it wouldn't be anywhere without you.

Words From The Author

Vanquish is the first book of three in the Triumph Series. Stay tuned for Angelica's story in Conquer, which I'm hoping to release late 2014.

If you enjoyed Vanquish please remember to leave a review. Reviews are lifelines for Indie authors, and truly mean the world to us.

About the Author

Born November 22, 1987, S.J. McGran is a new author with a penchant for writing, reading and reviewing romance novels.

She lives in Toledo, Ohio with her husband, cat and lots of siblings. She is a die-hard Detroit Tigers fan, and has a love for ice cream and pizza.

Connect with the Author

Facebook: Facebook.com/sjmcgran
Twitter: @SjMcGran
Website: sjmcgran.blogspot.com

Printed in Great Britain
by Amazon.co.uk, Ltd.,
Marston Gate.